THE DEATH OF
Donna-May Dean

Stonewall Inn Editions
Michael Denneny, General Editor

THE DEATH OF
Donna-May Dean

JOEY MANLEY

ST. MARTIN'S PRESS

New York

THE DEATH OF DONNA-MAY DEAN. Copyright © 1991 by Joey Manley. All rights reserved. Printed in the United States of America. No part of this book may be used or reproduced in any manner whatsoever without written permission except in the case of brief quotations embodied in critical articles or reviews. For information, address St. Martin's Press, 175 Fifth Avenue, New York, N.Y. 10010.

Library of Congress Cataloging-in-Publication Data

Manley, Joey.
    The death of Donna-May Dean / Joey Manley.
        p.   cm.—(Stonewall Inn editions)
    ISBN 0-312-07702-5 (pbk.)
    I. Title.   II. Series.
  [PS3563.A519D4   1992]
  813'.54—dc20   92-2630
                                                              CIP

First Paperback Edition: June 1992
10 9 8 7 6 5 4 3 2 1

For Jeff.
Hey.

To the following, in no particular order,
my thanks:

Yesho Atil, Don Hendrie Jr., Sandy Huss,
Kevin McClemore, B. K. Essary, Mr.
Stricklin, Cale Manley, Ami Mattison,
Mom, Andrea Cumpston and Elliot
Adams, Bruce Pitts, Dad, Dale Prince,
Russell Banks, and Cyn Riley and Lisa
Reddy.

Also, for recommending me: Ethan Mord-
den. For calming me down: Keith Kahla.
And especially, for bugging me: Michael
Denneny.

Contents

"Anne longed for the power of representing to them all what they were about, and of pointing out some of the evils they were exposing themselves to. She did not attribute guile to any."

—Jane Austen
Persuasion

THE DEATH OF
Donna-May Dean

WHAT WE SAY

I PUT ON PLAID FLANNEL SHIRTS, SPORT A WELL-defined mustache, grow apprehensive, solvent: Young Gay Manhood at last. No troll grabs my candy in the park anymore. I still go to the park—but just to tell stories. Sex here got boring and scary at the same time.

All of us come to the park, even so; but some of us are dead. Gone is the queen who would haughtily squat behind the bushes, with a cigarette stuck in the corner of a wisecrack. The three old men no longer wait outside the main entrance, bridesmaid faces averted one from another, hands churning modestly in trouser pockets. No shocked-up Mustang rumbles by, no beer bottle threat shatters on the sidewalk. We haven't been forgiven, though, for being what we are. The rednecks just don't want our blood on their hands, these days.

That is what we say, at least, and we laugh.

But you don't get AIDS so easily, here. It's just *not*, as Keller would have said, *done*. The very last faux pas indeed. This is Alabama—he would have insisted—this is northwest Alabama, and you have to be begging for AIDS, to dare get it here. The cheap, the lewd, the hopelessly prissy, he'd have said, counting on three deliberate fingers (he was all three of these himself): we are better off without them. Too many faggots in Genoa, he'd have gone on. Too too many faggots in all the world.

So it always has been. We have always had our self-hatred, we have always had our dead. AIDS is no new thing, just the latest face of the timeless: suicide and fagbasher, cutthroat trade and overdose. Our history, according to Keller, a long string of gaudy deaths, plastic beads to rattle and read. The Death of Harlot DeCarlo, Who Was Much Too Loud in the First Place. The Death of Little Nelle Helle, With the Polio Legs and Harelip, Who Should Never Have Been in That Truck With That Particular Redneck Boy Anyway. The Death of Donna-May Dean, in a Slightly Tilted French Hairdo. Our life is, according to Keller, a slow sad aria. "Lots of high notes toward the end. The end is all that counts. Work your skirts."

Keller called himself my mother. He taught me everything I know, every story I tell. But I am better off without him.

TO LOOK FOR
MY SKIRTS

THEIR HOUSE SANK TOWARD THE SIDEWALK on Confederate Street—a massy white Victorian, the smile of a widow behind a veil of twisty barren trees. I never knew what kind. Keller and Thomas: they took me in. "Ghastliness and glamour," Keller said, "and flawlessness. And fear," leading me up the cardboard-colored stairwell to my room, his hands tilted backward in the air by an imaginary headwind, "these will be our subjects of study. Not the proper names of trees." He stopped. "Oh. And Home Economics. Above all, we must teach you to be practical. None of this helpless Marilyn Monroe shit. And don't even *tell* me about your mother."

But I already had.

My new room, a sudden doorless square at the top of the stairs, smelled like a tree house: wooden, well-sanded. Keller made easily languorous tango-strides to the center of it, then a slow, full turn, gathering an invisible stole about his shoulders, as if the room were cold and objectionable, he had never seen such a room. It wasn't cold, though it looked like it should be: no curtain on the bent rusty rod above the window, no mattress on the single bed. "We set it out on the back porch," said Keller, "to air." He went to the window, bounced two fingertips of either hand on the sooty sill. "Donna-May Dean lived here. Poor thing." Then he snapped about to blink at me, small indigo eyes in a flabby and unindulgent face. "I mean, when she lived with us. This was her room."

I said, "Do tell," in a tone that meant, "Don't." I set my box of clothes on the bedsprings.

Keller inspected the soot on his fingertips, working his jaw catwise, to indicate hurt feelings. Indicate is all, he would have told me, if I had asked. Faggots have no feelings, we just appear to. We have been made to ask ourselves too often, "What do I feel? What may I show?" We put our feeling to sleep, an animal maddened by its time in the cage. We tell stories, learn to live within them, stories full of feeling—but not our own. Eventually, though, close enough.

He didn't have to tell me this. I had begun to learn my lessons already, and well. So I said nothing. I said, "Okay. What. No: tell me. You never said that he *lived* here."

"She. Lived here. This was her room. Her mother, you see, kicked her out of the—"

I was waving my hands, I had heard that story before. He was always revising it, I don't know why. To bring it closer to my own.

"Ahem," Keller said. We both turned to the door to smile, because there was Thomas, leaning into the room, his face low, in what could have been a leer, were he not so affable, dapper, corduroy-clad.

"Gossiping already?" he said.

This was his humor. He pretended—was encouraged to pretend—to be The Man of the House. Anybody else was nothing, was a silly queen. Except that Thomas cooked all the meals. And watched ballet on PBS. And called himself a poet.

We smiled, put our hands to our sides, waited for him to speak again.

He chuckled in his teeth, then stuck his pipe there. He kicked out of his way, gently, a red high-heeled pump, took one step into the room, slapped his front pants pockets, then his shirt pocket: being stung by invisible bees. "Anybody," he said, "got a match?"

"I was telling Mildred about Donna-May Dean," said Keller, slouching onto the windowsill in exasperation. Mildred was me. I hadn't wanted to tell him my name, the very first time we met. Later, he wouldn't allow me to. "You look like an Agnes to me," he'd said, waving one hand in the air to erase my words, "We'll call you Mildred."

Thomas hooked his thumbs to back belt loops, rocked onto his heels, waiting for a match.

Keller said, "Weren't you supposed to go in for a trim today?"

Thomas ran thin fingers through reddish greasy bangs. "You made me go there last week. I'm tired of that stupid barbershop. All those old men who spit on your foot and crack faggot jokes." He winked at me.

I laughed, took a sweater from my box of clothes (one of the few things Keller had deemed keepable), smoothed it against the bedsprings, with the most terse and pitiful hands possible, as if to say, My mother hates me now for a faggot. That was the story I had chosen to tell.

My mother's word for *lie* has always been *story*. As in, "Are you telling me a story?" But sometimes she'd be smiling, blinking approval, when she wanted to know. Is it still a lie when both teller and listener agree to believe?

Keller sighed. "The poor dear." Meaning me, or Donna-May Dean. "Eek! The roast!" He sailed across the room, stopped at the door, cast a mock distrustful gaze back at me, then sang his way down the stairs. Aretha Franklin. "Natural Woman."

I said, "The *roast*?" Keller had been with me for the past four or five hours; there was no roast.

Thomas shrugged, without moving his shoulders. He winked again at me.

I said, with Keller's unexpected voice, "Would you please stop that?" This scared me. Then my hands flew—Keller again—to my hair. Then I just laughed, took it in stride.

5

Thomas smiled, made two steps toward me, wearing his erection tucked to the right. A very conventional man.

He thumbed the bowl of his briar.

I sat on squeaking springs, lit a safety match, held it high, wearing eyes that were much too wide.

"What's a nice boy like you," he said, bending over me, to puff, "doing in a place—"

I said, "A place what? What kind of a place?" But I knew: somebody had painted a rose on the bed's headboard, in three shades of cracked and yellowing nail polish. Everything that I saw here was a queer thing. Which was, of course, fabulous. And also a new burden. To live up to that yellow rose, that red spangled pump.

Keller made kitchen noise downstairs, but not much. He rattled the silverware in a mostly empty drawer, opened cabinet doors, slammed them immediately shut. Just to let us know that he was down there, knowing, pleased. He must have thought we were fucking.

Keller said to me once, "Mildred? Does the sky *mean* to be blue?" His point: we are what we are. My name was never Mildred.

And I chose to be what I was, what I am. I was three years old, in my parents' bed, between them. "What does the Oink Oink Sack look like?" they said. "Who is the Hungry Worm?" They imagined that these were my imaginary friends.

I was the Hungry Worm. I'd writhe all day about the trailer, mouth open to nasty shag carpet. I'd finger the scummy underside of the toilet rim. I'd jam my tongue into the narrow aluminum tracks where the window screens didn't quite fit. Flies died there, lay on their sides, bitten wings bent. Smell of gunpowder, taste of old pennies.

I said, "He looks kind of like a pig," in a reasonable rational, rising tone. "He looks kind of like a worm."

They smiled, riddle-me-not. They smoked in bed, fire hazard, ashtray jiggling on Dad's tightly sheeted thigh. Dad was fat and hard. Mother was thin and loose all the same, within

6

her nightgown, two smooth crescents of breast too easily moving.

And I was the Oink Oink Sack. I'd go barrelling across the packed red-clay trailer park playground, my ears hot and thick and floppy, my forehead itching to grow curly horns, my hands in the air, my mouth shut, but screaming.

Mother took me swimming, where I'd stare and will him to come to me, the almond-colored teenage boy crucified to the side in the deep end, his flat hands on the concrete behind him: short cigarette, bent fingers. I held my plastic shovel and pail at him, devotion, shut my eyes tight to see red. He never looked back.

Then I was seven, "Almost a man," according to Dad. He took me hunting, I fell behind, slipped shotgun shells from his furry backward-pointing vest pockets, dropped them into high weeds, one at a time. They were yellow, they were hateful. Dad took me fishing, I was too loud in the boat on purpose, to warn the fish.

Dad sat, too heavily on my delicate bed, one hand on my forehead, the other flipping flops on his knee. He needed, he said, to tell me—he coughed, cleared his throat—about Life. He began, after a long breath, "A woman, son, has two buttholes."

I dreamed of a fat hypnotist, in a green-glistening black top hat, who made me drink beer, smoke, oink-oink, and shave. I woke hearing, but not listening to, the mystery of grunt and heave through the plyboard wall, through my clothes in the closet: Life. This had nothing to do with what I was.

I stood at the free-throw line I'd scraped myself, with a sharp rock, across the dirt. I held gravely in both hands before me somebody else's lopsided basketball. Even aloud, I said, "If I make this shot, they're right. And I am a queer the rest of my life."

They were the boys who sat in back of the school bus, cigarette behind one ear each, teeth often bared to show contempt, signs of rot, tobacco stains: rednecks in training who passed in my mind and in my dad's mind for what a boy should be.

7

I didn't make that shot. But I did try again, and kept on, I made it. I was glad, for the trying again, for the keeping on, for the wanting to be what I already was: the choice.

And I was glad nobody else was there to see.

I was already well-known in the trailer park, though. At least with a certain crowd of boys. Timmy came first, who had yellow bangs and freckles, chocolate kisses to spare, and sometimes real ones, in the culvert behind the store. Jerry held my face to his fly five minutes, then stopped laughing when I didn't fight back anymore. He ran away, he was going to tell on me, his dad. He came back alone the next day: "Could Jamie come out and play touch football?" That's me. That's my name.

("Faggots have no real names," Keller insisted. "A stepped-on cigarette in the street. We are nothing. We are abstract.")

There was Mitchell, who spent the night after church Wednesdays, who allowed me, more than once, to get a spat-upon finger up his tightening crack. He'd say that he liked it, then tell me to stop, it hurt. Mitchell told his brother Chuck, twenty-four years old, blond crew cut and wide ex-quarterback hands, who took me for a ride on his Harley, then bent me quiet over the seat of it, standing in the Southside Cemetery. I read the names and dates of the dead. *Faithful Husband and Loving Wife*. He sweated, swore, thanked me. I was loose three days with spunk and Vaseline, stepped thereafter with new, careful pride. I shat white goo, caught some of it on toilet paper, held it to my nose. I'd had a man, the smell was sweet.

When I was seventeen, I got my car, an Aqua-Velva-blue Toronado my uncle's girlfriend didn't want anymore, with a white vinyl roof and green rubber-smelling seats. I went to the park.

I'd just been waiting to get to the park, alone, at night. Everybody knew about the park. I stopped on the first curb I came to, got out, to lean on the hood, smoke, and pose, and smoke, and pose. I'd speak to no one.

Or I'd say that I came here to kill faggots. I was waiting for a friend, you see, and we were going to kill faggots together.

Now and then I'd check my wrist, run a hand through my hair, to pretend frustration: he's late. But I didn't even wear a watch. Nobody had to know. Nobody was looking anyway.

Killing faggots: I did it all the time. It was my favorite fantasy. I was both killer and faggot, would fuck myself, pressing heavy fingers to my own tenuous, trapped throat.

The park—backless aluminum benches, oil barrel trash cans, concrete walking trails peppered with nuts and prickly twigs. The lit tips of cigarettes around the fountain in the dark drifted, or not—lightning bugs at their first dance, too nervous and horny to blink or move. I sucked a dick or two, went home, jerked off sitting on the commode. I couldn't stand it. I went back.

Before long I'd established my own territory, a set of benches close enough to the bathroom building and the bushes, also close enough to my car. In case of rednecks, and baseball bats, and I had to get away. That was where I found Keller. I passed him by several times, hoping he'd be gone soon. I just couldn't bring myself to settle some other place. Finally he slid one hand across the seat beside him, an arc that ended with three imperious pats.

"Sorry I didn't have time to clean the living room," he pronounced. "We weren't expecting company."

So I sat, glad to have this chance to reject him and get him out of my way. Because he looked like a faggot. I was proud to be a dicksucker, but why look the part? What he wore: varicose veins, plaid knee-shorts, one cold-cream crescent under each eye, a yellow towel-turban.

"Do you need to piss?" he said. "Well, you look like you do. My name is Keller. You may call me Helen." He held out a mock-reluctant hand, to be kissed. I shook it instead.

"Well then," he went on, after my long silence, "what's in a name? Doomsday I'm sure. That's Shakespeare, darling, but don't worry about it. We'll think of something to call you." He laughed, lifting his face to bare the throat. "And what, pray, brings you out tonight? The Cum Trees are in bloom." He inhaled through his nose, exhaled through his mouth, with a shout, "Mwaah. The Cum Trees. That's cottonwoods to you. Live in this part of town?" He patted me on the knee, twice, smartly. "Talk to your mother."

That was when I looked up. I don't know what he must have seen on my face: "I mean," he said, "me."

An insult. I'd never spoken to such a faggot before. My contacts at the park were limited to trade, who dare not speak. Words might implicate them in the act. I loved the full responsibility, their sullen gratefulness, their plump and valued flesh between my teeth. What if one of them could see me now? Did they speak to one another? Would they like me anymore, if they caught me with faggots? Maybe that's what they expected all along. Maybe, to them, I was a faggot, too, a basin for their juices, a urinal, a commode. They'd be right, thinking this. But I wanted to have them fooled. I wanted them to think that I was one of them, just bored, just horny, or at least pretending just to be, surprised at whatever might happen.

I said, "I kill faggots."

"Won. Derful." Keller blew slow smoke over his left shoulder, away from me, with distaste. "Genoa has far too many faggots. All of Alabama doesn't need so many. The very world. So much competition, you know. Tell me: is that a baseball bat in your pocket or are you—" he flapped both hands away from his lap. "Oh, how does it go?"

I couldn't help it: "Happy to see me?" I giggled.

He turned his upward-tilted face my way, with the smooth-templed languor of a Pharaoh. "Of course I am, sugar-pie. Cigarette?" He lifted one from his pack.

I thanked him, but no, lit my own. Because his were menthol, his were 100's. I stuck mine in the center of my mouth, left it there. Camel unfiltered, damn him.

"Donna-May Dean was a drag queen," he began, then lifted his face to suck from the cigarette at the very ends of his fingers. "A bad one. Who lived and died in the Seventies, when faggotry flourished and attitude, *thank* you, abounded. The Village People were atop the charts, and Paul Lynde would always be the highest-paid Hollywood Square. A golden age.

10

You wouldn't know." He cleared his throat, two prim fingers pressed to orchid-colored lips. Were they painted? I leaned in closer, blinked. They were not.

"I'm not so young," I said. "That wasn't so long ago. I remember 'Macho Man.' " I said, "What was his real name?"

"Whose? Oh. Donna-May Dean. She had no. None of us do. Real! Name! The idea! I thought we'd covered this already. Miss Mildred. Miss Thing. We are all abstract."

"I'm sorry, that's bullshit." Then, because of his hurt face, "I don't understand."

"Donna-May Dean," he went on, "was a drag queen, a tragic one, but aren't they all. Who wore a natty and discontinuous fur coat—wolverine, I believe—and who killed herself in the bathroom. At her own party. To which she had not been invited. We did have social standards in those days. It was her birthday." He laughed. "And she just waltzed in, I don't *know*, and demanded to be shown the powder room. As ever, the gracious hostess, I waved the way, didn't wonder why. She must have had it with her and ready, that electrical cord. And: who can figure a faggot? What is a faggot anyway? A burning stick, a stepped-on cigarette on the sidewalk."

Donna-May Dean had, according to Keller, taken the cord from an electrical iron, had stripped away the cotton sheath, had untwisted the two wires, soldered safety pins to the ends of them. He stuck the safety pins into his nipples. He plugged himself in at the medicine cabinet socket. Keller called him *she*.

"She'd shoved her hairdo once to the left. That aesthetic of the Just Off that she was always touting, poor misguided thing. She did look dreadful."

I said, "He. He looked dreadful." Then this seemed to have been a very funny thing to have said. I didn't laugh. I scowled.

"Whatever. Who's telling this anyway?" As if surprised, he pointed five fingertips and a concave palm to his chest. "Me? Why, thank you?"

I said, "You're making this up."

He flapped a hand in the air, to show me that I was being disregarded, and to shut me up. "We just thought that somebody was fucking in there, the bathroom being locked and all, you know. Nothing unusual. Well! When we found her! You can imagine! Cast a pall on the social season. Ostrich feathers were in. After a while, though, we could laugh about it. Donna-May *Done*, we called her. Donna-May *Well* Done."

Silence fell, with a sardonic thud. We blew smoke a long time.

I said, "That wouldn't kill somebody." I didn't know if it would or not, but that's what I said.

"No? Well. Then. She was standing tiptoes in commode water." This part he spoke precisely, pinching some invisible baton between thumb and forefinger, as a conductor might, during an especially delicate, painfully important passage of a symphony. "I remember it well. Her twenty-first birthday. Nineteen hundred and seventy."

I said, "Um. I see. How old are you?"

"Never! You mind!"

I said, an accusation, "Why did you tell me this?"

"Just a story, to pass the time of day." He marched two stiff fingers across his lap, tilted his head, to watch them, to watch me. "Because," he said, "you said you kill faggots. And some faggots do need to die."

"I was kidding."

"It's not funny." He leaned toward me, to blink, so I could see that it was not funny. "Listen. Don't you know the drill? All that's expected of a faggot is that he die. Read *Giovanni's Room*, for God's sake. We're meant to be doomed and tragic and lovely. So what if we're not? We are made to be. We make ourselves be. The end is all that counts. Work your skirts. Hit the high notes. Take the flowers. Bow."

I bit my thumb to keep from laughing, then shook that hand, as if shaking water off, shaking away the small pain, but urgently. I said, "I don't have any skirts."

He slapped a brisk, dismissive hand between us. "Of course you do. You just haven't found them yet. You have much to learn." He nodded, once, to demonstrate profundity, and pleasure, in his point. "Someday you will be completely a faggot, and flawless. May God help us all."

So I walked away, to look for my skirts, I told him. I aimed myself at trees, barely missed. Each tree cut me off some, from his line of sight, his point of view. I gained the sidewalk with a shudder, not from fear, but as a child who has just left a room where something perplexes—the slant of light across an unmade bed. Not scary, just inconceivable.

For me, at that time, being queer was only the act itself. How sweet to suck sperm on my thoughtless knees. I had no need for drag and tragedy. That wasn't what I was.

What was I? I was standing barefoot under phosphorescent breathless hum, listening to leaves scutter past my feet on the sidewalk. I was laughing louder than I meant to.

Mother grew three sizes smaller in as many months, after Dad died, and white about the eyes, white at every knuckle, uncareful of dress. All I'd grown was a cold relief, hateful to me, a cancer casting roots across the bottom of my gut: now he'll never have to know that I'm queer. At the funeral home, I'd dodged into the bathroom, more than once, to check my tears in the mirror, not to see if they were real—that wasn't important—but to make sure they weren't sissy, that they didn't give me away.

For a while after that, Mother and I were always going to the grocery store, together, barefoot. Death in the family makes a body hungry. We kept the neighborly casseroles under tight Saran Wrap in the freezer, though: to fetch food was our need, to carry it home, under our arms, in heavy ripping paper bags. Nothing is so comforting as cans, bottles, cartons, to lock away, shut behind cabinet doors, to feel (we must be strong). Carrots to see. Collards for the blood. Milk for bones, fingernails, sharp shiny teeth.

One day, we came around the corner, to the Fruits and Vegetables aisle, and there he was, in a printed nightshirt, pinching passion fruit. He looked smaller, more serious, strange and masculine, more bald than I had expected, with a fringe of tight yellow curls, like ash on the tip of a fat cigar. Thomas, behind him, managed to putter about while standing

13

still. I didn't know Thomas then, his spats and suspenders, his black Polish cap.

Mother stopped, drew the back of her hand to my chest, as if we were in the car, I was still a baby in the front seat.

I said, "What?" But I knew.

"The town faggots," she whispered, as if there were only two.

I said, "There's more than two, Mother." I was watching my feet. She was watching me. I said, "There's lots of them."

She lifted one eyebrow, her Inspector Clouseau look, our oldest joke. "What are you trying to tell me?"

Keller said, "How do you know when they're ripe or not?" He thumped one, left a small snail-shaped impression. "Eeuh."

Mother, in an intrusive, nasal tone, "They're green, I think. The ripe ones. Excuse me, sir."

She was wrong. She just wanted something to say.

Keller turned to blink over his shoulder at us.

Mother said, "Green."

And I was hoping he wouldn't notice me, speak. I saw the earring in his right ear (which side the queer side? I didn't remember): delicate seahorse, thin plastic gold, with one imitation emerald eye. We were that close.

Keller said, "Thank you," to her, then, to me, with deliberation, "Oops." He turned right back around, because he knew that he was shameful to me.

I was glad. Glad that he knew. Also, a little, glad that I was ashamed. Yes, after all, this was not quite what I was. There may be hope for me yet. I would always be queer—that was fine—but also glad not to be one of the "town faggots." Glad that not just anybody, my mother, could pick me out at the grocery store.

Keller said, as if to himself, "I like Moon Pies. Thomas, do you like Moon Pies?" He waltzed away with an unseen, leading, partner. "Fuck this fruit," he said, sang, over his shoulder. "Let's get Moon Pies for dessert."

Thomas, careful, casually, made steps after him. He touched his cap to Mother, left his fingers there long enough to turn to me.

"We should wear shoes these days," Mother said. "AIDS."

"You don't get it that way."

"How," she said, "do you know?" It wasn't a question. She just nodded, didn't wait for me to answer. As if she had just proved something.

I said, "It doesn't happen here."

We pushed on down to Dairy, where the floor was gritty to bare feet, sedative, cool.

I said, "Anybody knows that."

She watched her hands push the cart, and smiled, as if she'd just stepped in something wet that wasn't supposed to be on the floor.

I said things, I don't know what. How we needed peanut butter. And look how much cheddar cheese had gone up since we were here two days ago.

Her mind had set, and her face had shut. I might have been talking to the cantaloupe in our basket, the kiwi, the kumquats, the corn. I laughed, as a child in elementary school sings the national anthem: off-key, and too loud, and without rhythm.

When we got back to the car, she fell hard onto her seat, snapped quick teeth once, a smile. "Tell me about your friends," she said. Meaning, the town faggots.

I turned away from her, to look out the window. "Who do you mean." I said, "Listen to you." I laughed. I said, "Shhh."

She scrubbed my scalp with her knuckles, to show that I was being difficult, and she didn't mind. I did—with most fierce resolve and reproach—nothing.

"AIDS is all I worry about," she said, quietly.

"How do you get it?" I said, "Do you really want to know? It's easy." I was screaming now. "You let them fuck you up the butthole, *Mother*. Scum you up and you're ripped and bloody." I smiled. "Easy as pie." I turned my smile in her direction. "I do it all the time."

She slapped me—tried to slap me—two fingers grazed my cheek, slammed onto the dash. She looked at me with narrow eyes, widening: indulgence had always been her plan. "Jamie," she said.

15

That's me. That's my name. But I said, "Just go. Just drive." And I felt nothing. Blood pressure beating in my hands and feet. I said, "Let's go."

Now and then, she'd turn to look at me.

"Look," I said. "See? This is how a faggot sits in a car."

She said, "Son." Meaning, I'm sorry. Meaning, Leave me alone. Meaning, Shut up.

"Watch the faggot," I insisted. "See it blink and breathe." And all at once, for the first time in my life, I realized: I sound like a sissy. And I always have.

Home—a new and dangerous place to be, and be queer. The windows showed bright, opaque, against the black bands of carpenter's tape between them. Air conditioner smell. Refrigerator's rattling drone. And there was nothing to do. I helped her put away the groceries.

Her knowing that I was queer—my knowing that she knew, that she wanted to talk about it—made me clumsy, fierce, giggly. I had always been queer, yes, but hadn't always had to think about it. Not here. I could sit on the couch, or sneak to the store for a cigarette, and not have to keep it in mind, my queerness. Now she'd always be there, to watch me, thinking, This is my son the faggot.

I slammed the English peas into place on the cabinet shelf. The peanut butter slid out, hit the floor, rolled away. "Damn!"

She touched my wrist, to hold me still.

I jerked away, stood, stepped back, folded my arms. "Okay," I said, all hostile fluttering lids and lifted chin, "Okay, okay. *What.*"

She smiled, to get me to. "I love you anyway?"

"Aren't you," I shot right back at her, then wished I hadn't, "strong and brave?"

I stormed to my room, to sit on the bed, wait for her to follow. I watched the door, so she would knock, but she didn't. I went to stand in the hallway.

She had jammed herself into a corner of the couch, watching nothing, watching her ashtray and elbow on the windowsill behind her.

The grocery bag stood sagging on the floor, half-full,

halfway between us. But she had shut the cabinet. She had set the peanut butter on the counter.

She lit a cigarette, flashed a look at me above the match burning. She waved it out. She turned to blow smoke out the window. Dad had never let her smoke in the house. I watched her thumb tamp once the nervous filter tip. This seemed a sad and characteristic thing for her to do, so I smiled. I watched the smoke work its thick way around her fingers.

"Listen," she said, "just tell me how to act, okay? I don't know what you want me to be."

"Don't worry about it."

"You've always pushed yourself away from me, from any-body. Locked up in your own strange world. Is this it? Is this why? It's what I've always been afraid of."

I said, resignation, "That I'd be queer."

"No." She blew a straight line of smoke at her feet on the floor. "That someday I'd stumble into your—magic kingdom. And you'd hate me for it. And you wouldn't let me play."

"It doesn't belong to you."

She said, "But you do."

That was what I finally couldn't stand. Because she was right. I went to the park.

The park was new by day, shot through with sunshine and heterosexuals. Even the walking trails had been swept bright white. A redneck, his beard too thin to be scary, had taken possession of my bench, along with his girl, his dog, his guitar.

It wasn't my bench at all, at this hour.

They watched with the arrogance of the dull as I passed. She rested her sentimental, pudgy hand on the back of his neck. At any minute, they might turn to kiss.

I hated them for that, that they could come to our place, feel more free even here than we could be.

I made my way to the bathroom building, where I imag-ined that whatever remained that was queer would have hidden itself until night. I'd never seen this building before, not really, how small it was, or its color—milkweed, with flaked-off irregular patches showing dry and gray. I leaned on one palm on the wall. Old women in pastel prints sailed past, chipper and determined and silent, pulling behind them toy dogs and grandchildren.

After a long while an old black man, wearing brown creased slacks and yellow socks and no shoes, came from inside the ladies' room to stand with me. He smelled of sleep, hand-rolled cigarettes, piss-water.

I allowed myself to believe that, standing there, together, we were thinking the same sorts of things. But I wasn't sure what those things were.

He blinked, turned away, muttering, shuffled with stiff dignity into the Men's. Change of scenery, I decided. We all need one every now and then.

I could sleep here, too, if I must.

I went to the fountain, leaning hard on my elbows on the rim of it, watching for a quarter or dime to glint through the scuzz. But nobody threw wishes into this fountain. I turned to sit, because a young businessman had passed for the second time. His wide-winged nostrils. His fat virile spiffy tie. I'd never cruised the park by day before, hadn't even thought that it was possible.

I said, "Hello?"

He just lifted his eyebrows, sat near enough for me to watch him test the inside of a cheek with his tongue. He smiled, spread his newspaper open in the air before him, snapped it three times until the spine held stiff.

I wasn't watching him.

Now and then he'd shoot a look my way, then duck, to spit.

I shook, but not much, and not from excitement—too many cigarettes, maybe. Or simple pleasure, that it goes on always, even under old women's noses and the sun.

He got up, a quick stare, to tell me to follow. I didn't have to, I felt as good as if I'd had him already. I shut my eyes, held my breath, until there was nothing left of me, except where fingertips pressed fingertips: five smooth points of pulse.

The redneck boy picked out painful chords on his guitar, but it didn't matter. Because here I was. Here, it was I who did the looking. Anybody who was here to see me, was here to see me be queer. Anybody who wasn't queer, who saw me, didn't matter, could go to hell.

I thought I might explain all this to Mother, while it all stood so perfectly still in my head. I made big steps toward the car, but passed it by. I was too scared, after all, now that I had had this knowledge, to let it go, and lose it. Like when somebody wants too urgently to make you come, and you're ready, but you don't, because this is yours. Also because you're not sure that it's real. You might embarrass yourself, screaming, "Here it is. Now. Now." Then nothing.

I stepped on across the street, into the dingy, moth-colored neighborhoods between the park and Old Downtown. Confederate Street. Robert E. Lee Lane. Wooden houses with wide, solid, shiny windows: I looked into each one, to try imagining what it would be like, to live there, to have to see always past this or that thing on the sill. A Coke bottle with a candle in it. A clay pot. A velour-textured cat biting the pads of its paw. I saw television sets laughing by themselves in empty rooms, somebody's hard black shoes left hanging on the line to stink, doors that had been open slammed shut, for dinner-time. The air moved about my face, brisk with young husbands' returns. Better yet—the possibility of meeting my own young husband at any corner, how he could bump into me, ask the time, take me away.

As I neared the river, the houses gave way to rough empty lots, intricate and straining with what Life is, any weed that grows to hold seed at the end, spread that seed, die. This seemed a reproach to me and my kind, and I felt it, but quietly. The sidewalks faded into red dirt and rocks—the road itself became a black uneven trail between the trees, poplars mostly, and willows that began, even a quarter-mile back, to lean to-ward where the water was. Then the river itself, and one wrong-headed rosebush, tending its own uselessness at the gritty edge, where no seed will take, no seed should have taken. I chose to sit beneath it, among pebbles and bottle tops and broken sticks and flaccid condoms. I inspected, for a long time, the surface of the water, fluted like old Saran Wrap. Or slick in petroleum lines after boats went by. The feeling that I had had at the park lost me. But I remained.

I didn't make my way back to the park until nightfall, after many nervy shifts of direction, random turns down unremembered narrow alleys full of cats and buckets, buckets and bottles, thin water puddles. I'd remember this mailbox, or this particular tuft of grass breaking its own cracks in the concrete, or this yellow house. But never this tree, with gothic limbs and hairy nuts. I stopped to think. I turned a full circle. Finally, from here, where I had not been, I found the park: two blocks down, one block over. Nothing could be easier.

Two lit cigarettes bounced in the wind, rolling and bouncing around one another, skidding across the intersection where I stood. The streetlamps threw on the sidewalk weaker yellow circles than I had remembered. The fountain, all at once, slapped off, except for the underwater lights, red and green in the otherwise leaf-dark and scummy basin. A slow Sunday night.

One quorum of queens—seven (I counted)—poised themselves on the corner, where my car was, each holding one scandalized hand to the side of his mouth. Rednecks had smeared with soap on the windshield: QUEERS SUX and PUSSY IS GOOD, and YOU ARE A FAGGOT AND FAGGOTS MUST DIE. The queens, near enough to be present, too far away to be spoken to (the eternal position of the catty), tittered, with gentle malice.

I slashed my hand through the air, tugged at my cuffs, I spat. Any butch, angry gesture I could think of, more for their benefit than mine.

They held stiff reddened faces back a little, touched fingertips to collarbones, to show delicacy, approbation. Or as if to say, That's what you get. Because I'd been seeing them here every night, would have nothing to do with any of them.

Later, I met some of the same queens at Keller's house. To a one, they had never seen me before, were delighted to make my acquaintance.

20

I didn't bother to clean the windows. Because it felt right, this message, this accidental truth. The justice of it: QUEERS SUX. Well, they do.

We do.

FAGGOTS MUST DIE. Hadn't Keller said so himself? What was his explanation? "It is how we make ourselves be seen."

YOU ARE A FAGGOT. This much is all they see, and all they need to, and all I need them to. This much is all I myself need to see and show. The rednecks, and the cops, and the Baptist steeple across the street, and I, were all in accord, at once. I shouted to the queens, by way of solidarity, "Begone."

I had found that feeling again, my power: my skirts.

I got in the driver's seat, and just sat there, my right wrist resting atop the wheel, left hand with a cigarette out the window. I watched the digital time and temperature on the side of the First National Bank slowly ascend toward morning.

One by one, the queens took themselves out of my sight. The last of them pushed a baby carriage, with haughty, presumptuous speed, directly by. I could have touched him, his brocade blouse, his bell-bottom attitude. I didn't even try, not yet.

I woke with my head on the passenger side armrest, my feet tangled in the steering wheel. Keller tapped once more, less lightly, two fingers on the window.

He said, "Are you dead? Are you ill? Did they hurt you?"

I didn't hear, didn't know what I heard. Later, I would remember having heard him, and would laugh, to think that he had thought such things about me. But just then, I wasn't laughing, wasn't anything, not even altogether awake. Only scared, and alive again, and stiff from too much sleep in hot weather. I lifted my hand, let it fall to my forehead, relaxed a finger or two enough to touch, hold shut, my lids.

"Oh dear. Wake up. Help, help," Keller whispered, as if almost calling the police, but too shy after all. He didn't believe that I was hurt. He did believe that I was pretending to be. Which was the same thing. That's what he told me, later.

Keller said, "*Talk* to your mother. I mean, me."

He held in one hand an ice cream cone, a Barbara Cartland romance in the other, which he set on the roof. Two chubby, narrowly blue-blooded women passed, on their after-breakfast constitutional. Keller blew imaginary hair from his forehead, to show them not to take him too seriously, this was nothing, not to call the police. "It's okay, darling," he whispered, shoulders hunched to show awkwardness, hand cupped conspiratorially to the side of his face, lips as close to the crack between window and car door as he could get them. "Your mother is here. You'll be just fine. Won't you."

I squeezed more tightly shut than before: my eyes, my fists. I rolled over, until my teeth met the vinyl armrest. My feet hurt. My left arm tingled, oddly, beneath me, no blood, sticky Naugahyde. My shirt and pants clung, in warm, frowsy, itching places. I cared, but not much.

I would be just fine.

Where was I? In my car. At the park. And why? And maybe I had been hurt, maybe I really was ill, maybe something terrible had happened. Would I be just fine?

And: why was he asking me? Only he—whoever—could see.

I blinked my eyes, painfully, twice, against the light. I said something, not much. And I don't remember. "Leave me alone." Or "Good morning." Or, possibly, "Mother?"

Who knows? We all embarrass ourselves at those times, half-awake, angry, with hard-ons in our boxers, matter in our eyes. I might not have said anything. I might have said, "Mother, listen—"

Keller—it is conceivable—nodded gravely over his ice cream cone, batted tiny, attentive eyes, took a cunning lick, well-pleased.

But I was already asleep again, dreaming again a story about my mother I had made up a long time ago: about what she wanted me to be that I could not.

Sometimes, when I was very little, Mother stood in my doorway, with a lit white candle on a jelly-jar lid, to watch me sleep. I was no doubt pretty, cheek on pillow, hand half-curled to the side of a shut smile, one eyebrow lifted from pleasant surprises in an otherwise too-long and monotonous dream. Sleeping was the only time she had seen me smile, I was a self-conscious, awkward boy by day. Or so it seemed to her. I am sure that she held her breath. That she bit her bottom lip. The trailer, as always, creaked and whirred darkly beneath and about her. She stood still.

Or she shifted impatient elbows, then her feet, with the caution of a mockingbird on a limb before morning proper, who already wants to sing.

She was even smaller than I have been used to seeing her: nervously pleased, fragile, blue-shining in her slippery white nightgown.

Sometimes she pretended to herself that this room was a new and dangerous discovery, that a door had appeared in the wall of the hallway as she walked past, by magic. This little boy had been dumped here accidentally, from Oz or the looking glass. Clean slate, pretty face, emptiness, subject to whatever unthought-of life she might wish to make for him. She could say he was a girl, and it would be so: raise him in dresses, send him to ballet, make little square cakes in a Barbie oven with him watching, learning. But no. She could whisper to him how he was an Elfin Prince sent to save her. Or that she was his big sister. Or his Fairy Godmother. Any of a hundred thousand possibilities, each of which would slam to, at once, if I opened my eyes, became again only exactly who I was, forcing her to do the same.

Safe now, she stepped to my toy shelf, on the shadow-puppeting wall directly across the window and the bed, as far from me as she could get, and still be present. The eternal position of the worried. She touched with hesitation this or that thing on the shelf, that I had mostly refused to play with: Lincoln Logs and Tinker Toys, still shrink-wrapped in their boxes; a Spider-Man doll, twisted in upon itself like a weak fist, its collar stretched down over both shoulders, as a strait-jacket, or a strapless dress; a red-white-and-blue aluminum xylophone, with rubber-head sticks neatly folded to the side, commemorating the Bicentennial.

23

Who was this little boy? she wondered, almost aloud. How much fun he must have. All these toys.

She sat on my bed beside me, balanced the jelly-jar lid on her knee, smiled. "Who are you? Whose little boy?" If I didn't open my eyes, she stood, went back to her room, lay herself restless on the bed against Dad. She didn't sleep, worrying about a son who was not—but she didn't know this—as unhappy as he seemed to be, as unhappy as she had every right to believe.

If I did open my eyes, she squealed with mock delight, held me, to cover her surprise. Sternly, "Who are you? What have you done with my son?" *Plunk*, candle and jelly-jar lid hit the inflammable floor. She tickled me, I was rolling rattling screaming, question and threat and thrill and fear: "You don't know me. You don't know me."

Then Keller opened the car door. My head flopped over the end of the seat, gravity compelled my lids down, open. He leaned forward, and was upside down, brought his hands to his ears, as to say, "Oops." He waved apologetic fingertips at me.

"Of course I do," he said. "You're Florence Henderson. I mean, Nightingale. Nooo. Lena Horne?" He bounced a slow knuckle in the air, to help him think. "Oh, I remember. You're the bitch who claims to kill faggots." He thrust two flat white undersides of wrist my way. "I've had enough. Do me in."

His ice cream ball plopped into the dirt, near the top of my head. He looked at the empty cone. "Shit." Then he lit a cigarette. "Good morning, faggot," he said.

I sucked on my teeth, ran my tongue's tip through the gaps in front. There was a cottony, bitter taste: bleeding gums, cigarette need. I said, "Hi," but my mouth fell more open than I expected, so it came out, "Ha."

"Well you may laugh," he said, "but some of us have a hard life." He pursed his lips, breathed out through his nose, crossed his hands over his heart, to show me what a hard life looked like. "Well you may laugh—" he licked the tip of an index finger, wiped, with agitation, the crusty sides of my eyes,

24

"But you gave your poor dear mother quite a scare. And what's *this*?"

He indicated the writing on the windshield, by lifting his eyebrows in that direction, lowering the edge of his smile.

"Getting yourself in trouble with the locals, eh? And, what are you doing here in the first place? At *this* very hour? A-sleep in a car, in-deed. At least it's yours?"

He half-stepped backwards.

"And, are you hustling?"

He drew an index fingertip across his cheek, to indicate the act of sizing me up. "Noo. Abandoned by a boyfriend? Kicked out of the house? *What*?"

He went walking around the front of the car, singing something wordless, tuneless, inadequate to his high opinion of himself, and made clean loops with one finger in the dust across the hood.

This bothered me, I don't know why, that he would move from where I could see him easily. I let my head fall back, I could see nothing now. I saw the green-gray sky, a couple knuckly ends of a tree branch. One thin power line slanted black, and straight, to the left, to meet a thicker twisted silver pair.

Keller said, "My, my, my. And what have we here?"

My erection, and my hand on it—I jerked up, rolled the driver's side window down, met him there, with my chin resting on folded nervous hands. He would see no more of me than this just now.

I said, nicely, using his voice, "Good morning, faggot."

He lifted back his head to laugh, but didn't. "Bitch." He patted me on the head with deliberately clumsy fingers. "I mean that as a compliment. It's not easy to be a bitch. You've learned quickly. Who was your teacher? The last and the best Bitch Thing of them all, no doubt. Oh, but she's dead, isn't she. I forget."

He bit his slightly blue bottom lip with his top three teeth, narrow corn kernels, white and sharp and square. He flared careful, delicate nostrils, twice. He took and twisted my earlobe between tight thumb and slippery forefinger. He pulled me up, hard.

"There's so much more," he said, with a lack of intonation, "to being a proper faggot, than bitchery. Next learn manners. Next learn grace. Don't sass your mother." He patted my cheek with his left hand, still tightening my ear to my head in his right. Musically, "I mean, of course: me. Apologize?"

I said, "But that's what you called me. That's what you call yourself." Slowly, as to a challenged child, I emphasized both syllables, "Faggot."

He said, "So? I don't follow. Relevance, please?" On *please*, he smiled, twisted harder, but lost his grip. I ducked back, bumped my head, then rubbed it. Rubbed my ear. Bit my thumb.

I said, "Sorry."

It came out wrong, too many syllables, high-pitched and inelegant, something like laughter.

"I do declare," he said, slapping his hands together, broadly, job-well-done, "you are the most laughingest faggot I've met in a long spell. In a coon's age. In a lifetime. It offends me. We have no right to laughter." He blinked seriouser eyes than before, "Tee hee hoo ha. Laughed enough?" A threat. "Come along before the day gets hot and Mother needs her nap." He minced heavily and without warning away, not looking back, still talking. His words clung to his face, like cigarette smoke, trailed thinly backwards: "Don't make me get mean. It's so boringly hideola. Mind your mother. Come along."

I said, "My mother? She's at home. She's not you. She has red hair, and shorter fingernails. And you were right, just a minute ago, how did you guess?" All in an unconvincing monotone. "She kicked me out of the house."

I started to say: Or I think she did. I wanted her to, she should have.

I said, "Because you were at the grocery store, and she knows I'm queer." Then I managed to raise my voice, but had nothing to say.

I said, "Listen!"

He just waved his hand over his head and said, with

disinterested zeal, "News flash." Then he turned operatically, sweeping from his way with one arm a heavy, invisible cape. "I do have to buy groceries. Now and then, you understand. Can't take to heart every little faggot who might tremble when he sees me, give himself away. Besides: mothers already know. Always." He turned away from me, and proceeded on the uneven path that sank toward the center, the concrete circle around the fountain. "Listen to your mother. I mean, me. I know."

He went on. Something about Donna-May Dean, something about Tuscaloosa, Alabama, something about mothers. He was too far away now, the rest was lost.

I said, "Wait." I scrabbled around the floorboard with my fingers, for my shoes, found nothing. I found a comb, a wrinkled apple core, Doublemint wrappers, and a pack of cigarettes. They were menthols, and somebody else's, and the pack was empty anyway. I tossed it out the window. I shouted, "Hey. You got a cigarette?"

He was gone, invisible past the curve. "Hey, wait! I'm barefoot! I'm coming!"

I shouted, "Fine!" Meaning, Fuck you. Then, to myself, more gently, "Fine." I sat back. I found my shoes. But didn't put them on.

I smacked my forehead with my palm, as to say, "I could have had a V-8!"

I sneered into the rearview mirror, to show complicity with my reflection, who had already been sneering at me. As if we were both saying, What is this bullshit, anyway? To get worked up over a silly old self-hating faggot. There was nothing I needed from him. I could always go home if I wanted to.

Except that I didn't want to, not yet. And maybe he had a cigarette to spare. Maybe he knew cute faggots. He might teach me something, pleasure or distress, or both, or not. He might teach me fear. I'd never been afraid yet, thought that I was missing something. All I had ever been was embarrassed. As if queerness were a harelip. Or the heartbreak of psoriasis. Compared to self-hatred, that seemed pretty puny. Maybe he

27

could teach what he claimed to know: the secrets of an older and more powerful way to be what I was. To be something else altogether, yes. To be too, too much, again.

I put on my red high-top basketball shoes. I cracked my knuckles, bit a couple nails clean. I smiled at my displeased reflection in the mirror, who had come to a very different mind about Keller and queerness, who didn't quite know what to make of me. I twitched my eyebrows quickly, one time, to show detachment, another time for humor. "*Oh* well," I said— an apology.

My reflection said, at the same time, "Oh *well*"—an attitude.

Then I went to the fountain, walked around it twice, no Keller. I ran a hand through my hair. I faced the basin, leaned forward to spit, for almost a yard away. I missed the water, splattered white on the concrete rim.

I walked around again, and there he was when I got back, propped exactly where my spit had hit. He slapped prim knees together as I passed. "There you are! What took you so long?"

"I was looking for you."

"No," he said, emphatically, "you weren't." Watching me, he pulled a string from his cuff, bit it off, blinked.

I said, "I was. I spat there. You're sitting where I spat?"

"No I'm not." But he stood, slapped the back of his pants. "Okay, okay. You caught me. I had to go to the pissoir, you see, and got entrapped there by sweet nostalgia. I had rather hoped you wouldn't follow me so immediately. Or at all." He nodded, held up a hand, "I know, I know, I told you to. Forget what I said. Lesson number one: always forget what I say. But *here* you *are!*" He struck a Carol Merrill pose, lifted arms and fluttering hands. "Ta! Da!" Then he lost his smile, let the hands fall. "Don't you agree, that a urinal is the most—I don't know—romantic? place in the world? I mean, the smell!" He took out a hanky, touched a corner of it to the corner of his eye, then whipped it in the air. He coughed up something rough, wiped his distant lower lip, folded the hanky. He tucked it between imaginary boobs down his collar. "Memm-ries," he sang, "from the corners of my mind."

I said, "Got a cigarette?"

"Of course not. I never smoke in public. Only at the house."

"That's not what you said before. You said you never smoke at the house."

He scowled, waved a hand, "Never mind what I said before. How many times do I have to tell you? Forget what I say. Oh. But remember that. To forget, I mean." Then he pointed an index finger at the invisible light bulb above his head. "I'll get you some cigarettes! Just you wait right here. I'll be back in a jiffy, yes ma'am. In a heartbeat. In a flash."

I touched his nervous shoulder. "Wait. No. You won't come back."

He looked at me, folded his arms, widened his eyes. Why did I care? he seemed to wonder.

I shrugged, held out my empty palms.

He looked at his feet, raised his lashes. "I'm an old charlatan," he whispered. "I work by intimidation. Anybody I know thinks I'm wise. A wise old queen. I'm not. I'm not even as old as I pretend to be. They think I'm wise, because they never follow when I tell them to." He slammed a firm, confidential hand on my knee, set all his weight there. "I count on that." He said, "Do you want to know a secret? I teach by bad example." He stopped, as if to spare my feelings, smiled. Then shoved me into the frog-colored water, and was his lordly—ladylike?—self again, standing above me, his hands in the air. As at the successful end of a rain dance. "I baptize you in the name of the flawless, and the ghastly, and the fearsome."

I came to the top, sputtering, but less offended than I wanted to be.

"What was your name again?" he stage-whispered. "No matter." In loud monotone, as an incantation, "Ag-nes An-al." Pronounced to rhyme with *banal*. The hands came down, flapped about, went back up. "No, no, no. Let's see now. Hmmm. Mil-dred Mis-o-gyny." He made flicking fingers at my face. "Piss on it. What do you *want* to be called?"

All I could think to say was, "Jamie. That's me. My name."

"How unfortunate for you." He sat, looking away from

me. I leaned over the rim on my crossed elbows. "We'll call you Jamaica. We'll call you Jamboree."

He helped me out of the water, his hands under my armpits, his face turned distastefully to the sky.

When I stood, he said, "Remarkable. You followed. You doubted. Were betrayed. That's all the tests and temptations I can think of. Can you think of any more?"

I said, "Now the cock has to crow."

We laughed.

He went on, "Hmmm. You have a name—several, for that matter. Never enough, though, never enough."

We were both slapping at my shirt and sagging pants, as if water were dust and we could make it go away.

"It's time," said Keller, as if checking off the most important item of a long shopping list, "to go home."

I said, "You left your book on my car."

He rolled his eyes: "So?"

I said, "I live on the other side of the river. You're going the wrong way." But I knew what he meant when he said, "Go home." I wanted to hear him say it. He meant, Be queer, be nothing but that. He meant, Come on to my house.

I said, "The passenger side door is open, still. The light, the battery—" The door wasn't open, I just said that.

Or maybe it was.

I looked back, but he said, "Now, now." He said, "There, there." He rubbed my belly, round strokes, as for luck. "Don't you worry about a thing. We'll be back shortly. I live just around the corner. You need dry clothes before you catch your very death. And no harm will come to your car. I don't believe in cars, anyway."

I said, "That they exist?"

"Exactly—it's a myth. It's your imagination." He boxed my ear. "No, silly. Such! A! Card! But I like that, yes I do. *That they exist* in-deed!"

I giggled, self-indulgently: once.

He nodded, chin to collarbone, left it there. "I have not been in an automobile in my life, never intend to be. And am the better off for it. Walking—best thing in the world for a faggot. I never knew a faggot with a car who didn't get himself in some sort of trouble eventually. Of course, I never knew a faggot walking who didn't, either, but that's another story. Besides, here we are already. See? Now wasn't that more fun?"

He stopped me, straightened my shoulders, as if he had just seen me, as if he had been up all night and morning, waiting, right here on the sidewalk, for me to come home. "Where! Have you been? We were worried sick? Just sick? You wait until your daddy gets ahold of you! And you're wet!"

I said, "My daddy's dead."

"That's what you think. You haven't met Thomas." He winked. "Last one in has rotten ovaries."

He laughed his way down the trail of unconnected stones that led through the trees in the yard.

Slow, and cold from my clothes, I followed, looking up. Looking straight ahead at this house—too large, too white— and at this porch, this heavy door, that Keller held open to the inside. I had always lived in trailers. My doors were flimsy, opened only outward.

On the porch, I stopped. "You live here?"

He hooted, disbelief, turned away from me, walked toward another door, other rooms. To show what an idiot I was. He called Thomas, holding two stiff hands in the air: frustration, exaggeration. "Come here right this minute. Come see what I've dragged in."

In just the one room, I saw straight-back wooden chairs, tasselled rugs on the wall, Sixties-style, and a crystal vase holding neat cigarettes, fanwise, on the coffee table. Camel unfiltereds. Yes. But I didn't go in. I held the door frame somewhere above my head with one hand, leaned sidewise there. I slid my hand down, easily. I bit some knuckles. I smiled. There was a red strapless high-heeled come-fuck-me pump for a paperweight on top of a stack of nevertheless windblown *Vanity Fairs*. A porcelain Scarlett O'Hara doll on the empty hearth. Three feathered flapper hats on two wooden hat racks. Another hat—an old man's gray fedora—cocked rakishly over the left eye of a deer head mounted on the wall.

31

Lackluster jazz percolated dimly from somewhere behind shut doors.

None of this had anything to do with me. And all of this was the queer life. These were the queer things. I would have to learn to live with them. After all—Camels. Maybe I was just too desperate for nicotine at that moment. Those cigarettes—my brand!—in this alien place, seemed comforting, surely a sign. Maybe Keller knew I was coming, somehow, and bought them for me. I really did belong here, after all.

Then, of course, Thomas showed up, took one, tamped it casually, possessively, on the tabletop. He connected it to his upper lip. He peered at me, to show that he wondered what I was doing here.

"Oh there you are," said Keller, gliding in. "Thomas, this is—oh, what's your name?" He looked at me, didn't give me time to speak. "What are you doing out there?"

He grabbed my hand, pulled me in.

"Ahem. Look what I dragged in." Then, to me, a whisper, "Stand up straight." He picked a soggy nit from my shirt.

I said, to Thomas, "Keller pushed me into the fountain." Tattletale. "At the park."

"So I see." He shot out a flat hand to be shaken. "Thomas Weaver. Pleased to meetcha. Yes sir. Pleased as punch."

He spoke with the blustery friendliness of a man in a neighborhood barbershop: a friendliness that has always put me off, that is designed to put off shy boys and strangers.

"Can I have one of those?" I said, with a nod toward his mouth, the cigarette sloping from it.

"What? Oh." Too loudly, "Sure, sure."

"You two get acquainted," Keller announced, "while I find *you*—" this word with hard stress, accusation and flirtation, "something dry to wear."

Thomas turned back to me with a cigarette at the ends of dry fingers. He smiled. As if he expected to fuck me soon.

Had I been set up? What if they weren't lovers at all? Was Keller some sort of procurer? Maybe it should have been obvious from the first, I just didn't know the rules, the language.

32

What signals was I sending even now, by taking the cigarette, putting it in the corner of my mouth, nodding thanks?

We didn't have a match between us, so we went to the kitchen to light our cigarettes on the stove. We stood for a while there, cigarettes flapping, as we shifted uncomfortable smiles back and forth. I felt like a fool, I don't know why.

Thomas pulled out a chair from the table, gestured with a hand cupped around his thumb-and-forefinger-pinching-the-cigarette. "Sit." A serious command. He narrowed his eyes, to show me: sit.

I did.

He sat himself down, leaned toward me, his forearms on his knees.

"Tell me," he said, with a swaggering shrug, "why are you here?" From the side of his mouth, with no malice, as Popeye, "What's your story?"

I told him. I said, "Well!" To indicate that it was funny, and difficult to remember, and too much to say. I setttled my fluttering hands in my lap, half-dead butterflies. I sat up straight. I said, "Welllllll," to indicate that I was thinking. I said, "Okay. I'm queer. That's the first thing, the first point."

I knew how butch I could seem. And I wanted him to know that I belonged here.

"You're queer. Hmm. And what made you think that?"

I wiped my hands down my thighs, twice. I laughed. "What is this?"

"I mean, who gave you that word?"

I thought of the boys on the back of the school bus, their heavy hams, their rotten teeth. "Oh, I see what you mean. Okay. So I'm—what word should I use here?" I winced. "Gay?"

He lifted his slow eyebrows, said nothing. "Whatever," he said. "Queer will do, if that's how you're comfortable. If that's what you are."

I just looked at him, to show that I knew he was making fun of me. That I didn't know if I liked him or not.

But I did like him. He had hair in his nose, a stiff stubby masculine set of nostrils.

33

I said, "So Mother kicked me out of the house."

"Is that all?" He blew relief, smoke, toward the ceiling.

I said, "Now wait a minute. I mean, that's pretty bad, to get kicked out of the house. Not the best thing that could happen to a guy, you know."

He chucked my chin with thumb and forefinger. "I'm sorry. It's just— You wouldn't believe what Keller brings in here sometimes. Escaped cons. Pot smokers. Pirates. Poets. Drifters. You know." He swooped his hands uncharacteristically, almost as Keller might. "Hell. Everybody gets kicked out of the house."

I was still thinking, what have I let myself in for?

I could always go home. Except that that would be embarrassing, to admit to the lie. To see either of them again, at the park, or anywhere else. At the grocery store, there I'd be, standing beside Mother, both of us barefoot.

"He thinks of this as sort of a halfway house. The Home for Tired and Wayward Faggots, he calls it. He's like my Aunt Betty, who could never leave a stray dog on the street. Everybody told her that she had to learn to turn her head. The house smelled like dog piss and dog rut and Alpo." He touched my knee. "No offense, you understand."

He crossed his hands behind his head, leaned all the way back, to point the cigarette in his mouth at the window behind him. I watched his throat, smoother than I had expected it to be, throb. "My Keller. He has a heart of gold." As if that were an insult.

He leveled a look at me. "But we had an agreement. I told him. No more."

He got up. "Something to drink? All we have is ice tea, sweet. And water, I guess."

I shook my head, no. He didn't turn to see, poured me a glass of water anyway.

"Glad!" said Keller, coming into the kitchen with much clothing folded over his arm, "to see you're getting along. I found— I don't know if it'll fit— Here, stand up."

He pressed something to my shoulders with sharp

thumbs. "Oh dear," he said, as if pleased. Then, in a worried way, voice rising and fading at the same time, "Oh *dear*?"

He turned to Thomas, who carefully gave no response. Who was looking at me like a sailor on a one-day shore leave.

It was a red taffeta dress.

"It's you," Keller said.

I laughed, tore it away from me, threw it on the table. "I'm not a girl. That's bullshit." I was ready to leave, I was walking away.

"P-shaw. Can't I have a little joke?" He tossed something at my back. It fell to the floor behind me. I stopped. I turned. Cut-off blue jeans and an "I [heart] my [dog's head]" T-shirt.

"The bathroom's down the hall," Keller said, pointing a bent finger to show me to turn left. "You might want to take a bath, too. That water was something ferocious scummy. We don't have a shower, though."

I was on my way.

"Listen," he called. "Soap's in the lotion dispenser, washrags stacked in the medicine cabinet. Oh, you'll find it all, I guess." He sighed.

I was already down the hall, and not looking back at him. The bathroom was exactly where I wanted to be. Then I stopped, I turned. "Jamie," I said to Thomas. "Jamie is my name."

But they were arguing, I couldn't hear, they didn't see.

The bathroom was cold, and small, and mostly white, except for pink plastic curtains on the one window, and black lines between the Scrabble floor-tiles. A porcelain tub stood on its own three claw feet and a cinder block.

I placed the dry clothes in the water-spotty sink.

I sat on the commode—no lid, just a hard round seat— pulled my cock past my sticky wet fly.

But I had left my hard-on in the kitchen.

I looked up, to see myself in the medicine cabinet mirror directly across. There, above the mirror, at the base of the light bulb, an electrical outlet, blasted into craggy plastic bits. Donna-May Dean.

35

I stood on the commode seat, steadied myself with my left hand sliding on the wall, reached with my right, to see if it could be done.

My veriest fingertips only made it halfway up the mirror. And Donna-May Dean had been standing in commode water—even further to reach. But that proved nothing. Maybe he was taller than I. Wearing platform pumps.

Keller *had* said, "Tiptoes."

The commode seat cracked, slid out from under me, skidded like a flat stone on easy water across the floor. I fell forward, hands grabbing at whatever, the toothbrush rack, and a plastic bottle of mouthwash, and a shaving cup with *Thomas* on the side, in the form of a looping lariat.

Which is what I was holding, looking at, sitting on the floor, when Keller knocked.

"Mildred? Whatever happened?"

I set the cup, the rack, the bottle, where they went. I looked for but didn't find the toothbrushes.

I said, "I'm fine." But that's not what he had asked. I opened the door enough to show him the commode seat in my hand. He took it, ran a worried, speculative finger across the broken edge.

"Oh, that's okay. Don't worry about that. We needed a new one anyway," he said. But ominously. And looked at me, as if to divine what I was about.

I heard a door slam somewhere else in the house. Keller didn't. Or pretended not to. Which was, for him, and for me, the same thing. "Thomas? Thomas, come see what our clumsy daughter has done this time." As if I had been here, breaking things, all along.

Then I took my bath, a long, manic one, kept losing the soap. I smoked, flicked ashes into the headless commode. I slid underwater, opened my eyes to the sudsy and the cloudy.

I came out in my new clothes, more beautiful than I had been in a while, because of the anxiety, I think, and because of the shorts, softer denim—more queer somehow—than I had ever worn.

36

Every door in the house was open. I walked into every room, barefoot on hardwood floors, leaving misty footprints. Queer footprints, queer floors.

I was singing, "If they could see me now." Meaning, Mother.

Thomas wasn't to be found. And I didn't really care to find Keller. What I found was a box of cigars, on a desk, in what must have been Thomas's private study. I looked both ways. I pocketed one.

Keller said, from the hallway, "Looking for me?"

I laughed, wiped my thieving hand on my shirt, turned to him.

"Yes, he was handsome in those days, wasn't he?" Keller came to stand beside me. Two-tone pictures in flat brass frames on the wall above the desk: Thomas in graduation robes and a beard. Thomas barbecuing, with a mushroom chef's hat on his head, some woman on his arm, whose face had been cut away by jerky scissors to show the green-felt backing. Thomas, dispassionate, with muddy hair, muddy gray T-shirt, holding a football with both hands above his head, buddies bright and indistinct in the background.

Keller was right. He was handsome in those days, with brighter eyes, even slightly firmer nostrils, a cleaner smile. Keller pointed to the headless woman. "My fag hag Brenda. I stole him from her."

I said, "Fag hag?" Then waved my hands, to change the subject. "I'm scared of beards," I said. I pointed to the graduation picture. "But this is nice—" The football picture. His bristly black flattop. Just like mine. I said, "I've got to go home. Pack my bags." I handed him the wad of wet clothes. "These aren't enough to live in." I stepped back, to show him, "And these are just a little too small."

"Ooh," he insinuated, tracing the outline of my penis with his index fingertip, "I like it." The voice startled me: all at once more cold, velvet and rhinestones. Later I would learn. Donna-May Dean.

I took another step back, two more, a third. "I'll be right back. In a flash. What was the word? In a jiffy."

37

"But you were kicked out of the house? Didn't you think about this before? Will your mother let you in?"

"She works on Sunday. Waffle House." This much was true, at least.

"Oh very well, then. Let me get my riding goggles."

We were on our way down the hall now, Keller striding ahead, me moving from side to side, to try to catch up with him. "You said you never ride in a car!"

This had been my last chance to get away from him, from them, before it was all too late and irrevocable. This had been my chance to think about it.

He snorted. "Did I say that? Pre! Posterous? Nothing better than a smart motoring jaunt with a handsome young fellow." He stopped, ran a hand through my bristles. "In a pinch, of course, a faggot like you will do. Relax, I'm only teasing. You have to learn not to take things so seriously, dear. Actually, I do have a somewhat minor phobia of automotive vehicles. But what the hell. Did I say that? *My,* my. Getting colorful in our old age, no?"

His riding goggles turned out to be glittery cat-eyed plastic sunglasses. He found them in a straw bowl on the kitchen counter, being worn by the largest cantaloupe.

Then he simply must find his pith helmet. "In case there's a crash of some sort, you know."

"I'm going," I said. I stalked to the door. I was even thinking, Here I am: stalking.

"Okay, okay, okay," he said. "Very well." He followed me outside, settling the helmet on his head—he had found it on a nail behind the door at the last minute.

Off the porch, he stopped. He looked at me. Fluttered the tips of five arched fingers to his heart. He sighed. "You have no patience with your poor nervous Nelly of a mother, entrapped in a *modren,*" he said, "*sic,* world she never made." He laughed. "I mean, me."

"You can cut the *mother* stuff," I said. "It's not funny anymore. Never was." If I was going to have to put up with this from now on, I would stop being shy about it. Maybe he would get mad, make a disinvitation. Which would compel my choices. Make me go back home to Mother after all.

He smiled. "Oh. Well in that case—." Took in a quick breath, as if to say something bitchy. Then he said nothing. He said, "Okay."

"Which way do we go to get back to the park?"

He pointed a hand to the left, followed it several steps. "This way." Then stood still, shook his jowls like that St. Bernard that Bugs Bunny is always picking on. "No, this way, of course."

And, of course, he was right.

He took his book off the top of the car. "See? Told you." He thumbed through it, browsing a wild fingertip across this and that page, random figure eights: Evelyn Wood on LSD. "Same book as before," he allowed.

I unlocked the door, opened it, stood there, smiling, a polite and horny beau.

He flapped the book toward the writing on the windshield. "But what about this redneck folderol? Don't you want to wash it off?"

"What for? It's the truth."

He sank into his seat, as into Calgon bubbles. "I guess you're right, aren't you?" He reached up to tweak my nose, but I was gone. "Of course you're right. You take after your mother. I mean—"

But I slid in place beside him, cut some dangerous eyes his way.

"Are you sure," I said, I smiled, I sighed, "you want to ride in this car with me?" Because he held one hand tight and white to the armrest, the other braced on the dash.

"What do you take me for? A sissy? Gentlemen, start your engines."

He snapped his resolute chin strap twice, then one more time. It held.

At every intersection, he screamed audacious murder.

"Keller," I said, "just stop it. You're going to actually make me crash."

39

"But that Chrysler, that very land barge, that that that half-ton of housewife-navigated machinery back at the light was about to blow through the red signal, and there you went. Like she wasn't even there. Like she was invisible. Or something other than a woman driver."

"She was going to stop."

"*How* you lie!"

I said, "She stopped, didn't she?"

"That's right. Argue. The facts," he spat. "As if that meant anything." He made haughty armfolding, he made headlifting *hmph*. "She stopped in-deed. You and Thomas, you're just alike." He may even have said, under his breath, contemptuously, "Men."

But this might have been my imagination. Or wishful thinking.

When we pulled into the Ponderosa Estates Mobile Home Park and RV Hook-Up, Keller blanched, for my benefit. "Oh. My? Darling! I had no idea you were white trash." He slapped my knee, reassurance: "But that doesn't matter. It's more fun this way, isn't it?"

"What? What's more fun?" I pulled in, threw the stick to park. I looked at him, blinked, blinked, smiled.

"The question was rhetorical. Now get out of this car and open my door before I slap you."

"I just want to know what you've got planned for me. That's all."

Then he made as if to slap me, so I jumped out of the car. Opened his door. Made a curt, passionate salute as he staggered out.

"Got to get my land legs back. Arrumph. Which one is it?" he said, pretending not to notice that we were parked square in front of the door. He wandered toward the Robertses' trailer on the next lot: "This sewage-colored one? Or a shiny silver bullet? Oh, tell me you live in a shiny silver bullet! When I was a little boy, I'd see those things and think—" He laughed, for no reason. As if to say, Look how out of place I am here. He said, "When I was a little girl, I mean."

"Watch out on the step. It's metal. If you step on it wrong, it'll shock you. There's a short circuit or something." I stood inside, leaning out to hold open the door. The trailer smelled of musty shag carpet and pinto beans and air conditioner. "Hurry."

I didn't want people to see him here. In case I had to come back some time, in case I had to face the Roberts family ever again in my life.

Suddenly, here, back in the gray, gray light of home, the old prerogative of secrecy grabbed hard hold again. I wished that I had listened to him, had taken time to wipe off the windows.

He clutched my hand in his mock weak one. "Sugar Dumpling, how does one step on it *right*?"

I slammed shut the door, waved him toward the raggedy couch. Somehow, by doing this, I hoped to keep him from seeing the Norman Rockwell prints on the walls, the brass spitoon full of potpourri on top of the television.

"I'll only be a minute," I said.

Mostly, I wanted him to sit and be still.

"Ooh. What's this?"

On the coffee table, beside her ashtray, her half-eaten Egg McMuffin, her empty Ronald McDonald Styrofoam cup: a shit-colored plaster plaque I had bought at a roadside souvenir shop on Mother's Day with her money, when I was a kid. I hadn't seen the thing in years. Why did she have it out now?

To one who bears the sweetest name/and adds the luster all the same/long life to her, for there's no other/who takes the place of my dear Mother.

It was the word *luster* that had sold me. Because I didn't know what it meant.

"Oh how sweet," Keller said. "You shouldn't have. It's going to look perfect in my sewing room." He held it in the air, to his left, as if to imagine it on a wall. "Right beside the needlepoint alphabet sampler and the tole painting of a fence post."

I said, "Stop. Put that down. Leave it alone. Why do you have to make fun?"

I went to my room, it was too small: why had I come

41

back? More for ritual's sake than anything else. Nothing I needed here. Nothing here but a bed, and a black-and-white TV on a red-and-green-painted card table for a desk, and coffee-colored stains on the ceiling, and some dark panelling walls. I counted: four of them.

I slapped my hands against my thighs. Nowhere to begin. I picked up a couple quarters from the table, and a bitten pencil, and a jumbo paper clip. I bounced them in my flat palm, as to guess their heft.

Keller, from the kitchen. "Look! Crocheted watermelon pot holders! Wooden geese on the wall! With blue bow ties, *no less!*"

I stood on the bed, took down the *Roll Tide* pennant from the wall. Mostly so Keller wouldn't see, get the wrong idea about who I was. It hadn't even been mine, or my idea. Dad had put it up there. It had been in his room when he was a boy. "What any boy's room should have," he said.

I'd always been afraid of it, for just that reason. And even more afraid to take it down. A small victory, then: I rolled it up, put it in my back pocket.

Then I jumped off the bed, looked around. Surely something else needed doing, or undoing, before I left. I took my box of comic books from the closet—four hundred fifty-two, mostly Marvel, some DC, and a couple hideous, unglossy Charltons. I dumped them on the floor, stepped slippery across, to the dresser drawers.

"Baby doll," said Keller. "Did you get your clothes already?" He stood in my door, taking more space than he needed to, elbows akimbo, feet mannishly apart. "Lovely." He clapped his hands before him, left them together like that, like praying.

But I didn't look at him. I tore out fistfuls of shirts, shorts, pajama tops, whatever, aimed them blindly at the box.

"Finished in a minute," I said.

He languished sideways into the door frame. "The trailer is of course: marvelous. Your mother must be quite the camp."

I didn't know what this meant, if it was good or bad, so I said nothing.

Keller pointed at my clothes box, at the clothes missing it, all over the floor. "Don't you think you could be a little more scienti-fic?"

He stepped over the comic books to help me. "Careful," I said. "Some of those are valuable. *X-Men* and stuff."

I don't know why I said that. After all, there they were, on the floor, where I had put them, had stepped on them myself.

He shot me a look. "Well?"

He parted my clothes on squeaky hangers in the closet, peered anxiously between them, as if they were undergrowth in the bush: button-downs, and Sunday clothes, and a full collection of *Star Wars* tank tops. "Mary Gawd."

He pulled out my yellow terry cloth bathrobe with blue trim and blue belt and monogrammed pocket. "We'll take this. To burn in the back yard."

He chose a thing or two else, at random, then folded them carefully over his arm, set them in the almost empty box.

All this time, I was pelting him with things from the drawers. He said, "I'm not much help, I'm afraid?"

I said, "Grab some of that stuff off the floor for me, will you?"

So he took up mechnical, indiscriminate armsful at a time, turned his face to the ceiling. More than once, he said, "Poly-ester?"

"I know, I know, I know," I said, as if I had already been worried about that. "Just put it all in. I want to get out of here. We can go through it all later. When we get back home."

Back home. Meaning, his house.

I stopped for a second, looked at him. He lifted an eye-brow, to show pleasure, and as a challenge. I laughed, because I had called that place home.

All at once, for no reason but that, it was.

We laughed. Then I stopped, he didn't, he laughed until he choked, choked until he bent over, bent over until he almost fell. The pith helmet hit the floor in front of him. Also the cat-eyed driving goggles.

I went to pat him on the back, but he pulled me closer,

as for support, coughed over my shoulder, backfiring a giggle when he could get the breath to.

I didn't even think, What if he misunderstands, gets carried away? I knew he would. He did. And I didn't even think, What if the neighbors see? Or, What if Mother walks in early from work? The neighbors may or may not have seen. Mother didn't walk in early from work. I wouldn't have cared.

This is how it happened: first, he stopped laughing. "Oh dear," he whispered, "I am overcome." He pushed me backwards onto the bed, for a joke. I lay there, lifted up on my elbows, to see. He didn't even take the shorts off, just pulled my cock past the curly white fringe where the jeans had been cut off. He licked the reddening head against my thigh, then looked at it, ironically, there.

He said, "Do you mind?"

I didn't say anything. I shifted some, to make us both more comfortable. Rarely had I been the stud, allowed someone to blow me off. Silence, I imagined, was the imperative of the suckee. I pressed my crotch just one more half-inch his way.

I allowed myself two silly words, a nasty command, a sneer: "Eat it." I might have added, "Faggot." And did. But just mentally. Keller was right. It was more fun this way.

Then he went down, and down, and easily down. It was as if he were falling face first through me, out of my sight. He was nothing. He was balding head and softness, a hungry worm indeed, scaldingly. He might have eaten all the way through.

I grabbed his wide ears, to pull him up, he was too far down.

His bottom lip, pressing the top of my sac, wiggled.

I made "Stop it" sounds, but pushed him down, after all, held him there, where he couldn't get away. He came up for froggy breathing nevertheless. Then down again, even further this time. It was as if he had no teeth, no tongue, no glottal stop: his recklessness, his gorging plunging.

This went on.

Then he pulled up, sniffed my bead of pre-cum, as a connoisseur. "I think you're just about ripe." He smiled, flattened one side of his face onto a frustrated fist. "You young'uns and your short ever-loving fuses."

He picked a careful couple hairs from finicky teeth. I was watching him, so he crossed his eyes. Which—myself again, no stud—made me laugh, and that threw me off, and I didn't come. As he intended.

"But no," he said, "don't laugh." He thumped my flat belly, watermelon sound. "It hurts my feelings. Not to mention wrecking hell with my role-playing." He grimaced, as a schoolboy over algebra homework. "I was pretending you were the SS man and this was my bribe. SS men do *not* laugh." He tickled me. He squeezed the base, and my balls, and just ran dry lips back and forth across the head-slit. My dick looked smaller than ever, down there, measured against his face, just as the moon looks smaller on a detailed horizon. I couldn't stand it, that smallness. I pushed forward, to make him take it in his mouth again and make it invisible. I hit his nose instead, then the top of an eyelid.

He pressed me hard to the bed with one forearm across my chest, burrowed his face and nose doglike into the crack in my pants. He bit my sac, once, tinily.

I really did pull him off this time. I looked him smack in the eye: "No."

He gave no sign that he had heard. I relaxed enough to allow him to go on. He sucked a while longer, most unconvincingly. He used my cock like a finger, up and down his lips, to make silly noises: "Rugga rugga rugga."

I coughed. This was getting boring. I laughed, but he didn't let me.

I laughed, but he went softly, too slurpily, all the way down, one more time. I yelled, like a little boy with his finger in a light socket, who wants to pull it out, who doesn't move. I grabbed his hair in one hand, slapped his forehead with the palm of the other. Then I tensed into a half-circle about his head, chestbone to his hairline, hands frantic up and down his back, or ticklish ribs, or the slippery nape of his neck, to press

45

him down, or not, or get him off me. Then: jerk jerk spit spit spit, a couple dry jerks, and it was over.

I was used to masturbation. I missed the mess, felt cheated somehow.

He took out my cock, looked at it.

Against my will: two more shots at his face.

Then it was really over, he was just blowing air through puffed-out cheeks, narrow mouth, to show relief, and job-well-done.

He dabbed my sperm from his lips and his cheeks, and from under his eyes, as with an invisible, expensive, silken napkin. Then he wiped the scummy fingers rude across my bedspread.

He cranked up my shirt above the nipples, spat what come he was holding in his cheeks onto my chest.

I said, because suckee etiquette demanded, "Thank you." But I wasn't sure that I felt thankful. I wasn't sure what I felt. I felt nothing but used, nothing but a real man.

I fell back, I was breathing high hoarse almost-wheezes. The urge was still there, to go and masturbate, just to let myself know that I could: this belongs to me.

"Let's get out of here," he whispered. "Out of this very mobile home."

I said, "You're right. You're so right."

I pulled my sticky cock into place with one hand, smoothed the shorts back down. With the other, I patted the small of his back, as to say, "Okay now. Let me up now. Okay now."

But he held me down with his elbows under my armpits. He ran a wide, violating tongue all over my chest, to smear the come, to make it evaporate and go away.

Before we left, we tore the place up. Not really, not badly. We threw the couch cushions on the floor, things like that. Left the kitchen sink stopped up and running. I don't know why. But we had a good time, a self-conscious good time, and silently.

I took a box of safety matches from the coffee table, where

46

Mother had left them. I patted my pocket: there was the stolen cigar, possibly bent. I slid the matches in sidewise, snugly. Next time, I'd be ready for Thomas.

When we got back in the car, I said, "Let's not talk about it, okay?"

He didn't say anything. I was afraid I might have hurt his feelings.

"Talk about what?" he said. But he knew.

"Right. Exactly. You've got the idea."

But there was something I wanted to know. Not that it bothered me. I just wanted to know.

"Is that what I have to do to live with you?"

"I thought we weren't going to talk about it," he snapped.

So I shrugged, I started the car.

Then he said, "I wouldn't put it that way. Just in those terms."

Then he said, "Yes. I'm afraid so."

We remembered that his pith helmet was on the floor in my room, and his sunglasses. But we didn't go back.

I said, "Oh well." Meaning something or another. Meaning, Oh well. I said, "I can live with that. Fine."

"Turn left here, darling."

We came this time to the house from the back. No driveway proper, just two red-dirt ruts that ran between other people's backyards, into a white rickety shed with a tin roof, and a decorative wheelbarrow upended beside the entrance.

"Have you talked to Thomas about this? My moving in?"

"Well!" As if this were the most obvious answer in the world, "No!" He laughed. "That's what you were supposed to do. Why else would I have left you alone with him? Surely you didn't think it took me so long to find something dry for you to wear?"

I said, "I don't think he likes me."

He rolled his eyes, and continuing the motion, let himself out the door. "You stay here. I'll check it out."

He was gone forty-five minutes, or forever, or two hours

and a half. Dead power tools glistened dustily on dark wooden shelves. I started counting elephants. Every sixty elephants makes a minute.

Seven hundred twelve.

Then Keller's face sidewise beside me, "I'm sorry. Forgot all about you!" He opened the door. "Come on."

"Thomas doesn't mind?"

"He was getting your room ready. Took the door down. It was rotten, you know. Took down the curtains, they were dank, they need mending. We set the mattress on the—you get the idea. I started helping, forgot why we were going to all this bother in the first place."

No grass in the backyard, just a swept grayness, interrupted now and then by one of those skinny leafless trees I had never seen before. A rain-spotty sandbox, and a high, rusty gallows of a swing set.

I stepped automatically through a bed of dead buttercups. My box was too big for me to hold and see Keller at the same time, so I followed his voice. But he wasn't talking.

I said, "These trees. Are they dead?"

I said, "What are the names of these trees?"

I said, "Why didn't you swallow?"

I tripped over the first cinder block step to the kitchen door, but kept my box level in the air before me. He put directly into my face a helping hand, foreshortened and large at the end of his invisible arm. His face pinched and impassive. A prophet of some odd effeminate God.

"There are more important things," he said, "than swallowing or not." Again, his voice, flickering and bothersome, somebody else. "There are more important things than the proper names of trees."

OUR BEST DEFENSE

THOMAS SAT BESIDE ME ON THE BED—THE BOX-springs, rather, we hadn't gone to get the mattress yet—puffed strenuously, smokelessly. His pipe wasn't lit well. Should I offer another match? No, that might seem too familiar, easy, might make him laugh.

What I liked about him was the tension, from the side of his straining mouth to the tube socks pulled too high on bony ankles.

He gave up, with a dry, wise look, set the bowl of the pipe on the windowsill, flipped it over onto its face.

I moved my knee half an inch closer, to touch his. He leaned forward, away from me, picked his teeth with a thumbnail, to show that he was thinking of something to say.

"I let you stay because you seem different. Less out to get something. I don't know. You remind me of me."

"That's what Keller says," I said. "About himself, I mean. That I remind him of him."

"Don't listen to what Keller says."

"I know. He told me that, too."

49

This was a good time to remove my knee before he noticed, decided that I wasn't so different after all. To camouflage the motion, I stood, and laughed, slapped my thighs. I flattened my palm above me on the wall. "I like it here," I said. "White walls."

"This room depresses me."

He laid his chin on the heel of his hand, index fingertip pressed to the middle of a clenched, reluctant smile.

"What exactly did he tell you," he said, and turned his face to the window, "about Donna-May Dean?"

I shrugged. "Oh, I don't remember. Oh, that? It wasn't important, was it? I forgot."

But he didn't believe me. And after a while we went to get the mattress.

What Keller had called "the back porch" was a shabby square of stones set into the dirt outside their bedroom door. The mattress was damp on the bottom, leaf-scummy, too stiff for easy riding up the stairs. Thomas did most of the work. I just watched him, his straining neck-tendons and eyebrows.

Then we—all three of us—waited for evening, and supper. I might have struck out on my own, walked to the park, or turned on the television. But it was nice, having them do nothing to entertain me—as if I were one of them. Keller settled himself daintily, weightily, into the chintz settee, with a Whitman Sampler box near to hand, *Anna Karenina* upright on distant, chubby knees.

Thomas shut the kitchen door, told me not to bother him. Keller, I guessed, already knew.

I walked about, trepidly, to look at things: the pictures on the walls, the milk crates of records on the floor by the stereo. But I kept bumping my shins, too many small tables. "Sit," Keller commanded. "You make me lose my place. You make me glower."

I sat, looking up, like a child his first day in the library, not reading, not yet, not books. Reading the room, and what everything in it implied. It was still the strangest feeling, that things here were queer things, that they could be solid here: the graceful curve of a wooden chair back. The drapes, bunched and yellow, shining to the sides of darkening windows. A line of ceramic elephants, tails-to-trunks, propping a door open.

I shut my mouth in reverence, sappiness. All at once, a pattern for life, beyond cocksucking and tragedy, had become possible. This is the living room I want to have. These are the things I want to own.

I went to the bookshelf, took down something thin, rag-gedy, chartreuse: *Madame Bovary*.

"Bonbon?" said Keller. He held the box my way. "Don't get the square ones. That's caramel. Those are mine."

"You'll ruin your dinner," Thomas called from the kitchen. "*Jamie*." I had the feeling he had given up on Keller long, long ago.

"Oh pish," Keller announced. "Thomas thinks he's your mother. I trained him to be butcher than that."

As I suspected, there was no roast beef. Instead, what Keller called "Thomas's company dish," meaning maybe that I didn't quite belong here as fully as I wanted to: ribbed pasta shells in a heady red wine and tomato sauce.

Then with a blink and nod and a wave, Keller sent me directly to my room. Conscious of how much I had eaten, I said, "I'll do the dishes."

"Nothing doing. Busy day tomorrow."

Timid child, I went.

"One of us will be up in a little bit," he called after me.

And I was thinking, Oh yeah. Forgot about that. No need to do dishes. I'm earning my keep.

Being done for my room and board had seemed fine, before. A lark, even. Now it began to strike me as a little bit dull. This, then, was how they saw me, how I belonged: just one more queer thing to place about the house as they pleased.

Keller said to Thomas, with no prompting, "Why, to tuck him in, of course. Whatever did you think? Dirty old man!" Then, to himself, "The little sweetstuff." He made a long sigh, to indicate transports of lust and concern.

Thomas left the kitchen—the scrape of his chair, his steps.

Keller went on to defend me anyway, at length. How it would be good, one more time, to have a handsome young

51

face on the premises. How nice I was, how well-behaved, despite what he called my "fetid upbringing." As if Thomas were still there, he scolded, "You should give him a chance. Get to know him better."

It was Keller who came up, with a porcelain bedpan, his mother's, decorated with flattened baby angels, harps and trumpets, written-on ribbons uncurling beneath their feet, something in Latin.

"Oh dear. Were you sleeping already?" He sat by me on the bed. "God is great," he translated, one finger tracing the Latin, "God is good." He said, "This belonged to the Phillips widow. She was a pious old pisser." He always called his mother "the Phillips widow." He said, "Episcopalian. Or is it Episcopal?"

I sat up, reached for the spiral-bound notebook on the table, propped it on my knees.

Keller rubbed my forehead with his thumb, hesitating circles. He scowled. "Mothers."

I said, "Yeah." I said, "Please."

What did we mean?

He said, "Your first night of your new life. What will become of you?" with perfect matching tremor in voice and thumb. His eyes lowered themselves—as from concern, or modesty—toward my crotch.

No light in this room. The bulb had busted earlier, when I switched the switch. What light there was, from the window, made fibrous glassy fire about the curling outer edges of his hair. He tilted his head, he smiled.

But I was looking at the notebook Thomas had given me, his own, from when he was my age. One word only, and that on the crusty cardboard cover: *Poetry*. The rest was empty blue lines.

I said, "Don't worry about me."

I stabbed the center of the cover with the bitten eraserless end of my pencil.

Maybe too easily, I said, "I'm okay. Life is good."

"Yes," he said, with difficult, hissing stress on that word, puzzled with himself to be offering it up. He said, in nervous—

52

not ironic, which is different—monotone, "Ah yes, yes. Isn't it, though?" He breathed out, through a stiff open smile, as to say: Yes it is, but how embarrassing.

I said, using his voice, "Listen—"

He shut the smile, made a dozen fast pats and tucks, urgently, to quiet me.

I said, "I'm just glad to be here. Thank you." I made wide eyes at him awhile, then turned away, as from too much feeling. Phony as hell. But that was what he wanted me to be. Faggots have no feelings.

The high-heeled pump, where I had placed it on the windowsill, spangled silhouette against the gray outside.

I said, "Do you have a thumbtack?"

But he waved five immaculate dismissive fingertips in my face. One flat vein throbbed through his temple. He blinked, once, as to regain concentration.

He said, "Thumbtack. Yes, of course. Yes, I'll get you one."

But he just sat there. But the circling rubbing on my forehead stopped.

"Thomas might come up tonight," he whispered. "Be gentle with him. It's hard, you know, to let him go, sometimes."

"Go?"

He shot mean eyes at me: You're not making this any easier. Play the game. "Outside the marriage. Because I do love him so." He puckered his lips, snickered, to show that he was mortified. Not because of what he had said, but because he had meant it.

I smirked, because I thought that this would help him. I made an angular smile, two degrees or so less oblique than his. "I'll take good care of him. Promise."

He said, to the invisible camera over his shoulder, "Oh dear."

He walked to the door, but stood there, pinched the bridge of his nose. Then he went two steps down. He turned me a backwards profile, the severity of a cameo brooch, "Don't overdo it."

I tossed the notebook on the floor, held the bedpan in my lap.

He took it away from me later, when he brought up my warm milk and cookies. He set it on the floor, kicked it under the bed. He leaned over my forehead, to kiss me good night, then stayed there, didn't. He tossed three thumbtacks, with a flourish, like jacks, onto the windowsill. He shoved a tube of K-Y under my pillow.

"My poor dear child," he whispered. "Are we abusing you?"

Which made me laugh. I said, "Yes?"

"But your mother. Loves you." And finally lowered dry lips to my brow.

I said, "You mean, you."

"Get some sleep. There's a party tomorrow."

"For me?" I felt like a child saying that. I felt like a child anyway.

"Of course not. Just a first Monday. Just a potluck. But a Coming Out Party. That's an idea." He said, more directly, to me, "Yes. It is for you."

He walked to the door, thoughtful finger tapping the pudgy cleft in his chin. He slapped off the light switch when he passed it. But of course, nothing happened.

Again, two steps down, he stopped. "Do you have on your socks?"

I did, but didn't say so. I shut my eyes, put the back of my wrist to my forehead, pretended to be asleep.

"Did you hear me?"

Then again, but less loud, as if to himself, "Did you hear me."

Then, with my dad's voice, any redneck's blustery intonation, "Boy?" He giggled. "Girl, I mean."

He went on down the stairs. "Girl, girl, girl," he said, as if to remind himself. Three *girls* to each hollow wooden stair, then one final, weary *girlfriend* and quick sharp linoleum steps across the kitchen floor.

I flipped the heavily patterned quilt from my chest, worked my knees until it fell to the floor. I was so hot I hurt: my feet, my nipples, tingled, the back of my wet neck. I peeled off each sock with the big toe of the opposite foot. I cooled four fingertips against the dry window pane. That bed was too narrow, too close to the wall, too far from the floor, too soft for sleeping in.

I scratched the line of hair beneath my sticky sac, then brought the fingers, sweet-scented, to my face. I was too much, too full of myself, for masturbation, though. Besides, Keller had already taken his share of my services. Where was Thomas? Keller, I didn't mind. Thomas, I consciously wanted.

No sound, nothing: a green-painted radiator in the corner popped, pinged. From the wall behind me came an easy, irregular scurry, a pencil working firm equations across rough paper. Or mice.

I listened past this, for Thomas on the stairs.

One slow car double-thumped, hummed, a heartbeat in the dark, across the bridge, across the river, several blocks away. I watched the ceiling. Here and there, the steady blue from a streetlamp directly outside. Otherwise, nothing, darkness: white. I shut my eyes, left them shut, opened them in time to catch the cutting spin of a headlight up the wall, more slow on the ceiling, then faster down the other wall, bulging crazily across the dresser drawers, the clothes box on it.

I turned onto my face. I reached my fingers to the floor for the notebook. I sat up, wrote, "Donna-May Dean was not real." Beneath that, "Here is his pump."

Nothing else came to me. My first poem, then.

I tacked it to the windowsill. I tore it down, wadded it in one hand, dropped it behind the headboard.

Who could write in the dark anyway? I walked across the room, to turn on the light, but remembered. Hand on the switch, delicately, I stood there. I breathed.

There was Thomas, in the kitchen, having himself a nervous cigarette. I didn't see him, just the back of his head, the back of his arm, one shoulder, his ankles wrapped tight about the back legs of his chair.

I saw the shadow of his smoke on the staircase ceiling.

55

I heard his grunting, shallow, reluctant cough.

From these things, I knew that he wanted me. I imagined that he was waiting to get his nerve up. Or waiting for me to settle in, sweeten myself up with K-Y or something. Or that he just had other things on his mind right now, would get to me later: an afterthought, an unimportant detail. This last thought in particular shook my knees a bit, made my cock push dully toward erection.

I held it in my hand, to cover it up, or to feel that it was there.

He might not like it, though, my waiting at the door this way, holding a hard-on. He might think I was too eager, a slut. He might think I wanted to be the man. That was how I understood sex at that time, somebody had to be the man. And I didn't want to, not with him. I was sure that that was exactly all he was good for.

I jumped back in bed. When the springs had settled from their bouncing squeaking, when my heartbeat calmed enough, when I remembered to think to, I listened again.

Something bumped into my window from the outside, then fizzed itself, with the anger of the itty-bitty, for a long time, to death.

Loud voices: the front door slammed.

I stood on my sinking-into-the-mattress knees, to look out the window. It was Keller, stepping out, with his feathered hat at a resolute angle, his gold-tipped cane cutting jaunty circles in the air before him, his lavender bow tie, his rubber galoshes. He turned, waved at me, then blew a kiss. Something lovely, nefarious and abrupt worked the edge of his smile. He went left, stopped, turned on a heel. He carried himself away, in the direction of the park.

My focus scattered, I was sleepy after all. In place of my reflection in the glass, somebody else. I didn't get to see it, though. It went away. I kept on staring.

And after a while, more distantly, there was Thomas, silhouetted in the reflection of the lighted door frame. I didn't turn, I watched him in the window.

He ran a hand through his anxious bangs.

I said, "Where is Keller going?" But I knew.

Thomas came to stand by the bed. He took off his clothes, one lanky thing at a time, he let them fall. He burped.

"Excuse me," he said. Then, "Where do you think he's going? To the park. Like always."

He winced, to correct himself. He kicked his pants across the floor: scoot sound, belt buckle jangle.

More easily, he said, "Like sometimes."

I said, "He goes there to smoke. He doesn't like to smoke in the house."

Thomas didn't dignify this. He curled into bed beside me, almost apologetically. He pulled me down. Careful, erection-less, goose-bumpy, he held tight to my back, face between my shoulder blades.

He said, "I'm cold."

But he wasn't. He couldn't have been. There must be something he wanted from me. I was too young, too butch, too hot for words. Cocksure and patiently, I waited.

But no: he went right off, into thin, uneasy sleep, his index finger pressed lengthwise, lightly, across my lips. Into my left ear he whistled a dim and intricate snore, like a slow song, like sweet nothings.

I tried to turn my head free, to hear the radiator, or the cars on the bridge, or the horsefly dying on the windowsill outside. But all night, I was held there, I was listening.

I must have slept, though, because: I woke. Sunlight on my legs, my disordered sheet. I tasted warm in my mouth. Otherwise, the room had gone cool. He was gone.

I stumbled to the stairs, but didn't go down. The question of what to do, what new morning habits to form, held me there. No matter what I did, it would be new.

I stepped into the empty kitchen, then across the squares of white light on the white floor. Dishes in a dirty sink. One neat, halved, hard-boiled egg on its flat face on a saucer on the table, its all-of-a-piece shell stuffed into a coffee cup with cigarette butts.

I'd have never noticed dirty dishes back at the trailer. I was proud of myself: I filled the sink, did loud dishes until Keller woke.

He pretended to yawn, batting his flat hand against open mouth, a Hollywood Indian. "Heavens," he said, but I remained to be convinced, "leave that."

"Good morning," I said. "Where's Thomas?"

"Getting a trim, I hope."

I rinsed the silver serving spoon, brandished it his way, like a sword. "What's for breakfast?"

He took four shuffling steps to the table, then, dumpily, sat. "Cocoa Puffs, I guess. What time is it already?" He looked at the ceiling, to express how difficult it was to be awake in the morning. He said, "Good morning."

"Where do you put this?" I said, held his china platter in the air above me, for him to see.

But he had set his face in his folded arms.

"I've got a surprise for you. Go into my bedroom. Tell me what you see there."

I did, stood outside the door. "Nothing," I said. "Your bed. Candelabra on the vanity."

He said, "What?"

More loud, "Cold cream!"

"Oh my God. I forgot where I left him. Look in the front room."

The coffee table had been pulled to the wall. A young blond slept on his face on the floor, wearing white hairless muscles, and cowboy boots, red bikini briefs down between his knees. One hand held his teddy-bear key chain. The other nuzzled in his crack, knuckles gently bent, fingertips pointing odd angles outward. A black motorcycle helmet on the sofa held wadded blue jeans, and a dirty white corduroy cap.

That seemed smart, to me: to travel so light, so neatly.

I called to Keller, "Um?"

"Exact-ly!"

I moved closer. Small freckles. Black brows, long unnecessary lashes. I said, for no reason, "He's pretty, though."

58

"I brought him home for you but you were, ahem, busy."

I knelt, just looking, as if he were a Christmas present I didn't want to unwrap. As if I wanted to shake him, make silly guesses, see what ways he rattled.

I ran a finger down his spine.

He turned over, opened his eyes, a flash of green, sexy laziness, then a widening: "You're not—"

I smiled, meaning, Be quiet.

He picked up on it right away, brought a fingertip to shush my lips, as if illustrating for me what I meant.

"Not good enough for you," Keller was saying. "He let me fuck him up the ass." Keller made an audible shudder. "Just another pussy," he said.

But I wasn't listening to his bullshit anymore. I whispered to the stranger, "I'm not Keller. Disappointed?" I set down the serving dish, touched him with ten drying fingers, here and there, nothing serious.

He sat up, shrugged, to show sleepiness, then one more time, to show embarrassment. "No, just confused. Who are you?"

"He picked you up for my sake."

"Oh yeah." He looked down, flashed a hand through his cowlick. "I remember now." He cupped my left shoulder in his hand. "Are you Mildred?"

We laughed.

I said, "Jamie. That's my name."

"Jimmy," he said.

I said, past his finger on my lips, "No. *Jamie.*" As if speaking to Tarzan.

"No," he said, and took the finger from my lip, thumped his chestbone, "Jimmy."

"Oh. How funny." Then there was nothing to say. "Hi, Jimmy." I said, with conspiratorial leaning-forward and hand on his knee, "He wants you to leave."

"Keller? No he doesn't. He's just putting on."

I said, "I knew that." But I hadn't. I started to say, "But how did you know?" But I didn't.

He slapped the floor on either side, to help him stand, then realized. He pulled up the briefs, scooting squeaky buns on the floor.

He said, "Do you?"

Then he said, with a breathless, serious look, as if this were the conclusion of a long speech beginning with *because*: "You have to be careful with Keller." And "I think you're cute."

My heart was beating in my nipples and asshole.

He took my hand in his, but I pulled it away: this was too much, too queer even. I was embarrassed for us both, for the three of us, for us all.

"This is a joke. Keller put you up to this. Things like this," I said, "don't happen."

But he just said, "Welcome to the world." Meaning, This world. Meaning, Get over yourself. Meaning, Anything goes. This time, I let him keep my hand.

"No," Keller was yelling, "I've decided you don't want anything to do with him."

We came into the kitchen together, still holding hands, still, mostly—both of us—naked. A sight to see.

Keller did nothing, though: he blinked.

"Keller, enough," Jimmy said. "We get the joke."

But I didn't.

Their familiarity bothered me. I stepped stiffly between them, all formality and joined Confucius-fingertips. "I think he wants breakfast," I said to Keller, with a bow.

But Keller kept smiling, smiling, smiling.

He said, "Of course." He set two bowls, too close together, on the table, slid milk and Cocoa Puffs and clattering spoons our way.

He sat in one chair, leaned on a flat palm on the other, leaving us one to share. We ate standing.

"But," said Keller, regarding us with a mockery of strict intentions, "he will have to leave. We do have errands to attend."

Jimmy held the bowl in both hands to his face, tilted back, shut his eyes, to swallow. Then he watched me.

60

Keller said, as if to get our attention, or express disgust, "Boys, *boys*."

We set our loud bowls empty on the table, went up to my room.

"Don't take long," shouted Keller. "Do the easiest thing! We've a party to get ready for!"

We sat where the light from the window was on the floor. I went to touch Jimmy, but he waved me away, hunched his shoulders, miming laughter, as if to say, Hold on. He took a wrinkled joint from his sock. He lit it.

Then I was embarrassed for having groped at him.

I said, "I forget how to act sometimes. Or I never knew how. I feel like an idiot. I feel like a kid."

He pulled my feet into his Indian-style lap. His eyes, slow but smart, and empty, and numinous, less green than they had seemed. "I know. Keller will do that to a body. But don't let him scare you. He means well."

I must have looked surprised. He leaned toward me.

"Did you think I was a stranger? I lived here before you did."

He made a hurting squint on the end of his toke.

"What happened?"

I'd never smoked pot before, but this was nothing. Cigarettes did more for me than this.

"I grew up. I graduated. He sent me away."

I said, "How sad."

"No it's not," he said, easily, without contradiction. "Listen. They know what they want from you. What do you want from them? That's what you're supposed to figure out. When you do—" He took my hand, where I was holding the joint his way, and directed it back to my face. "No. Hold it in."

I choked. He laughed. I threw the joint over my shoulder, because it made me mad, his laughing.

But I said, "Did you figure out what you wanted?"

He held out flat hands: I'm not armed, Sheriff.

He said, "Look. I'll come to the party, okay?" Meaning, I think I'll leave before this gets any more intense. "We don't want you to get into trouble." He shoved my feet to the floor.

I pulled my knees to my chin, hugged them, rocked back, to see where he stood. "Did you really do him?"

He chuckled, almost with contempt. But not directed at me, not exactly. "Don't you?"

He walked past me to pick up the joint, trimmed the sputtering tip on the edge of the table.

"Of course you do," he said. Sounding just like Keller would.

My face burned. What had Keller told him? No: he knew, that's all. It's what I was here for, anybody could see. At the party tonight, they'd all be knowing.

I said, to the floor, "Last night was what I meant. I meant, this morning."

Jimmy shrugged, stepped away, down the stairs.

I heard him talking to Keller: the open, rising tones of old friends: "That was fast," and "I'll be back tonight," and "Of course you will," and "My T-shirt. What did you do with my favorite T-shirt?" and "Give Mother a kiss."

Which one was I jealous of, for knowing the other so well?

I got dressed—same shorts, same shirt Keller had given me the day before. I stumbled pulling the shorts past my knees, I was walking toward the window. Then I stopped. There was the bent cigar. I stuck it between my teeth, to make the dry reefer taste go away. I didn't do anything. I lit the cigar. I opened the window.

I called his name when he stepped outside. His helmet was on, he didn't hear. He threw one leg over his motorcycle seat, revved the handlebars with loose fists, twice, before kick-starting the engine. I said, "How cute." I said, "Did you really let him fuck you up the ass?"

Then I remembered the listening Confederate neighborhood outside.

I shut the window, walked away, before he or anybody else could see me. Then I had to go back, stand there, brazen thing, to show I wasn't embarrassed.

He had been waiting on the street. He waved. But I couldn't see his face or his hand for the limbs of the trees. All I saw was his torso lift and twist. All I saw was his ass in the seat.

I didn't wave back. He puttered away.

Then I screamed recriminations, and giggles, down the stairwell.

Keller, as if mouthing the word over a caramel candy, "Mmmwha-at?"

"That was too too much," I said. I stepped once back, crossed my arms beneath an emphatic nod. As if he could see. "I'm pissed. I'm very very very pissed."

I realized that I didn't sound convincing, all those *verys*. I shouted, "Just pissed!"

"But darling," said Keller, his innocent blinking eyes of a sudden at the bottom of the stairwell, "I thought he liked you."

I sat, an image of sulkiness, poor posture, on the top step. "I don't need your leftovers."

Then, not as an accusation, but just because I wanted to know, "Why did you kick him out of the house?"

The kitchen door slammed. Keller turned a profile my way, another behind him. "Hello dear," he said.

Thomas breezed past, on his way to the bedroom, with a *Lucid Observer* folded under his arm. "Stupid barbershop," he mumbled.

Keller: "That's fine, dear." Then, to me, a vindictive whisper, "You're making a scene. What are you—pissed—about?" The word was funny in his mouth: *pissed*. With the tiniest hesitation, the earnestness, of a confused great-aunt, or grandmother, who only wants to see you happy.

I stood. I said, "You might be right, but—" I smiled, leaned backwards onto the door frame. "I'm not used to all this." I flapped my hands in the air. "What next? What now?" I turned my head, from rhetorical left to rhetorical right.

Keller patted my back as I took the last step silently down. "Next? We go shopping!"

He led me by my elbow to the refrigerator, poured a glass of cold water.

"Drink this. Sit here. Breathe."

I slugged it down. A couple of tears, but not from anything. I didn't let him see them. From the pot. From yelling.

He said, a command, "Better?"

I didn't say anything. I did hand him the glass. I did smile, and keep smiling.

"By the way," said Keller, leading me out the door this time, "Jimmy has the clap. Remind me to get that prescription refilled. Looky!" He scuffed the sidewalk with an indicative foot. "Somebody left a love poem!"

One red word, sputter of spray paint, across the concrete: AIDS. An arrow directed passersby to Keller's house. Our house.

I said, "You don't have it, do you?"

He snorted, the question deserved no answer.

We were making big steps down the street now. Keller waved at a rusty cluster of old women on one porch swing.

I wondered what they were thinking. They all smiled, only one waved back. *The old faggot has a new boy.*

"That's what this shabby, genteel neighborhood is made of," said Keller. "Widows and faggots. Widows and faggots and stories to tell."

I fell behind, watched my feet, smiled.

"That's what I need you for," he went on. "I have stories to tell." He whispered, sharply, "Listen—"

I said, "Do you have to walk so fast? Do you have to walk so prissy?"

Keller cut some sly eyes at me. "Mary God." Meaning, Please. Meaning, Go on. Meaning, Fuck off. "Now, where were we? We need potato chips," he said, "and party dip. Beer? Pretzels? Embarrassing headgear?" He marked off two or three more things with his pinky on an invisible pad. He pulled back his brows, scandal, then brought them down low, the better to see: "Cockrings? Pumice? Cabbage? I can't make this out."

He tossed it all over his shoulder, slapped his hands three sliding times.

"We'll improvise. How about fondue? How about an Ha-

64

waiian theme?" He squeezed my cheeks in one hand, to pull me along. "Such pretty eyes." He stopped. "Just like your mother's."

But his were blue. And mine were shut.

I said, because I wanted to change the subject, to make him stop touching me out here on the street for God and Anita Bryant and anybody to see, "What about those stories?"

As if I didn't know. As if I wanted to hear.

"Exactly," he whispered, a revelation. "The Deaths of the Drag Queens. Naughty cautionary tales for some silly Southern sodomites. Don't you think?"

Through forcibly puckered, tingling lips: "Think. What?"

He let my face go, followed his fluttering hand, a full three-hundred-sixty-degree turn. "Perfect theme for a party!"

I rubbed my jawline, a groggy boxer, a businessman in an electric shaver commercial. "Sounds gross. Why would anybody come to a party like that? Nobody wants to hear that stuff."

Keller, gravely: "My innocent." He took stern steps now. "On the contrary, it's all we ever want to hear. Our grand fatale fore-femmes. Rimbaud's perverse rush to silence, Africa, disease. Oscar Wilde, his spit and brass and suicidal polish. Even the bloody corrugated corruption-colored nipples of Donna-May Dean. All the dead faggots. Our favorites, all." In a droning whine, " 'Why, they couldn't help themselves,' we say. 'They weren't but faggots, after all. Tired old silly faggots, after all.' And nothing that happens is ever a faggot's fault."

He slapped his hands together, then held them out, as a magician, to show me: nothing.

"And everything is beyond us, is out of our pathetic hands. We must always appear to be victims, you see." In a more rough, realistic tone, with slower walking, to indicate change of tack, "Because—what is the threat we represent? Not that we're queer. But that we *want* to be. That's the insult, that's the threat. So what do we, can we, say to that? 'Lemmings,' we say, 'Think of lemmings.' To the hets, to *ourselves*," in Aunt Bea's mock-casual voice now, " 'Oooh. We'll be dead soon, anyway. Don't you bother about *us*.' "

He described a wide circle with his index fingers in the air before him, to show closure: "Self-hatred."

I caught up to him.

He smiled. In a weaker, warmer, reasoning tone, "It's our best defense. Far better to seem sick in the head than willful." He snapped a turtle look at me. "Don't you think?"

He nodded, once, with shut eyes, down. Then, brightly, with open eyes, up: "You're right. We'll go fondue. We'll go Hawaiian."

So we sailed into the Corner Fruit Stand.

"I know," said Keller, "isn't it a hoot?"

Smell of old magazines and rot-sweetening blackened bananas. The uneven floor shined earth-color through dull drying mop-water streaks. One old man behind the counter looked up from a newspaper, without moving his face or his unsparkling eyes.

"Barney," said Keller, an acknowledgement.

Barney tightened his dirty fingers. Turned his face left and right, as if to see who was there. As if to show us the hair in his ears.

We spent time choosing a shopping buggy, although the store was smaller than our own front room. Keller rolled each of them a few inches forward, then more slowly back.

First, we went to the magazines. Keller picked out a *Cosmo* and *Seventeen* and *Weekly World News* (MOTHER, 34, GIVES SELF CESAREAN WITH KITCHEN KNIFE!) Keller called, "Oh Bar-ney? Haven't you got that new issue of *Cocksucker Monthly*?"

I had to laugh. My legs were shaking. Oh my God. Barney knows. As if Barney mattered to me.

Keller said, surprised and hurt and amused, over his shoulder at me, "What? What?"

"You're asking for trouble," I whispered. "You do need to stop."

But Barney, shyly, around his toothpick, demurred. He hitched his feet one rung higher on his stool, settled in to ignore us for a long, hard read.

We got Hawaiian Punch, that was all, that was pretty much the "Hawaiian theme." Also the magazines. And canned pineapples. And a panama hat. And paper streamers, orange and black, left over from last Halloween. And Vienna sausages, because "Thomas likes them. Isn't he butch? Isn't it just devoon?" And several jars of Vaseline. And aerosol cheese.

Keller paid with a fresh one-hundred, folded longwise, at the veriest end of two straightened fingers. "Keep the change," he commanded. Then, "I'm only joking."

We pushed the cacophonous buggy on rough sidewalks all the way uphill, home.

Then Keller told me to take the empty buggy back. "We forgot Bufferin and Wheat Thins." He stuffed some bills, too many, into my back pocket, then slapped it three times. He turned his tight eyes away, pressed fingers to his temple. "Hurry back. Don't get lost. Talk to strangers."

First, I went around the park: nobody, nothing. I ran, pushing the buggy, then jumped on. I said, for no reason—but is there ever a reason?—"Wheee!" I followed one of the trails down to the fountain.

I shoved the buggy away, to see it spin. It rolled coarsely along, hit the bench where an old man was sitting. Who thumped from his soft paper bag, with hateful vigor, a dry boiled peanut at me.

I raspberried him.

He stood, folded shut his bag, tottered malevolently away.

I hopped up onto the rim of the fountain, ran around it, arms out: airplane. I made noises, until this got boring. I stopped, on tiptoes, brimmed my eyes with my flat hand, as Columbus sighting America.

There, stopped at the light on the corner, was a flesh-tone LTD, with a shallow shimmering-in-the-sun dent in its hood. I waved. Beautiful.

After that, a gray Volkswagen, bulbous as a full tick: Mother's.

Out of her rolled-down window came one straining elbow, the top of her face. "Jamie?" Strident relief to her, I don't know what to me. She honked her horn, flicked on and off her headlamps, revved her sputtering engine. The LTD, and the stop signal, impassive, remained.

How dare she? Because she didn't belong here, in this new world of mine. I'd expected her to have the decency to not exist. But of course not. She was worried. Everybody knew about the park. Of course this was where she'd come looking for me. How long had she been here?

I set my nose in the sky. I got my buggy. I marched, pushing it before me, to the opposite corner of the park, crossed the street there, just in time to have her cruise along beside me.

She was saying things. Where in the hell had I been? Or, She's sorry. Or, She misses me. Or, Get in this car this very instant, young man.

Or just my name. I don't remember. I didn't turn my head. I didn't hear.

At the next intersection, she pulled in to block me.

I went calmly around behind her. I was whistling. "Dixie."

Then she jumped out of the car. I swung the cart around, as a weapon, but it was too slow to hurt her. And why did I want to?

She had nothing, nothing, to do with me, now.

We watched each other above the buggy, no man's land. Her hands shut, then opened, at her sides. Her face: more flat than I remembered, like watching television sideways.

We didn't say anything.

She was breathing, like at the end of a marathon. I was breathing like nothing. I was hurting in my face.

She said, "I've been worried. Sick."

"I'm fine."

She nodded, a first-grader trying to memorize a difficult new vocabulary word: "Fine."

I said, "I'm fine. I'm sorry. I'm fine."

"Do you need money? My purse. Let me get my purse?" She leveled one hand at me, to keep me still.

I said, and it scared me, I never called her this, not since I was three years old had I called her: "Mama."

68

She didn't hear, though. She wedged her purse under one brisk elbow, tried to feel around inside it with both hands at the same time. Cigarettes, from their pack, fell. Then the pack. A pencil. A hairbrush. A Valium bottle, open, spilt, on the street. "Here. Ten dollars. It's all I have right now, but if you'll—"

I stretched one smooth hand over the buggy, snapped it away from her. To make her feel better. Why not?

Then the buggy—and me riding it—made a sudden, jarring break down the hill. I jumped off at the store, left it there sideways at the entrance, ran inside, stood by the window. My palms on the soda cooler. My teeth deep in my lower lip.

But she didn't follow.

But this would be a good place to be, if she came after me here: Barney knew.

But she never came, she didn't follow, I'd never see her again, I imagined. She didn't exist.

Barney slammed his hand down on the newspaper on the counter, left it there.

One quarter-second after, I jumped.

He pressed, hard, twice with a grimace, once with a smile. Then he slid dry fingers outward, with finality. A flattened cockroach fell onto the floor, straightened itself, ran staggering zigzag away.

"Whazzup?" said Barney, to me, with disinterest.

He folded the paper over two index fingers, then wadded, tossed it over his shoulder slam-dunk into the garbage can.

"Where's the Wheat Thins? Where's the Bufferin?"

I left the ten-dollar bill on the counter when he wasn't looking, to thank him for the safe place to be, and to make up for Keller's joke before, and to get, just get it away from me, I was crying. I shoved the door open. It hit the buggy, which went rolling slowly.

Barney said, "Hey!" He came to stand one half-step outside, held the ten as to throw it to me underhand, "Hey?"

I ran, with bright white bloodless fists, open mouth, mean, watery eyes. I was on the other side of the street already. Barney scratched his forehead in my direction. I waved. Then I was over the hill, and was gone.

The buggy, tinkling, rumbled all the way across the parking lot.

I skirted the park this time, went four blocks out of my way. Even so, I looked to the left, I looked quickly to the right, before ducking in the back door. I took a couple steps into the kitchen, then shuddered: close call. She might have taken me back. I might have allowed her to.

Thomas, bent over the table, stared down the barrel of a screwdriver at a rusty upside-down prehistoric fondue pot. I rattled my paper bag, a question. Without turning from his work, "In the living room."

Something small slipped from under his screwdriver, his gaze, tinked twelve times across the floor, into the corner. "Damn damn damn damn. And drat," said Thomas, turning sudden stares, respectively, to the fondue pot, his one hand and the other, the table, the floor, the corner. "Help me find it," he said. He held thumbprint and forefinger before squinting eyes, "About this big."

But I sidestepped to the front-room door. "Keller has a headache. I think." I lifted the Bufferin from my bag: mission of mercy.

He had already turned toward the corner, though, away from me, down on his knees and his feely, skimming fingers.

"Be careful," he said. "There's a drag queen in there. With some paraplegic invisible pussy."

I said, "Um. Okay." I said, *"What?"*

"Ha!" He picked at what was on the floor, pinched it up, held it in the air, too small to see.

"You found it?"

"No. Just somebody's earring." He turned, slid back against the cabinet, sat, smiled, "Looks like one I would have worn, in the old days."

I stepped over, he put it in my hand: one brass dirty faceted stud.

"I was a poet. I was a drifter. I was a pirate." He framed

me between the thumb-and-index tendons of both hands. "You'd make a good pirate."

Keller stood on one foot on the coffee table: tubby, straining flamingo. He held toward the light fixture, melodramatically, a paper streamer in one hand, Scotch tape in the other. Helplessness. Poise. "Oh? Fudge!" he said to his guest, who leaned more deeply into the divan with a smirk, lifted thinly noncommittal shoulders. Keller threw the streamer and Scotch tape directly down onto the table. They righted themselves, from the force. "I guess we'll just wait for Mildred. I told you about Mildred?"

The guest: dim, blue-veined, balding, two rough spots of rouge on acne-pitted cheeks, black velvet bell-bottoms with aluminum half-moons stitched along the hem. And a peroxide shock of wiglike hairdo. He crossed his knees, jiggled the curling, painted toenails of one sandalled foot my way.

"Oh," screamed Keller, "you have returned at last."

He put his other foot down, fell off the table, onto his toes, into the couch. "Whoosh. Not so young as we used to be."

He sat up, clapped commandingly. "Mildred? This is Bonanza Butt. And this" —he waved a distracted, extravagant hand toward a Victorian baby carriage by the window— "is Hell Thing."

I went to see. It was empty.

"I know," Keller said, commiseration, "I know. Isn't it sad?"

I said, "Yes. Sad. But what? There's nothing here."

"Of. Course! There! Is!" A warning: play the game. "Poor thing. Bonanza found it in the Dempsey Dumpster outside of an artsy porno theater in Atlanta. One of our road trips. How many years ago?" He turned to Bonanza, a distraction, whispered to me from the side of his mouth. "It's a legless cat. Pretend to see."

Bonanza secreted a cold moan. "I'm in love." He snapped up, pulled me away, backward, by the shoulders. "Little lamb," he said, "who made thee? May I fuck thee up thine ass?" We fell together into the divan, me in his bony, hurtful lap. He wrapped his whiplike legs tight about mine, set his narrow hands on my knees, slid them half an inch closer, half an inch more.

I tried to sit forward, act normal. Did Keller mean for this to happen? Maybe that was what the party was for. All these nattering drag queens, they would share me, or something.

I tossed the bag at the coffee table. "Wheat Thins," I pleaded. "Aspirin."

"Really," said Keller, past me, wearing passive, angry tiny eyes. "Such a display. Keep! Your hands off my goods."

I said, "I saw my mother."

"Oh, Donna— I mean, Helen. You always get the pick of the litter. 'S just not fair."

"I saw my mother."

Bonanza had his hand deep in my lap now, and my hard, despite me, clicked on. I squirmed, to keep him from finding it, but he thought I was pleased. He bit my earlobe, ran his other hand up my belly, to my chest.

Finally, I pulled away, stood. What if Thomas walked in?

And there was my hard-on, tent pole inside the soft shorts. They both stared, wearing exactly the same expression: open mouth, flared nostrils, squinty eyes. Keller as if offended. Bonanza mock-victorious.

"You saw your mother," said Keller, casually, monotone, as if I saw her every day. "And—?"

I shrugged. "And she gave me ten dollars."

Keller thrust his head back into the couch, "Hoo hoo hoo." He said, "I *am* overcome."

Bonanza, to sweeten me: "I just love a family man. A man who loves his mama."

"Gawd," said Keller. "Why? Do I surround myself? With tired, untrustworthy queens?" And, to me, clamping and unclamping clumsy fingers in the direction of the aspirin, "Gimme, gimme."

Then I put up the streamers, four strips, from the light fixture to each corner of the room. Keller said it wasn't good enough. He said to twist them. Then he flapped his gossipy hand in the air, turned to Bonanza, and had forgotten about me.

So I didn't bother, I went to the kitchen.

Thomas shut his eyes, to lean over the steaming pot of tea. He'd punched the earring into his lobe, where the hole had once been. He blew on a wet wooden spoon.

I sat on the counter beside him, swung my legs to and fro. I slapped my knees, to show I would speak.

"My mother didn't really kick me out of the house. She was going out of her way to be nice. I couldn't stand that."

I reached fingers to Thomas's lobe, touched it, slippery blood. I rubbed thumb and forefinger together before my nose.

Thomas didn't say anything, kept looking at his blood on my fingerprints.

He held the spoon to my dry, shut lips.

"Is this sweet enough?" he said. "Is this too sweet?"

I pulled back my head, and without tasting, "Perfect. It's good." I wiped my salty-tasting fingers across my face.

"So you kicked yourself out of the house?" He tossed the empty pot upside down atop the sink, then came over to put slow hands on my knees.

"Sort of. Yeah."

"Don't worry about it. I can keep a secret." He winked at me, boxed my shoulder. "Besides, what's the difference? Got kicked out—didn't get kicked out. I don't think anybody cares."

He wiped my lips with the backs of his loose knuckles.

Then, in a quiet, pleased, wondering way, "You were really worried, weren't you?" He chucked my chin, left his fingers there. He said, for no reason, just to get me to look up, "Okay?"

I pulled back, to bring him in closer. "Okay." I set my hands to the sides of his neck. The skin above his collar: old scar tissue, a dried powdery wrinkling tomato in the sun. He stretched his neck, jerked it *pop pop*.

Keller tiptoed into the kitchen, a sly show of being afraid to interrupt. "Mildred? I've some friends I want you to meet."

He turned back out the door, waved a broad coast-is-clear.

Thomas turned to the wall, abashedly, brushing his hands down his trousers. He stood there, watching the oven door, though the chicken and dumplings were done already. Just in there, warming: nothing to watch. He put his weight on one foot, on the other, as five queens, mostly older than Keller, walked a single-file circle from the door around the room.

They slowed once, with interest, where I was, then again, and more carefully, past Thomas.

They looked raggedy and splendid. Failed pageant contestants on final parade, averted eyes, improbable brows in the air, lips tight against their teeth. They settled, standing, about the kitchen table, hands perched on the backs of what were obviously their customary chairs. None of them was really in drag. Women's-cut blue jeans, Secret deodorant smell, Virginia Slims, things like that.

Keller handed me an apron printed with train engines and wagon wheels. I tied it on, wiped my hands on it, smiled, to show I was mad. I held the cloth in two hands toward Keller, as to say, What is this? I looked to Thomas, for help, but he was gone.

Keller stood, preening, at what became, by virtue of his being there, the head of the table. He allowed a weak, reluctant wave to his left. "This is your Great-Aunt La Gioconda."

La Gioconda ran a tongue inside his mouth around shut, puckered lips, but slowly.

Keller laughed. Then, clockwise around the table, "Your Great Aunt Retha Madness," a large man who shut his round cow-eyes, to show awe, consternation, at his name. "And your third cousin twice removed on your gramma's side, Wisteria Mercedes Magdalene. Also Scary Alice, her evil twin." They smiled: politesse, cattiness. Keller clucked. "And of course, Miss Lola Blow—" a stunning gazelle of a black man, who lowered yellow eye-shadow-colored lids, fingered shyly his fork. "And you've met," in a derisory tone, "our Bonanza."

Bonanza flared his nostrils.

Keller laughed loud, then said, hands open in my direction, Vanna White, "Our new houseboy. Mildred Piece."

74

Grand finale.

They snapped open or shut their eyes, to smile at me together, at once. I stepped behind Keller, but he betrayed me, went to get the dumplings.

"Charmed, I'm sure," said Retha, in a voice two octaves lower than I had expected. He clapped my hand in his talcum-slippery two. He bit his lower lip with sharp canines, a smile. "Good help is so hard to find these days." He said, "Do you know how to fist-fuck?"

Everybody laughed, tilted this or that way, to show reluctance, awkwardness, irony. The drag queen, it seemed, displayed his attitude in angles. The collective attitude, just then, seemed to be: indulge us.

Even so, my face burned. I pulled away my hand, wiped it on the apron. I poured the tea with hateful care, then stood behind Keller, at attention, for the rest of the meal. They didn't speak of or directly to me again. But everything they did was with me in mind.

For example: "Let us say grace," said Keller.

They bowed their heads, and said, together, with no pause, sweetly, "Grace."

Later I leaned that usually everybody laughed when Keller made the suggestion, nobody bothered on the follow-through, like the prisoners in that old vaudeville story, who have heard every joke in the world, and so many times, over and over again, that they tell them by number. "Thirty!" somebody yells, and everybody laughs but the new con and the guards.

But these queens were meaning to be nice. See our cleverness, they were telling me. We will slow ourselves down, just for now, to show you.

But I didn't care. I slouched against the counter, lit a cigarette. Keller snapped his fingers above his head, pointed to La Gioconda's empty glass: more tea.

"And then, she said!" whispered a scandalized Wisteria Mercedes Magdalene.

"But wait. This *is* the best part," said Bonanza, who clapped hollow palms together, silently, in anticipation, and to show that he already knew the story.

75

Alice reared back, three scattered fingertips to his throat, as if elegantly choking, "Can you believe it. Can you just see it."

"Brazen thing, she always was." Retha slapped his fork on the table, to show final judgement.

"And then," went on Wisteria, "she said—now listen—said."

And they all waited to hear. And I was waiting to hear, I don't know what, I don't know why. Wisteria, the moment's mistress, took a deep bewildered breath. As if that said it all.

"Draw it out, honey," said Keller, as to Billie Holiday on stage. He pressed Wisteria's wrist across the table with his supportive two hands. "I love the way you sling that story. You'd think we'd none of us heard it a dozen times before."

This went on.

Then Keller began, in a strange, guttural, urgent tone, "Donna-May Dean was a drag queen, but aren't they all, who—"

Then he stopped. And flashed up his eyes, much, much darker than they should have been. He was laughing.

The queens, as if scared of him, punched napkin corners, one-two, against the sides of their smiles. They stepped out of the kitchen, tittering, leaving behind dirty dishes on the table, purses slung over chair backs, dull lipstick smears on forks and napkins and cigarette butts.

Keller saw me looking at him. He shut his eyes, shuddered, opened them, himself again. He stood, clapped his hands above his head, left them fluttering in the air. "Very well," he announced, as if anyone were left to hear, "let the disco portion of the evening! Begin!"

Then he left me there, to clean up, I guessed. That was why the apron. So I sat, finished my cigarette, had another. I ate some of the food, but I wasn't hungry. The tea tasted funky of a sudden, but good enough all the same. I kept on and kept on drinking it.

"What's wrong?" said Thomas.

Because I was doing dishes too briskly, tossing wet silverware, hard, into the drawer, sloping my cigarette from my

76

lips at an angry angle. They hadn't even been eating. They'd put food on their plates just to put cigarettes out in it.

Thomas said, "They dance now." Just like that. Like the title of a poem.

"Houseboy! What's a houseboy? Who made me houseboy? And what's it mean? Butler? Maid? Butt servant?"

Thomas, his hands flat and comforting on my ribs, led me toward the common room. "Come dance with me."

I stopped at the door. I was holding a rubber spatula in one hand, a sponge in the other. He goosed my butt. He pulled me backwards, forearms tight around my collarbone, scrubbed his knuckles across my scalp. I giggled. Still, I stood there.

"Come on. Relax. You're not a houseboy. Keller was just showing off. He read that in a novel or something."

"What kind of a party is this, anyway? They're all so old." Then I said, "I didn't mean—"

I touched his shoulder, an apology. Which made it worse. But he just laughed.

"I know," he said. "Aren't they ill?" Meaning, disgusting. (We don't use that word that way anymore: ill.) He said, "The boys will get here later. The rest of the party starts in stages. Keller staggers his invitations by age-group and beauty. You'll see."

We watched them awhile. They weren't disgusting, just flaccid, just happy. They were gentle, they were dancing. But they hardly moved: shut eyes, serious smiles, vague, shifting, affectionate couples. They had been doing this, they had been dancing, you got the feeling, a good, long time.

La Gioconda lifted his arms akimbo into the air, to frame his profile. Lola made a shy joke into Retha's ear, who looked at the ceiling as he turned, to indicate cynicism and appreciation. He passed it on to Alice, who stopped, pressed a distressed hand to his forehead, left the room, came back holding a folded Kleenex to the side of his eye. "Oh, Mary!" he said, a thrilled and fed-up drone. Meaning, all of them. Meaning us all. I felt myself about to give in, but held back.

I turned to look at Thomas. "Disgusting," I said.

Wisteria, just off the backbeat, jerked his elbows. Then he stopped. He pointed a sudden finger, "You're the only one for me!" A threat. But it was directed over his shoulder, and across the room, more or less toward the umbrella vase, and he wasn't even looking at me.

Thomas tugged me by both hands out there.

The queens made an oblique, reluctant space around us.

Keller told me later he had never seen Thomas dance, not in fourteen years or so together. "Wasn't it beautiful?" he wanted to know.

And there was a sort of rough, embarrassed beauty to his dancing. He swung stiff arms from side to side, brought his brows low, smiled, opened his mouth, bounced a little at the knees.

"Get it," somebody said, "—girlfriend."

Which made him happy, made him bounce more deeply.

I didn't understand. I thought he didn't like them, I thought he didn't want to be like that. But there he was.

I pretended to be a less good dancer than I could have been, for Thomas's sake. I made circles in the air with my fists between us.

Thomas touched me at both elbows, to pull me closer, or hold me exactly where I was.

Gioconda put a slow squeeze on my shoulder, meaning nothing. Wisteria pinched my ass, to make me feel welcome. Bonanza hit the lights, but it didn't get dark. Just gray, just a little flatter in the room.

Keller cleared his throat. "Mildred," he said, "get the door. Please."

First I took off the apron.

It was two thin men, with matching black horseshoe mustaches, bomber jackets. Between them, an abashed Doberman. "I'm Cole," said the one with the leash, who put it in his other hand to shake mine. "This is Randy, and Topman, my dog and my lover, but not respectively."

Topman lunged against the studded red-leather leash toward the foyer, where Keller had wheeled Hell Thing's carriage.

I didn't say anything, just smiled, patted my thighs.

"Where's the party?" said Cole, as he suffered himself to be pulled inside. Randy, after a while looking at me, clicked the heels of his hiking boots, stepped on past.

"I'm Jamie," I said.

Topman nosed each urgent inch of the carriage, from the wheels to the tiny flat lace-fringed pillow inside. Cole leaned back, from the waist, as if to appraise a problematic, marvelous child. "Hell Thing, indeed. One of my favorite pussies."

"The party's in there," I said, waved a hand. "Follow the Yellow Brick Road." But of course, they knew that. There was the music. There was the hooting. And they had probably been here before. I said, "There is no Hell Thing."

Randy and Cole both blinked, smiled, moved on toward the common room. Topman followed on awkward, clittering nails. "Don't listen to her," Randy was saying. He made small pats on his lover's back. "Some people will say just anything, if it's scandalous enough." Cole's nose was well in the air by now, he already wasn't studying me.

I turned to shut the door, didn't.

"Who are you? Is this the party?" demanded a man with drunken Yankee suddenness, two blackened puffy blue eyes. He flourished short butch fingers at me: a diamond ring, brass knuckles, one bitten thumbnail. With the other hand, he grabbed his crotch, pulled up, then down, then shook. "You bottom? You like to get fucked?" He narrowed his eyes, to accuse me. "Who you belong to? Anybody here like to get fucked?" He jerked left and right, glaring past my shoulders.

I laughed. I shrugged. "Sure." Meaning, Somebody here likes to get fucked. Or, me.

"Yeah, yeah." He lit a used cigarette butt, touched the brim of his felt hat, shoved past. "Where's the goddam sissies, anyway?" He held his hands high and wide before him, as to throw open invisible doors. "It's supposed to be sissies around."

Then he was out of my sight: squeals of recognition.

"Don't call me that. That's not my scene tonight. Tonight, I'm butch."

Keller's voice, "Oh, Miss Monster! Just, please! You'll always be Cookie to me."

Then I just left the door open, went to sit on the front porch, over to the side, mostly in shadow.

Mother told me later that she saw me there, that she was, even then, driving around the block, too nervous to come and get me.

But I wasn't watching the road, I was watching the flower beds over my shoulder beneath me, outlined in circles of half-bricks, cinder stones, rusty tin cans. Soft, powdery, these flower beds, and empty, and black. If I stood there, I'd sink. I could put one foot in one, the other in the other, and stand there.

That was a silly thing to be thinking.

I could stand on my hands there, grit and grubs between my fingers. Except that I had never stood on my hands in my life. And my hands were tingling, just now.

I looked left and right, then again, more quickly, because that was all at once fun.

(Later I found out that Keller had spiked the sweet tea with leftover gin. "I mean, I had mixed the punch according to the Phillips family recipe, and there was this much left in the bottle—" He held out two straight fingers and a crooked half. "What's a girl to do?")

Another set of faggots bounced from their car on the curb past me, and into the party. Thomas was right: they got more aromatic, louder, cleaner-cut, as the half-hours clicked on. Some were holding hands now, even a couple in full high drag.

Four or five boys about my age set up a pot-smoking station on the other side of the porch. One of them, with no conviction, as in a foreign language class, said to me, "Hey, Miss Thing." Then he scuffed his feet, shuffled away.

I held my breath until seven more people had gone past, and two others had actually already left. And still no Jimmy.

Mother said she could tell it was a party, that's why she didn't come. She could see the dancing against the bright windows, she said. She stopped at the corner of Confederate and Elm, rolled down her window, to listen. There was a nice wind, she told me. She smelled cigarette smoke, more sweet and strong than her own, mixed with cloves and marijuana. She stayed there, until some other car got behind her, she had to go on. "I heard the music," she said. "All the way down to the river, to the bridge, I kept hearing the music. And somebody screaming. Like there was something happening bad. Or very, very good. That's why I didn't come in."

I might have seen her stop. The taillights dimmed at the corner, flashed off. I thought she was another queer, looking for the party. I started to run over, and say, "This is the party. The party is here."

Maybe I didn't want to move, or meet anybody else. Or I knew it was her all along. Or I never saw anything, imagined it later, after she told me.

But I do remember the screaming. That was why I went back inside. It was the brass-knuckle Yankee, Cookie, who had already lost his hard-pressed butch attitude, and was borrowing everybody else's clothes: weak, indulgent protests, eyes snapped past him across the room. "There she goes again," said somebody.

"I'm beautiful, I'm ripped," he screamed, his gravelly falsetto breaking low and painful on certain syllables, like Bette Davis, or laryngitis. "I'm too fucking much. The world the world."

He pressed half a dozen other people's skirts to his body, jumped up onto the coffee table. And was aghast, when he made gestures, to see the skirts fall. Eventually he tore my streamers from the light fixture, tugged them hard until they whipped loose of the corners, held them in his hands while he turned, and, lifting his arms and lowering them, turned. He fell dizzy drunk to the floor, stayed curled beside the couch, still screaming. Genteel applause. Those on the couch set their feet lightly upon him.

(The queen screams for herself, Keller once told me. Anybody who hears is incidental. Anybody else is always incidental. "But Cookie wasn't a queen," I said. And Keller, with a swoop of his lifted finger downward, "But aren't we *all*." Hard stress on the *all*. To show me, that for this once, he meant more than just faggots.)

81

But I wasn't thinking about Cookie, just then. I was thinking about my cigarettes: where had I left them? I was smoking too much in those days. It was important to me.

I might have gone back to the porch, to join the pot-smoker crowd, surely they'd have an extra plain-old Camel floating somewhere among them. But this party wasn't for me, despite what Keller said. And this wasn't the park, I didn't yet know how to be brazen here.

I went back to the kitchen, the long way, through Keller and Thomas's bedroom, to avoid the party. But my cigarettes were gone from the table, or I hadn't left them there.

Going back through the bedroom, I noticed the bottom dresser drawer was open, slick Technicolor magazines spilling from it, women's bodies on the covers. I got on my knees, slid my fingers through them. Why women?

Then Keller came in, with a quiet young man in tow, maybe the one who had mumbled "Miss Thing" at me on the porch. All at once, I recognized him: Richard Languster, who had sat beside me in algebra class last year. He'd make spit wads, never thump them, just line them in even rows on his desk, to dry. Then, one at a time, he'd put them back in his mouth, stare straight ahead with wild, nice, but slightly crossed eyes. His full lips. His pouty chewing. I hadn't recognized him right away for the queerness, the same queerness as mine, a new way to stand and be seen and be here on this earth.

I'd always thought he was cute. I'd always thought he wasn't tough enough. He had a John-Boy Walton face, the eyebrows and the mole.

I said, "Oh. Hey."

Keller: "Ahem."

"Just leaving." I stood.

Richard sort of nodded, then kicked his foot backwards, to hit the wall, but not hard. He was more embarrassed to see me here than I was to have him see me. I laughed, low in my throat, to show the power I felt. "Richard," I said, with Keller's most slow and bitchy voice, as if seeing him for the first time here. "Fancy meeting you."

"You know each other? How nice. How perfectly quaint.

Now, go and see how the punch is holding up. Check the fondue, if it's sludgy enough." Keller led me by the elbow out of the room, locked the door behind me. "You must," he was saying to Richard, "you simply must. Here. Try this on for size."

So: there was the party again, right in my way, I couldn't go back to the porch. There were the queens, there were the trade just beginning to arrive—mostly poor-looking, younger, silent. There were others, too. College boys, their Izods and Topsiders and little round Japanese glasses. A couple fat straight girls. Also, there was me. But mostly it was just queens, and the trade, an easy, palpable tension and a camaraderie of need. They were the show. They were what you saw.

Somebody opened the windows onto the flat black outside. Trade took off their shirts. Queens raised lustful offended eyebrows, fanned themselves—their lifted throats—with weak stiff hands. There was still no wind, not enough.

"Drag time," screamed somebody.

All at once, the dancing ended. The older queens settled in around the stereo. They stacked and unstacked albums, touched the covers with all five fingers, as if reverently.

"Ooh," said Wisteria, "I think I'll do Rosemary Clooney. 'Come On-A My House.'"

Alice countered, "But, bitch. That's my song. Has been since the Civil War."

"You mean," said Wisteria, all ice and collarbone, "the War of the Northern Aggression?"

The trade shrugged and flexed, hunkered near the windows, waiting for this art and nonsense to end, business to begin.

I sat on the couch, pulled my elbows in, smiled when smiled at, or not. I bit my thumb, looked at the teeth marks, bit it again. Something to do.

Gioconda broke fussily away from the controversy at the phonograph, came to sit beside me, then scooted much closer, slowly. Why was I so uncomfortable? he wanted to know. He held my thigh with long, dry fingers. "Let's do the nasty. I can pay if you like."

Thomas leaned over the back of the couch, bit my neck. "Leave the kid alone," he told Gioconda. "This one's mine."

Gioconda grimaced, twisted the end of an imaginary mustache. "Curses. Foiled again." He slapped my knee, meaning, Just friends. He slipped from the couch, and across the room. At the card table, where some well-built boys, future queens, were dipping fondue, he stopped, leaned on one languorous, demanding hand. "Let's bump uglies," he said to one of them, or to them all.

"Thanks for the save," I said.

Thomas fell face first over the couch, into my lap. I had never seen him so loose. "I'm serious," he said. "You're the only one for me."

But I was watching the door. What if Jimmy were to come in now, see me like this, Thomas in my lap? As far as I was concerned, and suddenly, Jimmy was the love of my life.

"Hey, hey," said Thomas. He sat up, tousled his own hair affectionately. "Why the long face? I'm not so old and ugly as all that, am I?"

I said, "Yes." But not like I meant it. "What's the deal with you and Keller, anyway?"

"What do you mean, the deal?" He leaned into the armrest pillows, put his feet into my lap, yelled at somebody above and behind him to play some kind of music, anything.

The queens turned as one, to demonstrate epitome-perfect nonplussed expressions.

Thomas said, "They're just not used to me like this. I might have had too much to drink."

Cookie Monster shifted and grumbled beneath my feet. Topman came over, to sniff, turn, settle in against him.

"How do you think of me? What am I to you?" I said to Thomas. "Am I a queen? Or trade? Or what?" I flicked my fingers toward the rest of the party, away from us.

"Why do you have to be either?" Then, to comfort me, "Keller says you'll make a good queen some day." After a short silence, "Maybe you'll end up just like me."

"And what are you?"

"Shhh." He leaned up, giggling, to tell me. "A pirate, still. I don't know. I think I might be straight. I've been imagining meeting this girl. Red hair, Heidi braids and all that." Then he leaned back, giggling like a sissy. "I'm so ashamed. You won't tell on me?"

This was, of course, too much. I said, "I thought—"

"That you were the only one for me?"

That wasn't what I was going to say. But I said nothing.

He went on, "I'm sorry. I wanted to make you feel better, you looked so sad. Besides, I could still get it up for you if you talk me into it. If you want it bad enough."

I started to stand, and frown, and lift my head, walk away: Barbara Stanwyck. But there was nowhere to go. And Thomas got his elbow and arm around me, pulled me to his side of the couch, pulled me tighter.

Then Jimmy came up, holding arms with a tattooed and balding and hairy leatherman: the first I had ever seen outside of porno magazines.

"This is my lover, Burt," Jimmy said, with a look that meant, Be cool. "He's in from Atlanta."

Burt had a wide brass ring in his nostril. He snapped shut his teeth—sharp, smart—twice, to show them, or to show sociability.

But I wasn't bothered. Maybe I thought I could steal Jimmy away from this guy, if I had to. He *did* have traces of ringworm. Maybe I was relieved. I had too much to think about already. Maybe I already knew, had known all along that Jimmy was nothing to me, was pretty much bullshit.

Thomas held out a flat hand. "Thomas Weaver. Pleased to meetcha."

It made me happy, to see this aggression again, to be on the safe side of it after just one day.

Burt didn't even notice. "Hidey," he said, "—doo." He looked at me with his twinkling eyes behind dark glasses. "And, Keller. I've heard so much about you." He took my hand in his studied, overbutch one, held it there. "You're younger than I expected. And much prettier."

I didn't say anything. Thomas just laughed. Jimmy didn't bother to tell him, either. They sat beside us.

"I was kidding," said Thomas, to me, "about what I said. About what I might be."

But I didn't believe him. I didn't believe that he was straight. And I didn't believe he was kidding when he said it. There was something else going on. I didn't want to know. I shut him out of my mind, snuggled in, closer, coolly.

"Kidding about what?" Burt wanted to know. "What might you be?"

Thomas said something friendly and dismissive, I don't remember what: not the truth, though. Burt didn't listen, anyway. He had his hand in Jimmy's lap, he'd flip it over, then back. As to warm it. After a while, he pulled Jimmy's cock out of the fly, said that if anybody wanted some of this slave meat, they were welcome.

It sloped, doughlike and thick, blue-streaked, away from me.

Jimmy looked embarrassed and happy above it.

Gioconda, from his side of the room, perked up. But Thomas glowered black sparks his way. We were our own party now.

Everybody was watching me.

"Slave meat?" said Jimmy, to me, "That's just a phrase. It doesn't mean anything." Then, to Burt, "He's new to all this. Don't want to freak him out, you know."

Burt said, to me, past Jimmy, past Thomas, "You know you want it. Go for it, Keller. Go for it, pretty."

I said, "I'm not Keller. I'm not pretty. I'm just the houseboy."

Thomas flopped his head back into the couch. "Jesus," he whispered. "Yes, you are. Pretty, I mean." He touched the back of his hand to my cheek, but shut his eyes. Was he thinking of how I reminded him of himself, or Keller? Was he thinking of girls? This didn't make me happy. Maybe it would have, before, at the park. If he had just wanted a blowjob. If I didn't know his name.

Then Wisteria walked to the center of the room, clapped

his hands, held them high, to announce the start of the show.

"A drag show? I can't stand this shit," said Burt. Still, he sat there. He spread his knees wider. He covered Jimmy's cock with one cupped hand, to take back his generous offer, I guess. To show disappointment.

"Don't feel bad, Pooky-Monster. It's not that they don't appreciate your gesture," Jimmy whispered. "It's just, they've all had me. That's all."

"I haven't," I said.

Jimmy looked at me with friendliness and surprise and reproach: "Don't you remember? In the bathroom at the park? You stepped on my foot after I came, you were standing up, you were nervous, and kept apologizing at me until I was already out the door. I didn't say one word. Because I could tell that's how you wanted it."

"Oh. My God." I was laughing. "I thought you were straight. I like to suck straight guys sometimes." Thomas pinched my ass, smiled: we have a secret. I said, "I *used* to like to suck straight guys sometimes." Because all at once, it seemed ugly and wrong. Because Burt bared his teeth, lifted his nostrils, laughed loud for a long time.

"Peo-ple! Excuse me!" commanded Wisteria. "Keller has informed me that tonight will be amateur night." He cast a glance at his compatriots by the turntable, who made mock grumbles, threw their hands in the air, as to say, "Hopeless!"

Wisteria—his *ahem,* his hands fluttering from shoulder height down, firmly—made a show of regaining his composure. Then, "Please welcome, in her first appearance anywhere, our *very* own! Miss! Roxy! Longing!"

Then, nothing.

Wisteria went to stick his head in the kitchen door, came back wearing a frazzled, deliberate, apologetic face. "Well. She's having a little trouble with the pumps, poor thing. We've all been there."

"Keller says there's no such thing as a straight man," Jimmy said. "Keller says anybody can be straight if you want him to pretend to be."

"Keller says, Keller says. Why do you kids fall for all his crap?" Thomas took a cigarette from the coffee table bouquet, attached it to his bottom lip.

"But you do love him," I said.

"Yes-yes-yes," he said, busily, as if he didn't mean it. Then, as if he did, "But I love him."

Burt lit Thomas's cigarette with a quick one-handed match. Jimmy tucked his cock back in, buttoned up, patted himself, all settled. He said, for no reason, *"Now."*

Wisteria, again: "Miss Roxy Longing!"

From the kitchen, high-heeled stumbling sounds. "I look silly. I feel bad. Keller, I just can't do it."

Then, Keller: "Oops."

In the common room, murmuring laughter of trade, queen's catcalls.

"Poor guy," said Jimmy, "they've been pressuring him to do this since he came out, two months ago." He added, slapping down his hand on Burt's, "It's sick to watch." But he was watching. "It's really hard to do, though. Drag. An art form."

I said, "Did you ever?"

He shot a look sideways, meaning, Yes. And to remind me that Burt was here. "Hasn't everybody?" he said.

Burt, carefully, didn't notice.

"Shut up," came Keller's voice. "Chin high. Shoulders back. Of course you can."

It was Richard, with big white shadowy hair, a shiny blue dress crusted with paste-on stars. He stumbled out, on Bambi legs, then waved his cardboard magic wand. He smiled, a nervous glance to Wisteria, there was no music. He stood there. They'd covered his John-Boy beauty mark with a star, too: blue, upside down, sparkling.

He smiled again.

Keller's arm from the kitchen shoved him one more step toward the center of the room. Then pointed a crooked finger at me: you're next.

Richard lifted his hand on a bent arm, brought it, full circle, down. As in Martha Graham. He straightened himself.

I wanted to leave the room, for his sake, because you could tell he liked it. His intense awkward naiveté. You could tell that this, despite his protests, was exactly how he had always wanted to be seen. Because he was shaking, he was lovely.

Wisteria remembered, and ran to the stereo, initiated some sluggish backbeat. Richard—Roxy—turned, lifted another hand, arched his back, to pretend to strain to hit a high note. "I Know I'm Losing You." Somebody tee-heed. Somebody screamed.

Then Richard went dancing, on the twisted sides of his pumps. But that didn't matter, he had the look in his hot, crossed eyes. Queens were wagging dollar bills at him. Even the trade, a dozen Wolfmen Jack, howled, lined up to pinch his toilet-paper tits.

He shimmied, he slunk, he was slinging. The dollar bills he held away from him, in tight fists, then let fall.

I went to the kitchen. I said, "No way."

Keller, smoking a cigarette aggressively at me from across the kitchen table, with an exhausted look, "Yes, way."

He tossed me a dress. Then, one at a time, with force, two red high-heeled pumps. Just like the one I had found in my room. Donna-May Dean's.

"I've been bragging about you. And now you want to embarrass me."

"What about me? Being embarrassed?"

"You're young, you'll get over it. Besides, it's your party. You can cry, if you want to."

"You said it wasn't," I mumbled. The dress, slippery soft in my hands, wadded with the pumps.

"Thomas picked it out," he said. "He's got his heart set on seeing you in it." Then, a change of tack, "It was Donna-May Dean's favorite dress."

I sat at the table, beside him, legs apart, dress spilling toward the floor between them. I looked at it there in my hands, but not in a mean way. I let it fall, wavy white against the dark tiles, printed with yellow roses, belted with a frail Naugahyde braid.

Keller said, "Here. Have some more sweet tea."

I said, "Donna-May Dean's? But you said he wore a fur coat and—"

He batted a nervous hand. "Not all the time. Well, maybe. It's hard to remember exactly, you understand. I mean, the fur was lost in the . . . ah . . . accident." Then, with a look at the dress, "No, not Donna-May Dean's, not at all." He stood, walked, skimming a fingertip along the edge of the table, until he came to me. Placed his hand on top of my head, like one of those little Jewish caps, then his other. "You think about that story too much, I'm afraid. It's not even all the way true."

But by now, I was standing, I was frantic, "Where's the wig?" I said. "I'll do it. I want it. Donna-May Dean's."

Wisteria stuck a pinched, giggling, distracted face in the door. "Miss Longing is just about finished unless there's an encore. She broke a heel. Her titties are lost and lumpy. After Richard it's this one. Roxy, I mean, after Roxy." He pointed a vague finger at me. "Right?"

Keller, "She'll be ready."

"Fine-fine-fine. Now, what's your name, darling?"

"Jamie."

"*Are*n't you precious." He flicked a businesslike gaze at Keller.

Keller said, past me, also businesslike, "Mildred Manhood. Mildred Piece. Mildred Juanita Clarice Pooh."

I said, catching on, "No. Call me Donna-May Dean."

I expected horror and scandal. But Wisteria just frowned, cocked an ear. "Ahh. Donna-May Ding? Did you say?"

I said, "Dean."

He said, "Gotcha." And popped a snap in the air at me, and was gone. As if he had never heard that name a hundred times before.

"I have created a monster," said Keller, to his left shoulder. Then, to me, in a tired way, "Come on. There's a mirror in the bedroom." He snatched up the dress, he bit his lower lip. He shut his eyes, let me lead the way.

Just to tease him, because I knew a secret, I pointed to the magazines. *"Penthouse?"*

"Yes," he said, pushing me toward the mirror. "There's a picture of Iggy Pop's dick in that one. Besides—Thomas likes to slum it sometimes. See how the other half lives." He put his arms over my shoulders, to hold the dress before me. To himself, "Belted, or no?"

I said, "The other half. You mean women, or straight people?"

He didn't say anything.

I said, "Do you ever worry about Thomas? Do you know what he's thinking? I mean, all of the time?"

Keller said, "Shut up and get in that dress this instant. So I can see what to do with you. We don't have time for makeup. A litt-le lip-stick may-be." He put some on for himself, sealed it with a tight pucker, smiled. "Thomas? He doesn't think. That's the *point*. He's nothing but a barbershop grin and a perpetual hard-on. Why? Has he been picking on you again?"

I laughed. "No. I think he likes me. I think he thinks I'm pretty. I think he wants to fuck me."

"Oh, I do doubt that indeed," said Keller, still watching his lips in the mirror. "But we can hope, all the same." Then he was watching his eyes. Then he was watching mine.

He capped the lipstick, put it away: "Not your color. Let's see. . . ." Then, "Thomas has to be reminded now and then, of what he really wants. That's what you're here for."

"Then you know about the girls."

"What girls? Ha! He wouldn't know what to do with a cunt if one came up and bit his nose off and spat it at him. He just likes to pretend. And I encourage him to. Because it's shameful, for a man so butch as he is—" Keller turned to face me. "All he likes to do is get fucked." A bitter accusation. "Surprised? So was I. It's been going on forever, for a long time, since I quit doing drag, as a matter of fact. I used to be a drag queen."

"I know."

He wagged a warning finger at me, allowed it to wander, distracted, to his dimple. "I bought him the magazines. To see if that was the problem. To see if that could help him get it up. He never does, you know."

I said, "You said, 'perpetual hard-on.' "

"I was speaking in ideals. It's what he should have, him being who he is and all, walking that butch walk of his. I imagine that if I say it often and loud enough, one day it will come true. That's my magic." Keller dropped his hands. "Come here. You've got it on inside-out."

I tried to help, but he said, "Be still."

He rolled the dress, like a rubber, up me, and off.

"And don't get me wrong," he said, "I love to fuck him. It's just boring after a while. Wrecks hell with my role-playing. He tells me to call him 'Rosebud' or something. He tells me to call him 'Pussy.' And that's a crochet dildo that he wears in his pants. I made it for him, special. Veins and glans and all." He slipped the dress back over my head. "No. Lift up your arms straight."

In the common room, loud applause. Richard was getting an encore, after all.

Then here came Wisteria. "Richard's worried. You won't tell on him at school, will you?"

I held my hands out, to indicate the dress on me. "What would I tell? Just look at me!"

Keller broke between us to apply my lipstick. "Now," he said, as if it were a military operation, "*pucker!*"

"I guess! You're right!" said Wisteria. "All the same, you should reassure him yourself. You know how silly, silly queens are." To Keller, "All your work has paid off. Quite a show, even without good tits. Richard was born to drag."

Keller lifted his nose, to show precision. "You must stop calling her Richard. You must stop calling her him. That one? She's a full-fledged coronated drag queen now." Then, more generally, "And I do know a drag queen when I see one, don't I?"

"Is that what I am?" I said. "Born to drag?"

Keller patted me on the back, commiseration. "Heavens, no. You're my butch daughter. You're the comic relief."

Which made me happy.

Then bothered me.

I looked in the mirror at myself. Keller settled the wig,

reverently, like a crown, down, then screwed it slightly tighter. He stuffed rough wads of toilet paper down my front, but I said, "No." I pulled them out.

"This is me," I said. I kept looking. It was, it was me. "Donna-May Dean."

"Donna-May Dean *fils*," Keller said.

Then we went to see the end of Richard's—Roxy Longing's—performance. "Start spreadin' the news," he pretended to sing.

"She's almost finished," said Keller. "You'll be doing 'Crazy' by Patsy Cline. You know the words?"

"No."

"Good. All the better. That's what a drag queen is for, to fake it."

There was Thomas, giving Jimmy a blowjob. Burt held the back of Thomas's neck, and shoved and shoved, as the final set of backbeats kicked, and Roxy tried to match them: bump-bump bumpadump bump bump bumpadump *dump*. On this note, the last, Roxy stomped too hard on his one remaining heel. It broke free and skittered, spinning across the floor.

Also on the same note, Burt held Thomas's head down hard, Jimmy made what must have been his I'm-coming-now squirm. Gioconda, from somewhere dark, blew a kiss to me, then wiggled the fingers: Hi, sailor.

"And now," screamed Wisteria, striding forward as Roxy backed off, "I'm pleased to introduce you to our very special guest. Put your hands together to welcome: Miss! Donna-May Dean!"

Thomas, with open mouth and narrowed eyes, sprang from Jimmy's lap. Jimmy shot accidental come all over Thomas's chin and throat. "Sorry," Burt said, then reached over with a paper napkin. "Let me get that."

Thomas waved him away, hunkered forward to me more intensely, with a haggard, bewildered expression.

I was awkward on my heels. I was smiling. Everybody stared. The dress moved air beneath my crotch. I'd never felt so open to the world before: this was more than naked. I held out my hands, then looked at them. As if to show everyone:

nothing in them. I walked a wide circle around the room. Then the music started and I couldn't think of anything to do. I swayed. I blew thin kisses through my lipstick, at no one in particular. I felt like somebody's ugly date at the prom, who has been left alone to dance by herself. I beckoned Thomas, subtly, with a quick wave, to my side.

"Crazy," sang Thomas, as he stepped, two full beats faster than Patsy. "Crazy for feel-ing"— he stopped, leaned back, made fists on the high note *feel,* then walking again, smoothly, lower—"so blue."

He grabbed my hands, twisted them together tight behind my back, leaned over me, bony, gentle, dancing.

I looked up at him.

We stepped with perfection from foot to foot, across left-over dollar bills and drink-napkins on the floor. Everybody watched. There was nothing else like us. Did they all know Thomas's story? How I was sent here to save him?

I felt quite the hero. Heroine.

So I licked his ears, I licked Jimmy's come from his throat, yes I did. There were tears in my eyes, scummy burning on my tonsils.

Some one person's loud, irregular applause, like a knock at the door, like the old fan in the window that rattles against its rusty frame. Then they were all giving us money, still quietly, stuffing it into our pockets, belt loops, socks, anywhere it might hold.

Then, the end. I took a low bow. Thomas caught me on the return, pulled me back, opened his mouth to kiss.

Keller said, to me, a command, "Get that."

Because I was wrong, it had never been applause, just somebody knocking all along. But not like wanting in. It was thudding knocking, with the heel of the hand, it had resigned itself not to be heard.

My dress, my attitude, the air of a star: everybody followed me into the front room.

There was Mother, with a gallon of cheap wine, half-empty. "I saw there was a party," she said, gesturing heavily up with the bottle. Wine splattered my feet. "So I drove to the Tennessee line." She held the mouth of the bottle toward me. "Want some?"

I moved back, she took a step inside.

I had never seen her drunk before, not really, not like this. It was good, though. She was smiling. I said, "Mother?"

She didn't hear me. Shut her eyes, held up a hand, to give her time to think. "Let me in. I just wanna say hello. I just wanna party."

I said, "Mother." I touched her shoulders, then, as if amazed, drew back.

She opened her eyes, made movements with her mouth for a while, then brought her hand up to cover them. Bitten fingernails, thin veins like hard, twisted satin. "Son?" She was breathing too fast through her smile. Then she laughed, with a serious face. "You're beautiful."

"So are you."

And she was, with no makeup, her hair pulled back straight behind a little-girl white plastic crescent. And red rings under her gray eyes. We held each other by the elbows, to see. "Wonderland," she whispered, with a look behind me.

Her purse dropped as she turned. It fell on the porch. She went running. I just stood there. I went to pick it up, I didn't find it. I found it, and was following her toward the street, but too slowly. I walked to the middle of the street, not where she was parked. Her red brake lights illumined me, my wig, my dress, demonically. I flashed open my eyes, tossed back my head, as to laugh: Donna-May Dean.

Mother had trouble starting her car. Then she was gone. At the corner, at the stop sign, she remembered to slam shut her door.

I held the purse in the air. I yelled, "Mother," with no emotion, only curiosity, as if we were on a hiking trip, and she had lost her way, but was sure to be around the very next dip in the trail.

When I turned back to the house, they were all on the front porch, even Topman, whining, even Burt. A solemn line of pixillated schoolboys after morning devotional. Keller ran down the steps, hands above his head, clapping. Then the rest of them: a rush and an ovation.

Keller clapped his arms around me, helped me up the stairs. "Some show," he whispered. "You little devil. You do your mother proud. Oops. I mean, me." He was pulling me back to the front door, but I stood on the top porch stair. "Some *kind* of show," he said, as if this would make me go on.

"She's crazy. What's she mean coming here?"

The crowd had already forgotten me now. They stood murmuring on the sidewalk, watching up and down the street, as if to see who else's mother was on the way.

"You must apologize to Roxy," Keller went on. "She says you planned it, you deliberately upstaged her. Which is, of course, the last compliment a young drag queen could give."

I said, "I'm going to throw up." But I didn't, not really: sharp taste on the gag-end of my tongue. I stepped past him through the door. "I need to be alone." I fell. I laughed, took off the pumps, used them to swat Keller away. "I'm fine." But my voice was shaking, the pumps in my hands were shaking.

The bathroom was locked when I got there. Somebody said, "Go away." Somebody else said, through a wet mouthful, "Who is it?"

I swallowed back the sick smell, taste of rotten oranges. Then I was fine, laughing quietly, sniffling. I went to my room. There was a boy in the bed, on his belly. One sock on, one sock off. His rib cage, breathing.

I tossed the wig on the floor, pulled myself out of the dress. I climbed into the bed. "Get out," I told him, with a cranky and effeminate voice, the graveyard cashier woman at a truck stop. "This is my place."

It was the lipstick that made me talk that way. I wiped it on the back of my wrist.

The boy didn't wake, but held tight to me, made scared sounds. "What's wrong with you?" I said.

"Boogermonsters."

Which anyone could understand. I decided to let him stay. His breath too hot on my face. I got the smallest corner of the pillow, turned away from him.

Once I woke to find him giving me head. I held—I tried to grab—his silky slippery brown crew cut.

Another time, he was on the floor, with the sheet in his hand in his mouth. I woke him, trying to get him back in the bed. "Fuck me," he whispered.

"I don't do that. I'm just the houseboy. I don't know you." I said, "I've never done that before."

He kissed me, pulled me toward him, on top of him, hard, to make it seem like I was kissing him. Then we wrestled. He was stronger than I, but kept making me win. He'd slip beneath me, and giggle, and squirm. He squeezed my shoulders, then down my arms, with tentative hands. Meaning, You're so strong. He lifted his knees on either side, to pull me up, and in.

His chest, smooth. His nipples, black and hard. Two hairs curling on the edge of one of them. Three hairs on the edge of the other, the right. I reached down to snip off the third with my incisors.

"What's your name?" I told him. I said, "Mine's Jamie."

His was something. Ricky. Randy. Rob. And could we be lovers? he wanted to know.

"Yeah. That would be nice."

I felt under the pillow for the K-Y, but he spat on his quick hand, darted it down, pulled me inside.

"I've never done this before," I told him again.

"Me neither," he said. Then, "Well. Sometimes."

He came without being messed with down there, without even touching his cock. I'd never imagined that that was possible. I had to pull out, and whack off, looking out the window, to think about that, him coming that way.

He snaked his hand around, to hold me, to play with my balls, but I pulled away.

His name was Rex. He had shiny green-almost-yellow eyes. He was gone in the morning.

Two weeks later I heard he was in the hospital. No visitors.
    Keller told me not to worry. The boy was a slut, he said.
"You don't just up and get it. Contributing factors. Hepatitis.
Alcoholism. Poppers." He even said, "As always, only the tru-
liest trashiest most worthless will die. The ones who actually
prefer polyester blends. The fist-fucking set. The Liza Minnelli
fans. The wrath of an angry God."

THREE

WONDERLAND

WONDERLAND: ALICE HAD TO SHRINK TO GET there, had to become less than she was. More and more, living with Keller and Thomas, I felt like that. In *Willy Wonka,* the movie, this greedy girl becomes a blueberry. I was three years old when I saw it, and terrified, and envious. Her expression, her eyebrows, her hair, turn inhuman blue. There is no hope for her, according to the Oompa Loompas. They sing their self-righteous song-and-dance around her, roll her pitilessly away.

To become something else altogether. To be left to the care of Oompa Doompa Diddley Doos. That was my life now. Keller and Thomas paid more attention to one another, less attention to me, as the days went by. "Clean the bathtub," said Thomas. Keller said, "Surely you don't need a second? Helping?"

But to go back to Mother, "Pardon me, ma'am," heart like a hat in my hand, was unthinkable. Keller bought me new clothes: polo shirts, corduroy slacks, a fresh leather jacket. I carried myself within them clumsily, timidly, by way of apology. As if, by seeming too small for this place, I might begin to be small enough. By seeming uncomfortable, I might be allowed to settle in and relax.

Or it might have been real, my awkwardness. Maybe I've told myself too often how self-conscious I was, how it was all a performance. I bumped my head on hanging plants. I left soap scum circles every morning in the bathtub. Thomas would kiss me on the forehead, after breakfast, pat me on the back. And remind me, again, to clean it up. And then again.

I broke Keller's crystal tea set, the Phillips widow's: I didn't mean to. Keller found me standing in the kitchen, barefoot, paralyzed by a thousand invisible glass shards. I was about to cry. He said, "How silly." He gave me the broom. But he was pleased. "Your snakes-and-snails-and-puppy-dog-tails attitude," Keller whispered, with no prompting, in my praise. He rumpled my hair, which was growing out curly from the crew cut by now.

But I just pointed into the cabinet, at what had scared me in the first place: a pickling jar, holding green fluid, and thick bubbles, and a bloated, floating, white-white penis.

"John Dillinger's," Keller snapped. He shut the cabinet door. "I stole it from the Smithsonian. Don't tell the FBI."

Thomas strutted past, with his hands in his back pants pockets. He wore a tight lifted superior smile.

I waved both my hands downward at the broken glasses, as if he hadn't already seen. I yelled after him, "Well, goddam it, I'm sorry."

I said, to Keller, more directly, tattletale, "He doesn't like me again, Keller."

Keller went to his chair in the common room, scolded us both. "Boys, boys." We should kiss and make up, he said. We should get over it. What was wrong with us? he wanted to know. We were supposed to be family. He couldn't even concentrate on his reading, "what with all the attitude flying about this house." He told me to go to my room. Thomas, he ran out of the house. "Go fishing or something butch like that. Go get your hair cut again."

100

Thomas would mope to the Corner Fruit, sit and spit with the old men on the benches outside. Sometimes, on my way to the park of an afternoon, I'd see him there. He looked away. I wasn't even allowed to wave.

Mostly, I didn't pass him at Corner Fruit, though. I didn't go to the park, didn't do anything. I sat in my room for hours at a time in my one chair. I watched the two pumps from my drag debut, where I had set them in the window, on either side of the old one, Donna-May Dean's. Now the differences showed. The original had a tight felt bow where the other two buckled. I crossed my eyes.

Donna-May Dean tipped out of the darkened window, winked at me, stepped into the room, over the sill, laughed. He lined his narrow eyes with righteousness, hard yellow mascara. Finished, and tired, and satisfied, as from sex, or labor pains, he leaned backwards onto the sill, with a long cough-interrupted breath. One foot, dull Rockette, he kicked without enthusiasm.

I said, resentfully, a question, "Mother called me beautiful."

He blew smoke from the side of his mouth, to show me his delicious worldliness, and that he concurred. "What the fuck does she know?" Then, "Beautiful indeed. You are. As are we all." He clamped his front teeth together behind a smile, a tease. "But how dare she see?"

I turned to my invisible mother, who sat on the bed, shyly, Indian-style, fiddling with her shoestrings like a schoolgirl. This is where I had put her purse, between flat feather pillows.

I lifted my eyebrows, nodded sideways, directing her attention to Donna-May Dean, to what he had just said. How dare she call me beautiful? How dare she pretend to understand?

Donna-May Dean flounced skeptically toward the bed, waved his cigarette holder through her, magic wand, to show that she was not as real as he. He puffed much lavender smoke her way. The evil, angular set of his jaw.

Then she was gone.

101

"She doesn't belong here," he scolded. "You have so much to jettison, still." This last he spoke with regret and nostalgia, a smile behind his sudden widow's veil.

He puckered thick lipstick into a parody kiss. Then pulled the veil aside, to let me see.

"This or that. Us or them. Let her go."

He sat in her place between the pillows. "Family. We're your family now. All the dead drag queens." His voice scared me, deeper than it should have been, more reasonable and ominous.

I said, "I guess you're right." But some childish part of me—the pretty little watched boy in his bed at night—stood back, shook its head, no no no. I said, "Family." That was just another one of Keller's words for queer. Of a passing stranger, he might intimate, "But Mildred. That one's family." Which meant that we probably should have nothing to do with him.

Donna-May Dean set his wig in his lap, picked at it with critical chopstick fingers. His real hair was too patchy and short, a newborn baby's ugly hair. Vanessa Redgrave in *Playing for Time*.

After a long while he stood, watched me from the sides of his eyes, above a long provisional smile. As if he would disappear again. As if to say, Just dare contradict me.

He prissed manfully away, down the stairs, he was gone.

But once, I heard him scream, from the common room, "All I demand! Is one! Little! Kiss!"

I ran downstairs, but it was only Keller, pretending to read. With delicate fingers, he pinched on either side the hinges of his glasses. Donna-May Dean could never have made such a tame, domestic gesture. And Keller could never have been screaming what it was that I thought I had heard. "Baby," said Keller. "What's wrong? What is it?"

I sat on the floor, leaned up to look at him past the armrest. "Tell me more about Donna-May Dean."

"Well, now." He folded the glasses onto his lap. "Let's see. What's there to tell? Did you know—? I'll think of something. Just a minute."

I looked out the window, where the dead trees had sprung,

102

over the past couple days, impossibly, blue buds. The mail-man—the cute one today, not the old man or the redheaded lesbian—stepped across the street, with the widow Nichols' hot bitch poodle Tutu humping his ankle. To know the names of the neighborhood dogs: I *was* beginning to belong.

Then Keller, more slowly, "Did you know she spent time in the madhouse? Donna-May Dean? Yes, she did. Her mother sent her there. For, ahem, the cure."

Keller shuddered once on the word *cure,* then one more time.

I snapped my attention from the window, bounced in place, happy boy, to show him to tell me more.

"Yes, the mad-house," said Keller, as Vincent Price, rubbing wicked eager hands together. Then he ran them down the armrests, pulled in his shoulders, to warm himself to his tale.

"They showed her pictures of naked men. They told her to look. Electrodes in her hands, you know. But they *told* her to look."

Keller shut his eyes, bit the insides of his lips, tightly, together. He didn't say anything until I batted my lids.

"A paper dress," he said, "and a swimming cap. Her mother's cologne. That was her wardrobe. In the mad-house. In Tuscaloosa, where she went for the cure. Her mother sent her there."

Then he breathed, folded his book with finality over his thumb. "You don't want to hear this." He boxed his hand through my hair. "It's a silly old story about a silly old queen, half-crazy, half-imaginary. It's been important to me, to my survival. But you, on the other hand. You don't need this." He was begging. "I don't want to tell this story anymore."

But I kept on.

He waved his aggravated hand. He said, an octave higher than he'd expected to, "Um." He laughed. "There was one window in her room. At night she'd sit before it, pretending to make herself up." He cocked his head. "Making herself up," he said, more thoughtfully. He rubbed slow fingertips into his cheeks. "Foundation," he said. His pinkies flicked a circle around each watering eye: "Mascara." He whispered, "Because there was the doctor, this handsome doctor, you see."

He turned his attention to his lap, opened the book to a random page, stared. "Go to your room." He might have been about to cry, the crack in his voice. He called me back. Resonantly, with closure, he said, "Donna-May Dean." He offered me weakly the backs of his hands, pale blue zigzag stigmata where the electrodes had been. But his face and his eyes were shut. No questions.

I said, touching his hands, with the confidence of the reverent, "Of course. Yes. Donna-May Dean." I had always known, I had already figured it out. I held up his hands a long time anyway, in the light of the reading lamp, to see and to see.

I went to the park, because I hoped Mother might be waiting for me. Then I was afraid to see her. I hid at the fountain, near the bushes, just in case.

She wasn't there, nobody was. Just Richard, who sat on the fountain's rim, leaning in, to look for quarters. Which reminded me of me.

"It's not that I need the money," he said, to himself. "Daddy gives me a generous allowance."

I said, "How much?"

"Oh!" He jumped away from the fountain, put three melodramatic fingers to his heartbeat. "Four or five or six hundred dollars a week. Daddy just says not to spend it all in one place."

His father was the assistant minister at one of the grungiest United Methodist churches in town. There was no way he'd have that much money to give to such a beautiful and silly son. I didn't say anything.

"And how much do you get from the fountain?" I said.

Richard flipped a quarter onto the concrete between us. (I remember once, my dad taught me the meaning of the word *oscillation* this way.) Richard said, "Enough to buy candy bars and Coke. Um. Coca-*Cola*, I mean."

I socked him on the shoulder. I laughed. "I knew what you meant."

He said, like a sorority girl, "Rilly?" He stood, lifted his head, shook back his hair. Except that he had none. Crew cuts were the thing that summer.

I liked that he was relaxed enough around me to be a sissy. He had never been such a total sissy at school.

He said, "I thought you ran with a wild crowd. I saw that crowd you're running with. La Gioconda and that leatherman and them."

"You were there, too," I said, "and *you* were in drag."

He lowered his flared nostrils, solemnly. "I don't live there." He paced before me. "And what about you licking Jimmy's sperm off that old man's neck? And you were in more drag than I was. And got better applause."

"But you liked it better than I did."

With guilt: "You've got a point there."

He sat beside me, close enough for our shoulders to touch, but they didn't. He said, "Are you a water sign?"

"What's that?"

"You don't know?" As if this were the most impossible thing to believe.

I shrugged.

"Good," he said. "Then you're not one. Then we can be friends."

I said, not a question, "Why did we never talk in school?" I slapped my hands in the air, to show amazement.

"I never talk to anybody at school. It's too scary, having friends. How much do they know about me? What would they think, if they really knew who I was? You know?"

"My mother found out," I said. "I still haven't figured out how."

"Rilly? Mine knows, too. She's flying in on her personal jet tomorrow, from Florida. Where she lives now. In a condo. I'll have to introduce you."

I offered my phone number.

He shut his eyes, disbelief, my rudeness. He walked away,

105

full circle around the fountain. When he came back, "Ha! I'll just bet you want to meet my mother. And we haven't even had our first kiss."

But this is Alabama, I wanted to say. This is northwest Alabama: everybody here knows everybody. Everybody here has met everybody else's mother. She was selling felt cutout Santa faces at the PTA Christmas Bazaar. Her hair, too black to be real. "Do you know my son, Richard?" she wanted to know. "Richard Languster? Maybe you could try to be his friend? He's lonely."

Mother pulled me away from her. "The town drunk," she scolded. As if there were only one.

Now she was at the rehab clinic in Pensacola again, drying out after the divorce. I started to tell Richard: don't even try. But I didn't say anything. Maybe she did find money in Florida. They do have a lottery down there.

"Mother says she loves me any-way," I said, tilting my head left and right on the two halves of that word.

"I don't know what I'd do if my mom or dad found out," said Richard.

I didn't bother to remind him of his story, how she already knew. Because he was looking so straight-ahead and serious.

I took two of his fingers in my hand. He let me, he smiled. We stayed that way for a while.

Then he pulled away, because a straight couple was passing. They didn't even look at us, but there was the weight of their presence, their possible disapproval. When they were gone, he didn't give me back his hand. Still, he was smiling.

He said, "What about that bitch Mrs. Sellman?" He meant our algebra teacher.

"Yeah. What about her?"

"I heard she licks cunt. I heard she licks your mother's cunt." He laughed, went running away. "Catch me if you can."

I didn't move.

He lost his balance, from laughing, from holding his belly. "You didn't catch me," he said to me, facing the ground where he fell. He sat up. But there I was, I was on top of him.

"Caught you."

106

We wrestled around, until our straight couple—an old man with black plastic science fiction glasses and a bent pipe, a young woman in a plain swervy-colored dress—passed again. They cleared their throats, to get us to look, so they could smile.

"We're from up north," said the woman. The man said, "We're liberals."

We threw our hands in the air, we screamed. We ran, like the Three Stooges, except minus one and much prettier. We poked along around the outside of the park, catching our wind and our wits.

I said, "We'll talk to each other? When school starts again?"

Jimmy got out of an old man's car on the curb. He stood inside the open door. He bounced and nodded and smiled. "Yeah," he said. "Yeah, yeah, sure. Right. Thanks. Right." He slammed shut the door.

"Come on," he whispered to me and Richard. He came between us, slapped our backs, pulled us more tightly together.

"I've got money. Let's go to Huntsville. There's a queer bar." He pulled a fifty dollar bill out of his pocket, snapped it crisp twice in the air, then folded and replaced it.

"What were you doing with that old man?" I said to Jimmy. I sounded like Richard, asking that.

"Hunh? Oh, nothing. He gave me a ride, that's all. My bike's in the shop."

Jimmy shoved us along, leaning his face forward, to show us to go faster. He scrubbed my brow with his fingertips. "What do you think I was doing?"

Which was either innocence or rhetorical, so I didn't answer.

Richard wasn't listening. "What if we get caught?" he said. "What if they don't let us in?"

I said, to Jimmy, "We *are* too young to go to a queer bar."

"What if the end of the world comes?" Richard said. "There I'll be in a gay bar."

Jimmy said, "So?" He snorted. "Where would you be

otherwise? Queer Park? Do you really believe that Jesus sees a difference? *I* don't see a difference."

He chuckled, went sailing between and past us. "What if the world had ended with you slung up in one of Keller's old dresses? You can get over it. Jesus can get over it."

"Don't talk like that," Richard said. "No: really." He held out a hand to protect himself. "It makes me scared. But okay. Anyway. I'll go."

"Oh no. Not if you don't want to," said Jimmy, a threat. "No, no, no." He wiped his comb through his hair above each ear, elbows up, carefully: James Dean.

"Please, let's go," said Richard. To me, "Don't you want to?" Then, to himself, "I've never been to a real bar before. With alcohol."

I said, "There was gin in the punch at Keller's party. And in the sweet tea, even."

Richard pressed three scandalized fingers to his lips.

"It's settled, then," Jimmy said. He slapped us anew on the backs, to point us to Keller and Thomas's. The old man, still cruising, followed us almost all the way.

"Keller and Thomas are what I'm worried about," I said. "If they'll let me go or not."

"Let me handle it," Jimmy said. "They can't say no to me. I've got my little ways."

I started to say, Let's compare notes. I started to say, Make them like me better. I started to say, Did Thomas ever fuck you?

I said, "How do we get there? Huntsville, I mean?"

"Easy," Jimmy said. "Highway 72. And didn't you say you had a car?"

I hadn't. But I said, "Yes."

"I wouldn't park *my* car at a gay bar," said Richard. "Even if I had one. I bet the police take tag numbers."

"Only if you're pretty," Jimmy said.

I said, "We are."

"Yeah," Richard said.

And there we were, stopped at the house. I looked back, but the troll was gone. Jimmy said, "Oh fuck you both."

I started to say, Please.

The kitchen air was brisk, an argument had barely ended: Thomas lay his face in folded arms on the table, Keller pressed hands more firmly flat on his hips. The toilet-bowl brush and a bottle of Mr. Clean on the table between them. Without turning to see: "Jamie? Is that you?" Keller said. "Thomas says you never did clean out the bathtub this morning."

Then he turned. There we were, Jimmy in front, Richard with hands in back pants pockets behind, trying to look harmless. Keller said, "Oh?"

"Can Jamie go to Huntsville with us?" Jimmy said, all in a breath.

Keller, in a singsong voice, cracking like a mother's: "But he's too young, Jimmy. You know that." Then, to me, "Aren't you? Too young?"

Thomas looked up. "Keller, let them go."

"But we have company calling," he said, a droning emphasis on every word. "But the bathtub. What will he wear?"

Thomas, to me, with rigid authority, "You can clean the bathtub when you get back."

Keller called after us out the door, "You're not going out wearing that?" And, "Don't keep him out late. You know better than this. You know how I worry." And, "Have a good time."

Jimmy crashed into the front seat beside me. "See? Wasn't that easy?"

"Do you think he was right?" I said. "Shouldn't I go change clothes?"

"Naah. They like them young and rough in Huntsville. That's exactly what they like."

From the back seat came Richard's whimper, "But I don't feel rough. Am I rough?" He giggled, to show awe. "I feel *bad*."

"You mean bathroom-bad?" I said. "You mean sick?" Because here we were, in my car.

"Oh no, not that. Just evil."

Jimmy laughed. "And excited?" he offered. He reached over the seat to paw Richard's thigh.

"I guess so," Richard said. "Excited. Exactly. And that's why I feel so bad."

Jimmy rolled eyes at me. Meaning, His pretty-boy-blue act is getting on my nerves. But I just blinked, defensively. I lowered my eyebrows.

Jimmy said, "Well, let's get on. Let's do it. So pretty-boy will have something to feel bad about. Let's go."

Because I hadn't started the car yet.

It hadn't been cranked for a week now, and it didn't want to be. We had to push it down the drive. There was Keller, watching us out the door.

Richard said, "I have to go to church tomorrow."

"It's not Sunday," I said.

"Revival," said Richard. "I'm supposed to sing a solo. In front of all those people. Who think I'm not bad. I mean, evil. Also, not a bad singer, I guess, they think."

Jimmy laughed silently into his hand.

"I'll go too," I said. "I'll be there to watch. So you won't have to feel bad." I turned around, to wink at him. "Okay? Will that be good?"

He nodded. Maybe that was what he had wanted all along.

Then Jimmy poked me, I had to turn back around to drive.

We took the new four-lane to Huntsville: a rough ride nevertheless, two and a half hours. Richard too nervous for words, jumping around like a toddler on speed in the back seat. Jimmy up front grabbing my crotch whenever he got bored. Which was every thirty minutes. And I liked it, but didn't know what to do. Because I was thinking about Richard, how it might be nice to know him better. And there was Thomas. And I still thought I might hear from Rex.

And what about this Burt, from Atlanta?

"Oh yeah. Oh, him. Did I use that word? Did I say we were lovers? He just wants me to say that. Part of his scene. I see him every two months or so. Nothing. No big deal. He turned me on to some things I never thought of. He's a chiropractor, you know."

Richard said, "I gotta pee."

"Can you do it in this?" Jimmy passed back a no-deposit Mountain Dew bottle, almost empty.

Most of what you see of Huntsville from the highway is new: The Space and Rocket Center, the Supermall, low-rise yuppie apartment sprawl. THE FASTEST-GROWING CITY IN AL- ABAMA! says the sign. "But think about it," Jimmy said. "How fast can that be?"

The bar turned out to be in the old part of town: a short flattop brick building, sharing its parking lot with Irene's School of Beauty and The Fruit Basket. A fluorescent light- box on metal legs at the access road entrance: THE LOCKER ROOM A PRIVATE CLUB. Posted with masking tape directly on the door: MUST HAVE MEMBERSHIP CARD AND PICTURE ID TO ENTER. And, NO DYKES. And, BEWARE OF DOG.

Jimmy reached past me to ring the doorbell. "Don't worry. That's just to keep the heteros out."

I said, "And the dykes."

"Oh. That's a joke. The owner's a lesbian. She just doesn't like them too butch, that's all."

Then the door was buzzing, Jimmy went in, stuck out his head, "Just wait."

Richard and I waited. We watched the door. We felt the disco backbeat and bass line in our bones and soles.

I said, "Still upset?"

He didn't look at me. He looked determined. "I'm fine," he said, more forcefully than he needed to. He said, "Sorry."

Jimmy ducked back out, gave his driver's license to Rich- ard. "Remember. Try your best to look like me. Then bring it back out for Jamie to use."

He showed us the back of his hand, a pink triangle stamped there.

"We should wait," Richard said, "because—what if they remember your picture?"

"Just go. It's Danny working the door. Don't worry. He'll let you in if you're cute enough."

Richard chose to take the compliment.

After he had gone in, Jimmy turned to me. "I see the way you're looking at him."

I laughed. "Jealous?"

"It's just, he's a fucked-up kid."

"And what are you? And what am I?"

"Yeah. Well. I'd be careful, that's all." Jimmy ran a hand through his hair, looked away. "Busy night tonight." Fourteen cars in the parking lot, plus one truck, plus mine. "For a Tuesday, I mean."

When Richard never came back out, Jimmy went in to see why.

Several queens gathered around the fluorescent light-box. The least thin of them called my name. "Long time no see," he said. "Donna-May Dean."

I shuddered a little. Then realized, he must have been at the party. So I smiled his way, but by now the queens were huddled and busy among themselves, as queens will be. One said, "Listen," held quick hands fluttering in the white light blinking from the sign, to indicate disdain about something, someone.

"Miss Thing!" they were saying. "Do tell!" Another of them passed a bottle of poppers from nose to nose. I recognized Wisteria standing there, and Scary Alice, but I didn't go over to speak. Because here I was, and there they were, and they were laughing.

I should have changed into long pants and a button shirt after all. Keller will be so ashamed, that they saw me here this way.

Jimmy came out. "He was afraid that they wouldn't let him back in, is what he said. He's dancing with some guy." Jimmy flashed me the license. "Wait a little before you go in."

Through the door, a dark-panelling hallway, no light, except inside the Plexiglas ticket booth. "Two dollars," said Danny toward the hole in the glass. He smiled, to show me his front-tooth diamond inset, to show me he was happy to be here, and that I should be, too. "What's the matter, darling? I said two dollars."

He didn't even ask to see the license. I shoved it under the opening anyway, folded inside the bills.

He picked it out, regarded me with narrowing eyes, a mischievous sniffle. "I've seen this before, tonight."

I said, "You've seen it twice before, tonight."

"Oh? In that case—" He shrugged. Meaning, I just work here. Meaning, It's too far gone to stop now.

I held out my hand to be stamped.

Inside, a sudden damp smell of cigarettes and dead beer, rose water, Vaseline. One square dirty mirror, frameless, with uneven edges, sparkled on each red velvet wall. No dance floor: just two pool tables, and an out-of-order Pac-Man machine, and half a dozen industrial wire spools, upended to hold drinks and flat aluminum ashtrays. The dancers were scattered, and too friendly, unenthusiastic: a weekday crowd, I gathered.

Richard leaned against a man who burped, then swayed. The man pressed a Budweiser to the small of Richard's back, with both hands, possessively.

A black queen with angry, glittering eyes held a drink in the air, to keep it from spilling. He winked at me, kicked elegant, brutal scissors across the room. I moved away, further inside, when he got to me.

I wondered if that was how he always travelled.

"Going through the motions," went the music.

Jimmy leaned backwards onto his elbows at the bar. I said, "Howdy stranger. I got in." Cardsharp, I flipped the license at him. It fell to the floor. He didn't look at me.

"Go away." He drank his beer. "They'll think we're to-gether."

"If I stand here," I said, "we will be together." I slapped him on the back. I collapsed onto one forearm on the bar. I looked up over my shoulder at him.

He said, "I mean together-together. We don't want them thinking that." With a cut of his eyes, finally, in my direction, and a smooth, resentful sip of his beer, he stepped away. "It's just not the way to work a bar. Man, are you ignorant."

I bent down to pick up the license, wipe it off with spit and fingers.

Somebody stepped to the bar in Jimmy's place. He had a beefy mustache, and direct eyes, no smile. "Smells good," he said. "What's that you're wearing?"

He shifted, nudged me with his arm, but not urgently.

"Old Spice." I had almost forgotten putting it on this morning. Thomas's.

"Old *Spice?*" He bit the ends of his mustache, distress.

I said, "Old Spice? Not me. Never. Just kidding. Aqua Velva. No, ha ha. Nothing at all."

He made a comfortable sound from the bottom of his throat: mmmmm. "Don't I wish?" His eyebrows jerked, up, and tinily up, while he watched my crotch. A parody of lust. I laughed. Then I smiled.

But when the bartender gave him back his change, he walked away.

Jimmy shook his head into his beer at me, across the room. Meaning, You dummy. Meaning, Follow.

I mouthed, "But I don't like facial hair."

Jimmy squinted his eyes: what?

"I don't like facial hair," I yelled. But, of course, he wasn't paying attention to me of a sudden.

The man passed through Mylar strips in a doorless doorway at the back of the bar. I mouthed, to Jimmy, with lifted palms, "Oh well." Defeat. I followed.

"Until I'm soaking *wet,*" went the music. Then stopped.

The back room had either been a gym locker at one time, or had been made to look that way: splintering white wooden lockers, rough benches against them, a concave floor centered by a grated drain. Four feed buckets of dry ice had been set out—rustic decadence.

One textured window shot wild rings of streetlamp light into the corner, where Richard sat, bent over into his man, who had his hand down the back of Richard's pants. He stuck beady eyes over Richard's shoulder, to watch what he was doing. A blond emptiness, a youngish businessman. He bit his lip, did something especially difficult down there, to see how his hand twisted under the denim, to see how Richard moaned and giggled. And writhed.

114

After a while the man took out two very dirty fingers, stuck them in Richard's mouth, went down in front, to suck. That's when Richard saw me, widened his eyes, tried to say something through the shitty fingers down his throat. He didn't seem unhappy, though. "Hey, Jamie," he might have said. "Come on in, the water's fine."

I had to laugh, after the way he had acted on the way up here. I didn't know if he was a hypocrite or just confused. I decided to go easy on him. "Don't talk with your mouth full."

But he didn't hear.

I sat down on the end of the bench nearest the door, across from my man. And that was it in the back room: just me, and Richard, and our two tricks. Except that mine wasn't a trick yet. I didn't know what he was.

He was staring. He sat with his legs wide, holding his beer in one tight fist between them. He'd been friendly enough outside, I wondered if I should speak. Or maybe you didn't speak back here?

Then I saw that the beer was moving, tinily, up and down the bulge in his denim. He lit a thin cigar. Which made me think of Thomas. I smiled. I said, "Hello again."

Silence. He smirked.

Then we kept staring at each other, until Jimmy came to get Richard and me. The police had just raided Atlantis, the other gay club in town, they'd be here next, he said. They always are. "Fuckin' pigs," he said. Then, like a queen, "You just don't *know*."

Richard was sitting up, rolling around on his guy's cock. He wiggled his toes further up the wall, laid back his head, tongue out, eyes shut. "But we're not drinking," he said. "They can't do anything. I want to stay."

The guy beneath him bounced up a couple times, so he didn't say anything else.

He said, like a child on his father's hobbyhorse knee, "Yah yah yah."

Jimmy said, "Fuck it." To me, "You want to stay, too?" An accusation. He turned up his collars. "I was just worried for you guys, anyway. I'm perfectly legal here, you know." He stalked back through the Mylar.

"None of us are legal!" I yelled after him. "Sodomy laws."

Still, I did see his point. I walked over to Richard. "Ah, Rich-ard? I think we need to go?"

He flashed me sullen eyes.

I bent past him, to address the man on his back on the floor. "Excuse me?" I whispered. "He's sorry, but some other time?" I wrapped Richard's arm around my neck, pulled him off. "Come on. You have to sing tomorrow, remember? And—where's your pants?"

We couldn't find them, they just weren't there. Maybe his trick was on top of them? We didn't ask. Because he kept on laying, humping, there, as if Richard hadn't been removed. He grabbed the bench behind him with both hands, tight blue knuckles. His cock bent backward, spat out, one two three, sudden wads. I was impressed.

"He seems nice," Richard said. "Let me give him my phone number."

There was nothing to write on. Richard repeated it seven times. "Did you get that?" he yelled.

The man shut his eyes: anger, or satisfaction, or sleep.

Richard repeated his number again.

Then I hustled him through the bar. It seemed twice as big a room as it had been before, holding three times the people. I thought that by keeping close, holding his shoulders, nobody would notice he was naked. Which was stupid. But, what to do?

Somebody hissed at us. Somebody else pressed a dollar bill into Richard's passive, clasping hand. A cluster of young and old gathered in our way, not because we were sexy. Because we were embarrassed: the novelty of it, *feeling* in a place like this.

But the scissor-kick queen stamped his spike heel on the floor. "Leave the poor childrens be." He snapped dangerous fingers twice in my face. "Come along, sweethearts." Then he cut us a pathway out.

I said, "Thank you."

"Wait a minute," he commanded. "Tell the truth. My titties. They look whomp-sided to you?" He thrust out his flat chest.

"No," I said. "Not at all. They look fine."

He spun about, to scream, "See? You sluts just workin' my nerves. Won't leave poor Harlot alone. Ahem. That's *Miss* DeCarlo to you."

Harlot DeCarlo? But when I turned around to see him better, the door was shut, he was gone.

Jimmy slid off the hood of my car, slapped his thighs to congratulate himself. "I knew you'd come." He looked at Richard, who still held tight to me, an injured athlete coming off the field. Jimmy said, silently, with lifted eyebrows, "?"

I shrugged.

Jimmy opened the door. I dumped Richard inside. "Ooh. Naugahyde," he said. "Sticky, sticky."

Then the damn car wouldn't start, and the parking lot was too small and full for pushing. Jimmy said he'd go find somebody with jumper cables. "If the cops come, lay low," he said.

I told Richard to get his naked self down on the floor, cops or no cops. "Just in case," I said.

"It's Wendy's hamburger bags on the floor. It's Pepsi cans."

He'd been in dirtier places, I told him. "More germs on those fingers than you could imagine."

"But they were my own germs," he said. "Besides, I think I loved him."

I told him to shut up, just shut up. I was shaking. I was smoking. I said, "Mr. Jesus Freak. Mr. Innocent."

"Hey. That's not fair." He stuck his head up between the front seats. "I don't deserve that."

"Oh shit," I said. "Get down. It's the cops." But it wasn't. I smiled, stubbed out my cigarette. "They've got out their billy clubs. And their mustaches."

"I'm scared, Jamie." Then, with a rising, pitiful, curious inflection, "Mustaches?" He wanted up, he wanted to see, but I told him no.

That was when I decided to call home, I don't know why. Just to be doing something. To let them know I was fine. I went to the phone booth by the beauty shop entrance. First, I called Mother.

And this was funny, I didn't remember the number.

I called long-distance information, seventy-five cents, then she wasn't home anyway. I called Keller.

There was Jimmy, standing by the car, with another man. They knocked on the window: no Richard, nothing. "Tell him it's okay," I yelled. "Tell him I was lying about the cops." Then I hung up the phone, walked over. It was my guy from the back room.

"This is Gerald," Jimmy said. "Turns out he's from Genoa, too."

Gerald chucked my chin with gentle fingers. "Small world."

Jimmy, ingenuously, "Then you've met?"

"Mmm. I wish."

Which confused me. I started to say, You had your chance. But I didn't, just breathed out once. I got Richard out of the car, gave him two hamburger bags, "Use this to cover up-front. And this to cover in back." I don't know why I specified.

He did exactly as I said. I led him by the elbows, following Jimmy following Gerald.

Richard said, "No cops?"

"Not yet. Don't give up, though."

"Quit teasing me. I don't like it. Not much." He added, "I have to get up in the morning." He nodded, sternly, as if that made everything clear.

"I know," I said. "Remember? I said I'll be there."

He gave my hand a squeeze between his elbow and his ribcage.

"Cops," I said. "Never can find one when you need one. Or their billy clubs. Where's the Vaseline?"

Richard pulled his elbow away. "I said, stop."

And I said, "Slut," but in a nice way.

We got into Gerald's white Corvette. He took down the

T-tops, looking down at where I sat in the backseat. "Nice night," he said. Then we peeled rubber out of there.

I put my head back. He was right. A nice night, a clear one. I whispered to Richard, "Too many stars." He set his forehead on my shoulder. I held on to him.

"I think. I'm cold," he said.

But nobody heard.

Jimmy, up front, lit a joint. I didn't want any, thanks. Richard took a toke, passed it up to Gerald. I lifted my brows at Richard. He shrugged, burrowed more close to me. Sperm on his breath, and smoke smell, a suburban autumn.

I kissed him, a long time, didn't shut my eyes. There was Jimmy's hand on Gerald's crotch. Gerald cranked up the country music station.

"Were you ever scared of the Oompa Loompas?" I yelled toward Jimmy and Gerald. "Were you afraid you might, did you burn to become, a blueberry? You know. In *Willy Wonka?*"

They didn't say anything. Jimmy held smoke in his mouth, tight lips, to show he wanted to laugh. Gerald said, slowly, "You're a strange one, aren't you? But that's just fine."

Richard was singing, though: "Oompa, doompa, diddley doo. I've got a new riddle for you." He marched two fingers across my chest, the Oompa dance. "Oompa, doompa, diddley dee. If you are wise you'll listen to me."

His tenor: unremarkable. I hugged him anyway, patted him, twice, where my hand was already touching naked buns. As to say, I'm happy.

And maybe I was.

I said, "*You* remember the Oompa Loompas."

He tweaked my nose with his Oompa Loompa-dancing fingers. He held the tip of his thumb between them. He said, the way you tease a child, "Look. I've got your nose."

"The Oompa Loompas," I went on. "They were know-it-all bastards, weren't they? No telling what they did to that poor girl. No telling where she ended up."

Richard looked at me, wearing some pitiful eyes. "The squeezing room," he whispered. "They took her to the squeezing room. To get the juices out."

119

"Oh yeah. How terrible."

"Squeezing can be fun." He locked his hands together behind me, tugged. Then he turned his face into my lap, said he was warm enough, he guessed.

"What about in the morning?" he mumbled to himself. "Will they let me sing? Will I be pretty? Will they know?"

He slept the rest of the way.

Once, he said, "My butt's dry. Jamie, the wind!"

Which made my heart thump, once, deeply.

Jimmy, despite his rock and roll attitude, the NEVER MIND THE BOLLOCKS button on his collar, sang along, with the radio, and the Jordanaires, and Loretta Lynn, and Gerald.

"Can't you turn it down?" I said. "Can't you see he's sleeping?"

Jimmy turned, cupped his ear in one hand, but didn't let me talk. "If you're lookin' at me," he yodelled, "you're lookin' at country."

I burned a look his way. But he was right.

Then we had made it back to Genoa. Gerald said we should come to his house. It was out on the shoals, he said. He could show us dirty videos. He could show us the moon over the dam.

But I had to get back home.

"Yeah," Jimmy said. He laughed. "Poor little baby's gotta clean the bathtub."

I didn't say anything.

I said, "They must have waited up for me," when we pulled up. Because there was the front room light on.

Gerald shook my hand, he didn't turn around. "Good night."

I held his hand there over his shoulder. "Why didn't you talk to me, in the back room?"

"I'm a shy kind of a guy," he said. He turned around, winked, shrugged.

Jimmy said, stress on the second syllable, "Good night, Jamie." Then he settled in yet closer to Gerald.

I slid from under Richard, I was gone. I turned, at the front porch, but there was nothing to see. Richard lifted his

120

backlit head from the seat, then shook it, scratched it. Gerald peeled rubber all the way to the stop sign, then all the way out of sight.

In the tone of somebody losing an argument, I said, "Well, okay. Okay. Good night."

Still, I watched the street awhile, where the car had been, as a movie camera might. One cat crossed on hunched, unliquid thighs.

I rang the doorbell, then remembered where the key was hidden, inside the aluminum mailbox nailed to the door frame. I rang the bell again, damn them, as long as they were awake.

I was singing, "Oompa, doompa."

I gave up, let myself in. I was drunk, but not from drinking. From Richard's head on my shoulder, maybe. From the wind through the T-tops.

Mother, on the settee, in the common room, spread her flat hands atop the pages of Keller's family album, nodded. Keller, his back to me, leaned toward her, forward. "That's Harlot DeCarlo," he said, his most scandalized, confidential tone. "Uppity high yellow. She killed a redneck once with her spike-heeled pump."

Mother lifted her tightest smile, as to say, Why are you telling me this? Danger behind that smile: Keller didn't notice or care. He leaned back, slapped his knees. "Self-defense. She went to prison anyway. Came out with a new tattoo, some felon's initials inside a wobbly blue amateur heart on her wrist."

One lamp above Keller's head made a soft circle of shine about the two of them.

Mother set her hands on her hair, which had fallen over one shoulder. "And this is how you live, then?"

She saw me, my shaky smile, my standing still. I said, "Um. Hi."

Keller turned, slapping his hands in the air, exaggerated difficulty. "Oh, hello. We didn't see you there. Do come on in."

"Her titties," I said, as I stepped, angry opera entrance, holding my hands palms-upward, high, "did she wear them whomp-sided?" My voice broke on the "whomp." I covered,

121

by clearing my throat. Then I apologized: "I mean, Harlot DeCarlo's? Titties, I mean?"

I nodded a mean smile at Mother, to show pity.

"You know," said Keller, "I believe she did." He bit his pinky-tip, speculatively. "Of course she did. And simply all of us *told* her. She never would listen, though. She never believed. How did you know?"

I came to stand directly behind and beside him, settled a hand on the chair back. "I met her tonight. I mean, him."

This last directed, with lifted eyes, at Mother.

Keller waved a hand at me, then returned to his story. "Where was I? Oh yes." He took a breath. Directly to her, but with an eyebrow lifted in irritation my way, "Harlot DeCarlo is dead. You see, they let her out of prison, even though she never wanted to leave. So she stole the mayor's television set. But the prisons were full up in Alabama, they shipped her to Tennessee. Where she died of heartache. Or a knife in the throat. I forget. Same thing."

Mother kept looking at me. I rolled my eyes, as to say, Don't believe anything Keller tells. Then I turned to Keller, I nodded: go on.

Because I was beginning to enjoy showing off our grotesquerie.

"They say that the felon—nobody knows the name, you understand, and even the initials from the tattoo were illegible, that's the nature of story time—still beats his meat into her old cage every morning and noon and night. Young love."

He flicked dry tears from the sides of his eyes with speedy fingertips. He sighed.

I sat beside Mother, reared into the armrest, stared her down. She turned the album on its face on the coffee table, folded meek hands in her lap, blinked at them.

I felt myself begin to soften. I didn't show it. "How nice," I said, with vicious primness, "to see you here."

Keller, stunned by my venomous attitude, whispered, "Now, Mildred! Please!" Not because I didn't have a right to be hateful. But because I had interrupted his story, broken his concentration. He took a breath, as to finish or continue his Harlot DeCarlo story. But then he said nothing.

I laughed, but not much this time, not brutally. "No," I said. "I mean it, I mean it." I touched her hands, then decided not to. I wiped my palms on my thighs, as if they'd been burned. "Nice to see you," I said, more quietly. I whispered, "What's up?"

"Mildred?" She touched her cheek, then touched mine. "Mildred." Tentative on the first syllable, solid on the second. Just trying it out, this new name of her son's.

Keller straightened his legs, stretched luxurious toes, then snapped right back up. "Jamie, I mean." Louder this time, and with authority, as if he had said nothing before, "Now Jamie! Please! Don't be ugly!"

I had a hard-on, for myself and my new life, and that she could see me. My skirts. My power. She nodded, as if she understood, holding serious wide eyes on her lap.

"How can you be here?" I said, in a tiny amazed voice. I meant, How can you be here in this queer place? How is it that you don't disappear in a puff of lavender smoke?

But Mother and Keller thought I was mad. They both jumped forward, they were explaining, at cross-purposes, together. Collaborators.

"Now, Jamie, don't," said Keller.

Mother held up her hand. "Let me tell."

But Keller went on, "We're both worried about you. How you break things. How you sit in your room. How you talk to yourself up there."

"No," I said, heavily, as if he were an idiot, "It's Donna-May Dean that I've been talking to."

Keller shot a look at my mother: You see?

Mother exhaled: It's worse than we thought.

"We both want what's best for you," Keller offered.

"We've just been talking, me and your friend—."

Keller said, "Keller. But you can call me Helen."

And Mother, "—me and—Keller? Is that your name?— we've been talking." She rubbed the flat palm of her hand against one of mine, back and forth, as to start a fire. "Are you happy, son? In Wonderland?"

I looked at Keller, a question. Meaning, Why have you betrayed me?

He just said, "Well. Are you?"

I couldn't stand it, they were both watching me, both my mothers.

Keller breathed heavily out, stood. "Diana," he said to Mother. "Can't I get you something? Wine? Sweet tea? Wheat Thins? Tea cakes?"

Mother smiled. "No, thank you."

I said, to Keller, with resentment, "It's not Diana. It's Diane."

"What-ev-er." He went bustling to the kitchen. "I made the tea cakes. You'll love them. Phillips family recipe."

"He's lying," I said. "Thomas probably made the tea cakes."

She said, "Listen to me. I mean it. Listen."

Then she didn't say anything.

I said, "That's funny. Listen? Keller's favorite word."

She said, she was laughing. "I *know*. I've been here since two or three hours ago. I know."

Then she went on:

She was late for work this morning, she said. She hadn't slept well. She hadn't been sleeping for a long time. Not that it was my fault. She didn't come here to make me feel bad.

It was partly my fault, she said, but not all. "It started before you left, even. My not sleeping. You remember."

I nodded, because she sounded so sure, though I had never known.

She said, "It's no big deal." In a tone that meant, It is.

The sheets would get wrapped around her, that was the worst part of it. "You can feel how dirty they are, because I haven't been doing laundry either. Gritty and sweaty and you can even feel it in your sleep. Except that I wasn't sleeping."

I didn't say anything. What did she want from me?

This morning, she said, she was out of bed in plenty of

time to get to work, but what was the point? She kept watching Donahue.

"It was about you people. About—what do you call it? Gays? And you know what? None of them had last names. Randy and Linda and Ricky and stuff. One of them was just a shadow on a screen. His voice came out like a computer, like Darth Vader. Somebody from the audience said something about mothers. How you loved your mothers too much. Or the other way around. Is that what it is? Is it my fault?"

I said, "Don't be silly. No." I didn't sound convincing.

She nodded anyway, good girl. "That's what he said, the Darth Vader guy. That mothers have nothing to do with it." She laughed. "And you know what? That bothers me a little bit, too. I mean, it's what you are, right?" She swallowed, to show that this was a new idea, at once, that it was awkward in her mouth and throat, but she was fine. "Maybe I wish I did have something to do with it. That might make me feel better." Then she added, "Might not, though. Might not." Because she didn't really want to hear me say, "Yes, you did this to me."

But maybe she did. I didn't say so. Who knows?

I was thinking, What's keeping Keller? But of course, he was doing this on purpose, letting us talk. Because this was all his game.

And I was thinking, What is his game?

I nodded to Mother, go on.

She pulled herself up, fuller of gumption than she realized. She was even angry. "So what? So I got in to work late today. No big deal. That was just tough titty." She was just *wanting* her manager, Martin, to say something about it. She's their oldest waitress, has the star on her name tag to prove it: fifteen years.

Martin didn't look happy, but he never does. "I think his wife beats him," she said. "He comes in sometimes black-and-blue."

All he said to her was, "Nice of you to drop by." Smartass, that Martin. He's twenty-eight, he reminds her of me. He also

125

told her, "Somebody called. He left his number. Name of Keller. Said it was im-per-a-tive that he speak with you." Martin hit the word *imperative* with swishy stress, as Keller must have.

Mother, as if reciting a memorized version, shut her eyes. I could imagine her practicing, on the way over here. "Martin didn't let me call until my break. We were busy, he said. And I had been late. And no personal calls. When I did finally call, you had gone to Huntsville. Keller told me you were fine, not to worry. He had made some tea cakes, he told me. Would I like to come over and have tea cakes? He was worried about you." She said, "You're not mad at me? For being here?"

I said, with affection, "Keller's a real bastard. He lies like a rug. Thomas made the tea cakes."

"I know. You told me that." She said, "Jamie."

As if there were something I hadn't said already.

The first time she ever came to the house, the night of the party, she had been brazen, had knocked on the door, because she was drinking and didn't care, because she imagined that nobody would answer. She had followed me home from Corner Fruit, had cruised several hours around the block, had finally broken away, relieved, ready to put it out of her mind, only to go to the Tennessee line, come back, be pathetic.

But this time, she'd been invited. And she wasn't sure she had come to the right place. The paint was too white for faggots, peeling patterns up the walls. The Daughters of the Confederacy might have meetings in a house like this. The John Birch Society.

How could her own son be living here?

So she stood back, looked up and down the door, timid and angrily. She checked one more time where she had scribbled the address on the back of her employee dinner discount check.

Maybe she should go back home, change clothes? Because she was still wearing her waitress uniform, plaid shirt and skirt

126

and French cap and kelly-colored apron. Not the proper attire for Wonderland, she said.

So she just stood on the porch, pressed the sides of her sore feet together, a trick every waitress learns, to make herself keep standing when she must. She bent her knees slightly. She breathed. She crossed her arms, uncrossed them, smiled, lost it, smiled again. Rang the doorbell, at once, simply because she hadn't noticed it there before.

Then she heard nothing. Some bird in the trees behind her made a sliding, flutelike trill. Meaning, Trouble. Meaning, Rain. Or maybe she was just being paranoid.

Keller pretended not to have been expecting her. He lowered his bifocals, blinked above them, three times. He said, "Yes?"

"I'm his mother," she said, meaning to sound stern, coming out friendly instead. She said, "Hello."

"Of course." He cleared his throat, "So am I," opened the door wide, continued the sweeping motion with his hand, to show her the way. "His mother, I mean." She didn't move until he took a half-step backwards and a bow. "Delighted to once again make your acquaintance," he whispered.

She walked toward nothing, inside, on nervous tiptoes, as if he might bite. "So this is it?" she said.

He didn't seem to understand. She didn't say it again.

"You realize that we have a problem," he said. He steered her elbow toward the common room.

She suffered herself to be set in the settee.

"Coffee?" he wondered aloud. "Tea cakes?"

She said she was fine. "Why did you call?" she said. A nervous, absurd caution in her wrists and eyes, as if she were negotiating with the Queen of Hearts.

What Keller told her was this: they loved me. "And yet—" He sat, allowed the second word, with a spin of his hand, to trail into unspoken possibilities.

"I never meant it, when I said we should wear shoes at the grocery store. When I said, 'AIDS.' Is that why he left me? Did he tell you about that?"

She ran a hand through her hair. Keller lifted his eyebrows. The stringy color job.

She said, "I never meant to know he was—he was—"

Keller said, "There, there." He patted her knee. "Not your fault for finding out. Mothers know. They always do."

"It was his daddy who told me."

Keller grimaced. "How improper. You must never repeat this." He said, "Shameful, even. His daddy, indeed."

Mother lit a cigarette. "Do you mind?" She said, "I mean, I think he hates me or something. I just wonder how I was supposed to act. I was trying to be nice about it. I just wanted to talk to him. I guess I'll shut up, though. I guess I sound stupid."

She waved out the match, sent an arc of blue smoke sputtering before her face. It lifted. She watched it until it broke on the ceiling.

Keller tactfully slammed an ashtray from the bookshelf behind him before her.

"He told us that you kicked him out of the house."

Mother lowered her face. She said, "Hm." She laughed. "Did I?"

Keller smiled, slapped his hands on his knees, sat. "Of course you did. Because that's the story. That's what mothers always do."

She said she didn't understand.

"What's the truth?" Keller said. "The truth is what we choose to believe. Am I right? And your son"—here he stopped, to lean forward, inquire with lifted brows, to see that she followed—"our son believes that you kicked him out of the house. Or he claims to believe it, which is the same thing. Listen." Keller beamed now. "He doesn't hate you. He just wants to."

Mother, catching on, "Which is the same thing?"

"Exactly."

She said, "I see," airily, as if she did not.

Keller clapped quick palms together, holding his fingers stiffly separated, as a child.

"But why does he want to hate me?"

Keller shrugged. "It's not even that simple," he said. "It's not even that he wants to hate you. He wants to hate himself. You're an easier target. He can't stand it, what he is. He can't stand it that you know. None of us can."

Then he smiled.

"I don't mean just faggots. But I do mean faggots in particular."

He stopped. He stood. In another tone of voice, to indicate a greater degree of honesty, "Listen. About what I just said? About not being able to stand what we are? That's a lie, an old attitude, a romantic yarn. It's just something I like to say. It sounds so tragic, don't you think?"

He took down a picture album from the bookshelf.

"I have too many stories of pathetic faggots to tell. None of them are true. Because, listen—*The Boys in the Band* got it wrong. There's no such thing as an unhappy homosexual. We're all just pretending."

He lifted his face, as to laugh, then he didn't.

Mother protested, without vigor, against the complicated turn of the conversation, "I'd like to have my son back."

Keller snapped a finger in the air, to obliterate such a callous possibility. "Trust me. He's not ready for that yet."

He shoved the album her way, with lifted chin, squinty eyes, puckered lips. He said, "Donna-May Dean," and angled a cynical pinky at a picture of himself: fifteen years ago, high school graduation. She recognized nothing but the eyes, rounder and less crafty, touched in drab watercolor blue.

"But that's you," she said.

"Donna-May Dean," Keller went on, with insistent whining, "was a drag queen, a tragic and sad one, but aren't they all?" He turned the stiff page. Here was Keller's prom picture: Wally Cleaver in powder blue, with a visible lisp, dateless.

The facing page, the Phillips widow, eleven cracked and fading inches by fourteen, labelled on the scalloped border in a meticulous cursive, *Bitch Thing*. She wore a high, blunt hairdo, a white lace collar on black, an overbitten smile.

Keller pulled away the plastic cover, tugged loose the picture. He put it in Mother's hands, turned it over. On the back, a long story: *Bitch Thing got a wig,* it began. *Bitch Thing got a brooch. Bitch Thing got a God. Bitch Thing lay in bed all day, with her bills and her pills and her hot water bottle. Bitch Thing got a son.*

"So you see," Keller said, "a faggot's mother must learn to be careful. You wouldn't want your son to turn into Donna-May Dean."

"What are you talking about? I'm sorry. This is too much. I don't get it."

Keller said, to calm her, "Listen." He turned to another page, said nothing, stopped, breathed out. Frustration. "Because she needs her mother. I mean, Donna-May Dean. Because every faggot does."

He licked imaginary sweat from his upper lip. To stall, he threw the picture album back at her.

Here was Thomas, younger, naked in the kitchen, except for sunglasses, eyebrows lifted at the camera, a clumsy beer bottle tilting from his grin.

(This would have been one of the parties. Before they got tame. Before they turned potluck.)

Behind Thomas stood silhouettes, immaculate, hands in the air. Like deco details on a vase. At Thomas's feet, on either side, entwined, was a drag queen. His dick hung toward the one on the left, who smacked dry, sly lips, one eye watching the bulbous head, the other trained, ironically, on the camera.

Keller said, "Donna-May Dean." He whispered, "Happy? So were we all."

Donna-May Dean wore a fur coat and a jockstrap, fingered with his free hand a pearl choker necklace.

Mother said, despite herself, "Where's the tragedy? You said lovely. You said tragic."

"Yes, yes," Keller said. "Wait a minute." He flipped through the pictures like a madman. Now and then he stopped, read what was written on the back. He said, "I don't want to talk about it." He offered an alternative, a distraction, as a sideshow barker, "Harlot DeCarlo!"

*   *   *

"And that," said Mother, "was when you came in."

I waved my hand, annoyance, lit a cigarette, put it out. "He makes it all up, you know."

I was thinking, How much of it does he make up?

"I know," she said. "He told me. And he said it doesn't matter. That that means it's all the more true." She spoke with the gravity of a recent convert. "What is it about his mother?" she said. "What was he trying to say?" Then, "Why don't you like me?"

As if this question were an answer to the first two.

Keller broke in here, holding the tea cakes on a silver serving tray above his head. To Mother, "I've always wanted to be a waitress. Is this how it's done?"

She laughed. "No. On your fingertips. It balances better."

I was embarrassed. He was making fun, and she didn't even know. Or maybe she did. Or maybe he wasn't.

Keller grimaced. "I'd best not try." He swooped the tray down, set it atop the picture album on the coffee table. It slid, sloping, stopped. Tea cakes bunched on its rim, some of them fell on the floor.

We took a few.

Mother said, "These are good. You did a good job."

One-note Jamie, "Thomas. Thomas did a good job."

Keller, to me, "Thomas is sulking. He likes you, after all. He said to me, 'You're not going to send him back?' He's curled up in bed with his thumb in his mouth. I told him, I said, 'But Mother's china. The toilet seat. Donna-May Dean.'"

Keller sat. To Mother, "Thomas was the one who answered the phone when you called the second time. Thomas doesn't count. Ignore what he said."

I said, to Mother, "What did he say?"

Keller said, "He was rude, was what he was. He called her 'lady.' He said to her, 'Look, lady. Don't come here.' He didn't know that it was my idea. He didn't know that I had called her up. It's my house, I can have whatever company I choose."

131

Mother said, "I had to work a double shift, that's why I called." She set down the tea cake: two tiny, bitter bites. "I had to, Martin said. I could make up being late. What could I say?"

Thomas had told her not to apologize. That it might not be such a good idea to come now. Or at all. "Look, lady," he said. Then he couldn't think of what to say. "He belongs here with us. We're his family, now. Don't think you're going to waltz in and take him away."

Mother reported this with a good go at Thomas's mock roughness.

Keller slapped my knee across the coffee table. "Isn't your Mother the very End?"

But I was thinking of Thomas, I was smiling.

Mother said, "I told him that that's not what I wanted. To take you away. But I said that I could." Her voice: low and level and vindictive, "The law is on my side." She wasn't speaking to the imaginary Thomas, though: she was looking directly at me.

Thomas had said, "I'll tell Keller you'll be late," then hung up on her.

Keller took over the story from here. "He came looking for me. He said, 'How old is Jamie anyway?' I threw a third pair of pants on the bed. What to wear? Middle-class kitsch? Dreary faggot decadence? Calvin Kleins? Sears Huskies? Thomas told me that you"—he waved a hand at Mother— "would be much later than you thought. I told him, 'Good.' I sat on the bed."

Keller stood, crossed over, to pantomime the scene on the couch. In his own Thomas voice, less rough than Mother's imitation, more accurate, "Why did you call her, anyway?"

Then he scooted to the other armrest, fluttered his hands, to show he was impersonating himself. "Because I'm sending him back. Because he's driving me crazy." His tone, deliberate overkill, to show he was not so determined now as he was then.

In his own voice, but with Thomas's nod, "Yeah." Then he said, "Oops." He moved back to what had been established as Thomas's place on the couch (the bed). He deepened his voice by clearing his throat. He said, more definitively, "Yeah."

Then quickly, flouncily, back, "I just don't think he's got what it takes to be one of us. A proper faggot."

He stood. He looked at us. In a more direct voice, "Then Thomas folded his hands on my shoulder, set his chin there. What did I mean, he wanted to know. What is a proper faggot? And I told him that I still don't know, that I wish I did. I said, 'I should listen to you? My greatest failure.' "

Keller made a poised and sad face, to show the performance was over. He accepted a moment of inaudible applause. Then he went back to his chair, but didn't sit. "He told me not to give up on him either. I mean, himself. I mean, Thomas. He pulled me down. He held me there. And then? And then, he fucked me."

Keller took two theatrical steps, held up his hands, meaning nothing. "I said, 'I give up. How old is Jamie?' And he said, into my ear, he said, 'Shhhhhh.' "

Keller put his own finger to his lip, to show us where Thomas's had been, and how delicately.

Mother, despite herself, choking a little, "That's beautiful. I can't believe you told me that." She covered her mouth with a quick stiff hand. "Where's the bathroom?"

Keller went on. "And then the phone rang." He sat. "But whoever it was, the bastard, hung up."

"That was me. The car wouldn't start. I wanted to tell you, though, that I was fine."

"I know," Keller said, "how fine you are, boy."

I told Mother how to get to the bathroom. She grunted, humor and helplessness. Then she left.

I shrugged, went to my room. Donna-May Dean was not to be found. Mother had turned out to be more real than he was after all. I came back down with her purse.

Keller said, his old, gossipy self, "How old are you, anyway?"

I opened the purse: Spearmint gum smell, lipstick tissues, fresh, sweet, broken cigarettes. I said, "She always goes to the bathroom to cry. Runs in the family."

I leaned forward. I hissed. "How could you call her here? She doesn't belong here. I hate you."

"No, you don't." He set his hand on my knee. "You should talk to your mother. You shouldn't have just disappeared. I have a lot of sympathy for her. You should love your mother."

I said, in his voice, sarcastically, "Oops. You mean, you."

He blinked. "That's not what I meant, this time. But, yes. And also, no."

"I'm legal," I said. "I'm eighteen."

Mother, standing in the doorway, with a tissue wadded to the side of her mouth, "He's sixteen." She looked at the tissue in her hand, an apology. "I'm sorry. Just nervous, that's all."

I said, casually, to Keller, "So? I'm sixteen." I gave the purse to Mother as she sat. "I'm old for my age." Her eyes were red. "Let me stay." I looked at Keller, "Please."

"We only want what's best for you," Keller said. "We'll see." Then, to her, "Is it hot in here, or is it me?"

Mother shrugged.

"We should go for a walk," Keller said. "Go to the park. You can see how we live."

"She's already been there," I snapped. I said, "No." Because I was ashamed. Keller was bad enough: what would she think of the trade and the trolls? What if Bonanza Butt cruised through, with his bell-bottoms, his invisible crippled pussy?

They voted me down. We went to the park. And: why did I care, anyway?

No cars at the park—even two blocks away we should have seen, we should have known to turn around. One of the first lessons Keller had taught me: never be alone in the park at night. The fountain was running, but lightless, invisible. Just the sound of it, eerie in the total black. The Firestone building across the street, an air-conditioned cage of glass and steel, fluorescent security lights left burning bright until morning, hummed. From the highest dormer window of a party house two blocks away, nervous red and blue strobes, the bodiless thud of rock music heard from too far. It was so late that the birds who nest in the church eaves woke when we passed. They flew, irritated pepper against the slightly brighter sky.

Keller, upon stepping into the park, whispered, "Odd," the first word any of us had spoken since leaving the house. Mother and I jumped. Then there they were, on the corner, waiting at the light:

"FAGGOTS HOMOS FUCKING COCKSUCKER PUSSYBOY BASTARDS—" A bottle burst and spread at our feet. "QUEER PANSIES FRUITCAKES FAGGOTS HOMOS FAGGOTS FAGGOTS FAGGOTS." Then they were gone: a jacked-up Mustang with racing stripes, fuzzy rearview mirror dice, no license plate.

Keller bent, to sift the glass through ten fanned and shaky fingers. "Look," he said. "A love poem." He said, "Diamonds."

Mother held her elbows in her hands, as if she were cold. "Wonderland."

I told her to shut up. She was getting tedious, I said. I bit my hand, the soft pulpy web between stretched thumb and forefinger. I said, from the pain, "Shit." I wasn't even upset. I turned into myself, examined every place in my body where emotion usually shows: heart and hands and head. Nothing. How funny. I said, rising on each syllable, "Keller, let's just get out of here."

"Oh pish. They won't be back."

All three of us breathed, as if Keller—his magic—had settled the issue.

He took Mother's arm in his. He pulled me to his other side.

"Besides—never let them see you run. It's an invitation."

He strode us stiffly down into the park.

"We'll have to go through to the other side, cut behind the Post Office. We don't want them to see where we came from. Follow us home. Now, do we? Not that they would, of course. Not that they're coming back. No, sir. No, ma'am. Never, never."

And there they were, we heard them, we turned. They stopped in front of the church.

Keller pulled us in, toward the fountain. He sat us on the

135

wet, rumbling rim. He said, "Be calm. Be silent. Stay." He paced before us, hands in his pockets, head back, eyes shut. He mumbled something: magic spells? A prayer? Our backs got wet. We sat there.

Keller said, brightly, "Cigarette?" Then put them back in his pocket. "Never mind."

Slam of a car door. Somebody stood silhouette, sluggishly, in the headlights. "Faggots!" he screamed, as if to himself. "I just hate faggots."

Keller said, "Juicy Fruit?" He held a stick of it in my face. I jumped.

I said, "Thanks."

The redneck, impossibly far from us, banged his fist on the hood. Several fisted hands out the windows, assent: how many, though?

It was almost as if it didn't matter. We chewed our gum.

Then the voice was swooping, hateful falsetto: "Faggots? Ooh, faggots? Pretty pretty pretty?" Like calling a dog who knows it needs to be spanked.

I said to Mother, "So now you see. This is how we live." But this was a joke. She didn't laugh. It wasn't a joke anymore. I said to Keller, an accusation, "Tell her." But I didn't give him a chance. "Welcome to the world," I said. "Welcome to the fucking magic kingdom." I spat, but not at Mother. At the ground. I said, "Give me one of those cigarettes."

Mother grabbed my arm, Keller my shoulder, as if I were a drugged animal at the veterinarian, I might bolt. What was in my face? Had I been screaming?

Keller said, "Darling, behave."

I kept looking into those headlights, wide-eyed. "Fuck you!" I screamed. They held me tighter. I didn't care. I screamed, "Naa-naa-naa-naa boo boo!"

The redneck might have been beating his chest, alternate fists, like an ape. It was hard to tell. He might have been sexy.

I hated having thought that.

Then I kept on: he might have been blond, he probably had a big cock, hair on his balls, tight crack, smooth thighs.

He jumped back in the car. It went around three times, faster and faster. Then they were gone.

I was patted all over with four motherly hands.

Keller laughed. "Talking back to the bashers. Aren't you just Miss Butch?" He fixed my collar for some reason, briskly. He ran a hand through my hair. "Aren't you *just?*" He sighed.

Mother lit a cigarette, blew smoke at a sharp angle from her face. She looked bored, of all things. Bored and beautiful.

I said, to both of them, "So have you decided yet, what to do with me?" Less loudly, "I can take care of myself."

I walked away, but not with conviction. I went around the fountain and toward the bathroom building and past it. I came back when they didn't plead and beg and call after me.

Keller, back to business, took our elbows. "This is kind of fun, isn't it? Comrades in arms."

We matched our steps to his, but I stumbled. He pulled me up brutally and kept walking to the other side of the park, where we crossed the street. Keller's plan held, to cut behind the Post Office. He wasn't taking any chances, he said.

He kept saying it.

Also he said something else, under his breath: "Listen to my heartbeat." That was the last line of a Laurie Anderson song I had played for him, the only part of the song that he had paid any attention to. Or maybe he didn't say anything at all, just moved his lips, breathing through them. Then he said, for sure, "Listen."

Because there was that car—at least a block away, from the sound. Surely they were on their way home.

They came up slowly behind us.

Keller said, "Don't look."

But I did. And I was right. How cute he was. A short cigarette sloped from the side of his contemptuous, taut, un-shaven face. Smoke curled up and around then away from small, hard eyes—the color of tin on a roof on a cold morning, those eyes.

We kept walking. It was like being shadowed by a great white shark and you're just a school of tuna.

Four others in the car nodded, bit their bottom lips, shined beady hateful eyes.

Mother screamed.

But Keller stopped her, didn't let her, squeezed her wrist. We'd almost made it to the Post Office. Delivery jeeps lined in a row, puddling oil. We stepped between them. I imagined that we might be safe once we got inside. We could pretend to be checking our mail. We could pretend to be buying stamps from the machine. It's funny what you think of at a time like that. Nobody would hurt us, I imagined, if we were just buying stamps from the machine. We could say that we weren't faggots after all. Keller and Mother could confront them, holding hands. We could lift Mother's shirt, to show that she was real.

But then I shuddered.

"I'm talking to you," said the driver, with elegant patience, except for the hoarse and maddened syllable *talk*. His quietness itself was sexy. His eyes like crosshairs on the back of my neck. I caught myself offering a snivel, a cowardly smile. I shuddered, shook it off my face.

"Fuck you," I whispered, but not so he could hear this time.

Keller, with dignity, lifted his head, stuck out his foot, came down on pointed toes. He pulled back his face. His eyes were as self-contained and mortified as a Church of Christ housewife's at a tacky Pentecostal tent service.

Then he broke away, with fisted desperate awkward hands back and forth above his head: temper tantrum, shaman magic. He didn't say anything, ran directly toward the car.

Then he got there.

He said, surprised with himself, and quietly, "Begone?"

I didn't know if he meant himself or them.

Then he slammed his flat hand on top of the car. But they didn't disappear. He crossed his arms. He smiled. He turned to wink at me. He slapped again the top of the car, with more reluctance, as if it were soiled. He shouted, "Begone!"

They jumped out of the car, with no baseball bats, just rolled-up sleeves and dirty hands and cowboy boots. Just a tire-changing tool. Keller fell into their closing, almost affec-

tionate circle. They might have been dancing around a may-
pole.

I took a step, two more stumbling curious steps. Mother
whispered, "Don't go over there." She fell on top of me, held
me down: savagely. Breathing. My forehead struck the concrete. I smelled blood. She bit my collar. She held me there.
"I won't let them hurt you."

Which made me laugh. But I didn't. I was quiet, I was
calm, I was just trying to get my head up. All I wanted was
to see. If they were hurting him. No: *how* they were hurting
him. And how cute they were.

A thud, a thud, a continuous rattling gurgle. I recognized
it by the rhythm—Keller, laughing. Then a dratted interrupt-
ing thud. Even more slowly, he took up his laughing again.
Trying to pronounce the distinct syllables, just like nothing,
just like always: "Tee hee hee. Hoo *hoo* hoo ha." But something
caught in his throat. He said, carefully, "Urk."

I heard them stop. I heard, all at once, nothing. One of
them said, as if apologetic, as if to justify himself, "Fuckin'
faggot. What's a fuckin' faggot for?" Meaning that no real man
could help himself, in the presence of a faggot. Meaning that
it was Keller's fault.

Mother let me lift my head, turtle to her shell.

They made nervous chuckling. Maybe it was their first
time. They looked down, with solemn smiles. Maybe he was
bleeding. Of course he was bleeding. Maybe he was lovely.

Then came sputtering groans. A fat ridiculous cow stuck
in the slaughterhouse chute who won't die, who keeps on
straining against the swung blade, muttering blood.

One of them said, "It's Miller time." He winked at his
own joke, touched the brim of his cap. His cheeks burned red
through the whiskers: adrenaline and, possibly, guilt. He
scuffed his feet. As did they all. His lashes were long in the
light from a cigarette match. He blew wide, thoughtful puffs,
passed his pack of Camels. My brand. Cigarettes got lit all
around.

Another of them, an older man, somebody's weathered
alcoholic father, whispered, "Jesus." He let drop the tire-

changing tool. Then stepped on it, to stop the metal oscillating clang and echo.

There was still Keller, but we had all gotten used to that sound.

Another one, leaning back to watch the sky, with proud thumbs in front beltloops: "Yeah. Jesus."

"Maybe we should call an ambulance?" said the first one, the driver. His voice more quick and broken and postcoitally small than it had been before.

They bowed their heads, they scratched their necks, they tried to think, but with hateful leisure.

A car turned from another street toward us. The rednecks jerked alive and bright-eyed like animals in the headlamps' slow glare.

"Oh, man. The cops!"

But it was just a timid troll, his gray Buick. I'd seen him a dozen times here before. He stopped half a block away, leaned forward over his steering wheel: rabbity nostrils, blinking eyes. He did a three-point turn, quick as the pencil point on a Spirograph.

The rednecks, real men again, laughed, slapped each other on thick shoulders, on the back, on the butt.

Mother let me up, then let me go. I stepped into their circle. They smiled, made humble room for me. I lifted my nose and fairy fluttering powerful hands into the air. "Be," I whispered, "gone."

This time it worked.

I still didn't look at Keller. Mother came behind me, touched my shoulders, the back of my neck, held her face there, said something hoarse and indecipherable.

"Is this how you live?"

I shook her off again. I stared. "It's not our fault," I said.

But that's not what she meant: her hands clasped before her. She meant that she was worried. She meant that she was scared. She meant to be in awe. I felt sorry for her, but didn't say so. I turned back to Keller.

His face lolled from side to side. Maybe he was still struggling to laugh. Then he said, in his most rational, unbroken voice, as if he were sitting in his common-room chair, "Don't be silly. It's always our fault."

He spat some blood. He laughed.

I lifted his throat back, checked the tongue. I don't know why. Because that's what they do on TV. His tongue was there. It was bitten. It was blue. I said, "Keller, are you okay?" Which was stupid. "I'll get an ambulance," I said. I picked up the tire iron. I tossed it, caught it, was walking. "You stay here. In case they come back."

Mother laughed. "Jamie. What could *I* do?"

I kept going, more calm than I should have been, shakily, two blocks down to the phone booth. Each thing I passed on the way glimmered with nervous meaning: the stoplights, trash in the street, an open manhole. The texture of the sidewalk. The lack of stars in the sky.

Keller called this phone booth "Dial-A-Queen," he had made me memorize the number. He said that somebody was always walking by, on the way home from the park. "You can get a date that way on slow night," he told me.

Scrawled above the door, in Magic Marker: ABANDON ALL HOPE YE WHO ENTER HERE. And sure enough, it was ringing.

"Do you have a tight, greasy asshole? Because I've got a hard, horny cock."

I looked at the receiver. I said, "Cookie Monster? Is that you?" Then I realized. "Thomas?"

Then the click, then the tone.

I slammed my hand holding the tire iron into the glass beside me. Nothing. I kept on. I kicked the aluminum base. I winced. Relief. One more time. My hand broke through. I dropped the tire iron outside, screamed.

I decided not to call the police. What would they do? Arrest us for loitering, probably. I called the hospital.

Blood on my knuckles, shining black on the dull gray receiver as I placed it quietly in its cradle. I leaned back, crossed my arms, watched with wide horrified eyes, until it rang.

Should I answer? Should I tell him?

"This never happens," I told Mother, "except in Keller's

stories, maybe." But, of course, she wasn't there to hear. And when I did get back to her, I didn't dare speak.

They let us ride in the ambulance, with the driver, up front. A thick black layer of gum and dirt on the floor-boards. A naked girlie air freshener swaying from the rearview mirror.

Mother held my hand and my shoulder, comfort, and to keep me from turning around, to look through the window at what they were doing to Keller.

She said, "He's fine. He'll be fine."

The driver lifted his eyebrows, twirled the cigarette in his mouth—redneck apology—after a loud and smoky burp.

Once, I did look back, but saw nothing. I saw arms in white sleeves moving an urgent dance about his body. I saw a red IV tube, looping down, jerk.

The emergency room smelled of Lysol and worked nerves and mine and Mother's cigarettes. Mother smiled, put hers out into an empty dunce-cap paper cup.

I couldn't stand it, that she had protected me. "They were looking for faggots," I explained one more time. I thumped my chestbone, mouthed, "Faggot."

A passing, frilly, male nurse tossed back his piss-elegant locks, snorted. I guess he thought I meant him.

Mother said, "Jamie. I just didn't want you to be hurt, that's all. Any mother—"

And I knew she was right. But still, "I could have stopped them. Killed a redneck with my spike-heeled pump."

"You're barefoot."

"It's a metaphor."

She shut her mouth, made a serious Walker Evans dust-bowl mother profile.

I laughed, ran a hand through her hair. "Rough night. Don't listen to me. I'll be nicer tomorrow, to everybody. I'll try to be nicer to you."

She didn't accept this, though. "Who do you hate?" she said. "Is it just me, or is it all straight people?" She lifted her

142

chin, set it back on her hand. "Because, you know what? I'm beginning to see why."

I went to get a sip of water, but couldn't find the fountain, had to drink from the bathroom tap. When I got back, she was gone.

She waved me over to the nurse's desk. "He's fine," she said. "The nurse said he wants to see you." A short, quick grin. "He wants to see Mildred. They thought it was me."

I wiped the water from my chin. "Aren't you coming?"

She looked down, to look up at me. "Do you want me to? Can I?"

I stepped back, clicked my dull heels, held out my hand, as to say, After you.

Keller lay covered by a neat paper sheet, except for his face, his swollen lip and eyelids, the clear tube clipped beneath his nostrils. I held his hand on the safety rail.

"Bumps and bruises," he said. "I'm a tough old sissy."

Mother, peeking over my shoulder, "Hey?"

Keller shut his eyes, turned away. He tried to lift an arm, to show her: I hate to have you see me like this. Then he laughed. "I suppose you'll want him back for sure, now."

Mother didn't say anything. Meaning, Yes. Meaning, Probably.

My heartbeat shook in my shoulders, shot down both arms, into my fingers. I squeezed his hand. "I'll come back tomorrow."

He squeezed back. "They're going to be taking tests," he said. "Bring a couple number two pencils?" Then he coughed, he wanted to stop, he waved impatient hands. A sudden nurse wadded paper to the side of his mouth, he spat red into it. He took it, looked. He set it, folded, aside.

He said, "Well."

Mother tugged at my shirt, stepped backwards.

I yelled from the door, "Keller, bye!"

He flapped a hand, he was coughing: go on then, go on. He said, "Hooey," to show exhaustion, and humor, and because he wasn't coughing anymore. "Somebody light me a cigarette."

Outside, down the stone steps, a cool wind in our faces from the river before us. The bridge was just beginning to pick up and shine with morning traffic. Past that, my neighborhood, Keller and Thomas's. I even picked out a couple familar stop-lights: one at the park, one at Corner Fruit. And over there, a block from where that big tree sent wide branches in a very particular pattern above the horizon, was my house. Keller and Thomas's.

She said, "What now?"

"We walk, I guess."

So she did, but I kept standing there. I said, "Got a cig-arette?" Had she ever seen me smoke before? I ran to catch up with her. She slapped her pockets, her purse, shook her head. She gave me her last cigarette, the lit one from her mouth.

I said, "I belong with them now."

We crossed the bridge on the narrow walking lane, smack in the middle of traffic. The protective rail twisted inward, violently, on either side of us, in places. We stepped more carefully, there, over the things in our way: one entire flawless windshield, the arm of a baby doll, an open, broken compact mirror. There was the hollow sound of something dangling against something metal, the sound of a flagpole and its cord in the wind. Halfway across, Mother stopped. I looked past her: a square metal hole, where some worker had left the trapdoor open. A thin ladder jutted three abrupt rungs down. Then nothing. Green and hum and darkness. Scummy leaves and bright bits of paper spun figure eight whirlpools on the water, impossibly far. I shoved her shoulder, she looked back at me. "Let's go," I said. "Jump. I'm cold."

But she held the rail in tight knuckles on either side.

I pointed a finger, though she wasn't looking at me any-more. "It's not fair, if you make me come home."

She turned, scratched the sides of her mouth, tugging them down with spread thumb and forefinger. Her lipstick smeared, a Mardi Gras frown. I sat down. She squatted, grace-fully, looked me in the eyes. "You're my son. I miss you. That's all."

"So we'll get together now and then. We'll do brunch."

I meant to be funny, not brutal: but there were her eyes. I said, "I'm sorry."

She stood, brushed her skirt clean with a firm, humorous hand. "Never mind. Sorry I mentioned it. Bastard." But she touched my cheek, my chin. "Bastard, bastard, bastard." But lovingly.

I said, "Bitch. I mean, me. Call me bitch, I mean. You'll catch on."

A scream. Wild teenager hands came slapping out the window of a passing car. We jumped. Then we laughed. Then we went on.

"Don't let them beat you up," she told me. "Don't get AIDS. Don't turn into Donna-May Dean."

I said, "Promise. Promise. And promise." Easy enough. Because who wants to get beaten up? And AIDS doesn't happen here. And I had already turned into Donna-May Dean. But what I said was, "Never. Never. Never."

Then it was raining.

Thomas didn't come to the bedroom door when I knocked. I creaked the slow door open, took myself on tiptoes inside.

He had pinned a haphazard quilt to the window, to block out the light. Hard white around the sides, burning sepia through the patches, sparse cotton clumped like smoke shadows within.

He lay on his fist socked deep into the pillow. A glass of water atop one of Keller's high-tone magazines turned to the crossword on the chair. No answers filled in, no pencil.

I set the water and magazine on the floor, reached delicately down, spread fingertips, between his shoulder blades. That was all. He didn't wake. I didn't want him to. I watched a bug spinning madly into the long-dead exposed light bulb in the ceiling. Force of habit, I guessed. I was shaking: wet clothes and wrecked, melancholy nerves.

My hand, as on a first date, made sticky sweat. I lowered the palm all the way, gently, down.

145

Thomas stirred, looking sleepy daggers at me from one straining inch above his pillow. "How did you get in here? Where's Keller? Is the bathtub clean?"

He blinked, squeezed the pillow into a ball, threw it at the headboard, hard, then crawled grudgingly after, put his face down, again, into it.

The radio alarm clicked on. I shut it off. I left the room.

Opened the front room windows, and the ones in the kitchen. Then I shut them, cleaned them with Windex and old newspapers. I sat in the sun at the kitchen table.

I slapped my hands together, Keller-wise.

I made a dark pot of coffee, poured it out, failure, started another.

I put away last night's dry dishes, set a saucer of milk on the back cinder block step for stray neighborhood cats.

I went to the common room again, straightened the cigarettes in their holder on the coffee table.

I went to the bathroom, cleaned out the bathtub.

Richard's number ringing in my head like a commercial jingle, from hearing him repeat it so many times in the back room. So I called him. "Richard, please."

"Who is this? What did you do with my son?"

I didn't say anything.

"He was supposed to sing," said the man, as if begging me to know, to tell, where Richard had gone.

I hung up, laughed. But really: where was Richard? He'd be fine, though, I decided. Jimmy would see to that.

Then I thought, Maybe not.

I went to bed. Thomas woke to the scorch smell. He stood over me, shook the blackened coffeepot. "And what about Keller? What have you done with *him?*" As if I were the most amazing, the most laughably villainous thing.

"I washed the windows. I put away the dishes. Don't be so mean to me." I said, "I didn't do anything to Keller." I pulled the sheet to my collarbone, protection. "Keller's in the hospital. Rednecks. But he's okay."

Thomas set the coffeepot down on the sill, touched it with two or three fingers. He said, "Keller."

146

"Richard I'm not sure about. Richard, I don't know where he is." I was wrecked and sleepy, not thinking right. And I was finally crying—roughly, heaving, tearless—until Thomas left the room. And I felt silly, crying alone, with no one to see.

So I stopped.

I watched Thomas out the window, he stalked down the sidewalk. He came back. He slammed the front door shut. Then he came back again, called a taxi, waited in the kitchen. He made loud steps, to show me not to come down, that he was mad.

Then he stood at my door. "Here's the taxi. Do you want to come with me?"

I didn't say anything.

"Fine," he said. A threat.

"It's not my fault." I jumped up, stood on the bed. I yelled down the stairs, "Don't you slam that door again."

He did. Then he opened it, slammed it again.

Then he put his head back in, called up to me, "Jamie?" With a sinking, fallible inflection. "Hey, buddy? Hey, Jamie? I'm sorry."

Donna-May Dean, from the windowsill, wagged a smart-ass finger.

The phone rang, it was Jimmy. "Wanna go get your car? My bike's fixed now."

"I need to sleep now." Then I said, "No, he can't come to the phone. He's in the hospital. Not that. That doesn't happen here. No. No. No. Just nothing. Just rednecks. Yeah. They were cute. How did you guess? I know, I know."

I said, "What did you do with Richard?"

But before he could answer, I hung up the phone. Because I didn't want to hear.

FOUR

FLAWLESSNESS
AND FEAR

JIMMY DIDN'T GIVE ME TIME TO DREAM, HE WAS knocking on the door. I set him down in the common room. I scratched my head. I made hot tea. To sound more jaded than I was, I called from the kitchen, "Oh, he'll be fine."

I sat opposite him. I crossed my legs.

Jimmy, with a grumbling, nervous cough, leaned forward, put his cup in the saucer on the table, left it steaming there. "It's getting worse," he said. "At the park, I mean. Friday night they were throwing water balloons filled with piss." He slapped his knees, disbelief. "Why do they bother? What is their deal? And anyway—what's ours?"

Which would have been Keller's cue. In his absence, something oracular and unlikely left itself unspoken: I can't imagine what. We lowered our eyes, as to listen. We lifted them again, on the sly, to show how silly we were.

I said, "The nature of the beast."

"You mean rednecks or faggots? You mean, that they beat us up, or that we let them?"

It was too much for me. I waved my hands, as to say, I'm not Keller. But the gesture itself was his. I stood, slapped my butchest hand to the wall, held it there. How much of Keller had taken me over? Or was it just an innate prissiness shining through? How much of Keller in me was inevitable? How much of Donna-May Dean?

I said, "Where's Richard?"

"Oh that." Jimmy smiled, showed me his tongue in cheek. "He went to sleep on the floor in Gerald's bedroom, while we were undressing. Gerald has a water bed, we were having too much fun, didn't even bother to wake him. Then it was daylight. He wouldn't go home. Said his daddy would kill him. We kept trying to get him to let me drive him home. I said, 'Maybe he'll send you to military school. You know what happens to pretty boys in military school?' So he's thinking about it. He wants to move in with Gerald, though. Gerald doesn't know what to do. I told him, 'Give him a good spanking. Send him on his way. That's what to do with a boy like that.'" Jimmy smiled, crossed his arms, fell back in the chair, to show me how he had all the answers. "I was one, once. A boy like that."

I said, "What are you now?" Then, "I guess Richard could move in here, couldn't he?"

"Oh, no. Keller never takes two at a time."

"I'm thinking of moving out. Going back home." Which was a lie. Then, after I said it, I thought: yes.

Jimmy said, "Can't." He laughed. "Did Keller tell you to leave yet? I really don't think so. You don't look like a total faggot. You don't look flawless enough. Not yet. To me."

I came to lean over the back of his chair at him, on crossed elbows. I smiled, kitten, coy. "Maybe Keller just hasn't noticed yet. Maybe you haven't either."

"Maybe. Maybe. I don't think so." He stood, walked, watching, toward me: lion tamer. "Keller said I have to fuck you at least once before you graduate."

"How much did he pay you?" Then I was sorry I said it, I waved my hands, to change the subject. "Will you give me a good report?"

149

He, all at once all man, wide hands on my hips, "I'll give you a report."

Then we just laughed, we didn't go to my room. We went to get my car instead.

I rode on the back of his motorcycle, hands and arms tight around his waist, as if I meant it.

My chest did beat wild adrenaline against his back, but not from love, not from anything. From the wind in my eyes, the motor razzing in my ears. I said, "What if it's gone? If they towed it away?"

Jimmy hunkered more distantly toward the handlebars, patted me some backwards reassurance on the thigh, heavily, meaning, It's not gone. Or, I'll handle it. Or, Just wait. Or to tell me he didn't hear. Maybe he thought I was flirting again, this was a chance to cop another feel.

I sighed, pressed the center of my forehead to his backbone, hard, until it hurt. I shut my eyes. I tightened my teeth, to feel the road grinding there, the rough repaired-pothole patches. I left my teeth together, my eyes tight, my forehead firm, for the entire two hours and a half.

We didn't go to the bar, not right away. First we went to what Jimmy called "the Overlook," a new concrete circle, smooth as a fresh-peeled Eskimo Pie, on the side of what Jimmy called "the mountain." A cruisy place, he told me. I blinked my eyes against the bright white and dizzy sky. "I don't want to cruise."

"Shut up," he said, but in a sexy way, smiling. We sat on one of the limestone blocks on the edge. The four-lane directly beneath us, humming, descended toward flat purple and nothing and horizon.

"There's the Space and Rocket Center," Jimmy said. "And there's my favorite restaurant. Mexican. Do you want Mexican later?"

I tried to see what he was pointing to. It all looked like Lego blocks and random chance to me.

"I heard they put Alpo in the enchiladas. But don't believe it." Jimmy wrapped his legs around mine, but I pulled away,

150

forward, embarrassed. He said, a command, "Chill." Then he tugged me back in, to press his chest and chin and crotch against my back. "This," he told me, slowly, another command, "is our date. Remember?"

"I don't want a date. Too too much on my mind."

"Exactly. That's what I mean." He kneaded the base of my neck with slow palms, thumbs touching tips at my spine. I held still, despite myself, to hear the joints in his fingers popping. He was working so hard for me, just for me.

A spotty old man stepped out of his Cordoba, hiked up his plaid slacks by the belt in the back. He stepped nonchalantly near, in Florsheim flat-soles. "Lovely view," he said. His twinkling eyes. I blinked. The eyes—no colored—locked on Jimmy's behind me. He nodded.

"Gotta pee," Jimmy whispered. He scooted off the rock. "Right back." He slapped his thighs to clean his hands of me.

The old man, on tiptoes, hands in front pockets, waited at the beginning of the trail until he knew for sure Jimmy was on the way. He went whistling "Dixie" into the trees.

Jimmy came back with an apologetic shrug. I said, "Fifty dollars?"

"I don't want to hear it. None of your business." He said, "What you do with Keller and Thomas? That's exactly the same thing."

I didn't argue. "Couldn't you have waited until another time? I was just out here alone, that's all. I was bored." I pulled a knee forward, wrapped it in my arms, bit it, unsuccessfully: teeth slide on dry denim.

"One of my regulars." He lit a cigarette, held it there in his smile. "Don't want to hurt his feelings."

"I just don't see how you could—" I nodded toward the man, who was returning, satisfied. "A regular?" I shuddered. "Eeugh." The old man sat on a rough red bench at the mouth of the trail.

"You don't think about it. You shut your mouth and mind, pull down your pants. An art, I guess."

He took my hand, squeezed my fingers tight between his,

playing Mercy. "You can't deal with it—fine. You're just a kid." He scuffed the ground with his shoe. "I didn't want you to know."

"I knew, though. I think."

"I know. I know." He lifted his palms to me. "About Richard, you were right, I was jealous. But he *is* a fucked up kid. And so am I, and so are we all." He stood away, to look at me. "And I do want you."

"Don't be silly." I pulled him in, laughed at his serious face. "You've got Burt." I waved a flat hand at the trail, "You've got this man, this regular—" I rolled my eyes, stuck a finger down my throat, to show disgust: not to be cruel, but to make a joke. He didn't laugh. "You're right," I told him. "I am just a kid. I want to be loved." I stopped. I laughed. Where did that come from? "You know that's the first time I ever said that? Keller would die. Keller would laugh. But it's the truth. I want to be loved." The words sounded unconvincing, so I said them again, "I want to be loved, I want to be loved," which made it worse. I said, "Or not. And you don't want me. Not really. Not at all." I took a breath, as to say, "Don't I talk a lot?" I batted my eyes, as to say, "So you talk now."

But he hadn't heard a word. He held my chin and cheekbone in his hand, as Mother would. "Why do I want you? Hmm, let me see. You've got a nice face? You remind me of somebody?" He kissed my forehead. "I don't know?"

I stood, threw my Julie Andrews *Sound of Music* hands in the air. To the old man, or nobody, I yelled, "I do want I want I want to be loved!" That made me laugh. I looked down at Jimmy. "I want to be fucked. Can you do that for me? Did he use you up or what?"

Jimmy said, "Sure." And "Okay," and "Not at all." He shrugged, held out his hands to help me fall, "But I thought you had too much to think about."

I said, "Oh well." Meaning, Never mind. But he paid no attention, we went up on the trail together, holding hands. I raspberried the old man as we passed. "I get it for free."

He shot a kind smile at me. "Young love," he whispered. Hands flew to either temple, hurt feelings. "I've been with my

152

*huth*band thirty-seven years, and forty-one years with my wife. It's hard. It's worth it. Good luck to you." Then we were gone. "Bitches!" he yelled.

I said, "So much for a good customer."

"Where's your manners," Jimmy said. "Keller will be furious." He pushed me face-forward onto a sloping rock, my knees bent forward, my elbows locked, palms flat. He lay atop me to help me down. He wiggled his hands into my front pants pockets. I was hard. He found it, played with it that way, pressed it bloodless against the limestone, rough pocket hem scraping up and in on either side: loose change, and cigarette pack, and keys. "You little shit," he whispered, "you'll get yours." He flipped me onto my back, struck a heroic pose, undid my button-fly with one practiced indifferent finger, pop pop pop. He stabbed his knees on either side of my waist, pulled out his own cock (freckled, white), leaned forward to slap my eyelids, my face, each side of my nose. Then he fell back, rubbed his cock against my chestbone. His buns rocked with calm smoothness above and too close to my own straining cock in my briefs. His buns, they touched cotton fibers, brushed them back, touched down again. Or just nearly. I thrusted up, to settle the issue, it was suddenly urgent, but he didn't let me. I grunted, fear: no doing, he seemed to say, a smile, a shake of his head. But it was good. I lifted my head with puckered goldfish lips, to suck, but the angle was too sharp, I couldn't reach, I couldn't breathe. Jimmy told me to lift my butt so he could slide my pants down. I did, he did, then again, awkwardly.

But there was a funny feeling. I said, in a matter-of-fact tone, "Just let me up." I pushed him back, so I could see. "Oh." He loosened his guilty passive muscles from about me, looked down, grinned. There was the old troll, and two of his buddies, grins and whispers, watching. I walked toward them with angry purpose.

"Hey, Jamie? Hey, I'm sorry? I didn't know?" Jimmy called after me, but not as if to convince. As if trying out what he should say. But I didn't mind. He buttoned his pants. He tucked and he patted. He followed me.

153

I said, backward, "It's okay." I lifted one hand behind me, to hold him there. I took a couple longer, more slow steps forward. The other hand I lowered before me, I turned my palm up, wiggled greedy fingers. "You have to pay for watching. You have to pay me, too."

But then Jimmy had lost it, couldn't get it back up. We had no K-Y anyway. I tried to pass out refunds, but they waved rain-check hands in the air. I was too funny, they said. I was wonderful. They touched my hands and my thighs and my waist, and my shoulders, and the insides of my thighs, but not lecherously. Just to see that I was real, that I was there: doubting Thomases. Just being girlfriends. Even to show relief. To say good-bye. Then they went one at a time away, to see what other show was on, further down the trail: giggles and lifted hands, eyes batting to signify heartbeats.

I returned to Jimmy—flat on his back and ashamed on our rock. He passed air through ballooning cheeks. "You really don't know how to work this game, do you?"

But I spread the bills like a fan before my face, winked and fluttered. "What? They were nice. You never told me they were nice."

He shut his eyes, to show me there was no hope, he was giving up. I cuddled into his armpit. He pulled away without moving.

No cars in the parking lot at the bar now, so we decided to push, see what happened. I watched Jimmy's face in the rearview, forgot to pop the clutch. So he pushed again. His eyes were wide with effort, empty, green. When I did remember to pop the clutch, there I went, hobbledy hobbledy onto the highway. He waved, ran after me. I don't know why, I gunned the gas pedal, in the sudden direction of home.

Out the window, I carried a cigarette. But the smoke didn't follow, it blew back in, twirled mad strings in front of my face, I couldn't see. I was breathing, ugly, urgent, scarily. This was what I had read about in supermarket tabloids: something felt wrong, something felt terribly wrong.

But then, at Keller and Thomas's, there was nothing but wind, and nobody home, and a note on the door, cardboard with soft, ribbed, fibrous edges:

You said you'd come see me sing. I guess I wasn't there.

Beneath that, in a smaller, much more careful hand, sloping its own angle:

I never heard that about Mrs. Sellman and your mother. Made it up. I like you (haha). But I'm going away to live with my mother. So never mind. I guess you're thinking how silly I am.

A final addendum, running up the right side of the cardboard, ninety degrees to everything else:

I bet you're in there. You know what Keller told me one time, that night he was getting me up in drag at the party? We are the world, he said. We are the children. Now I know what he means. This morning I became as queer as I will ever be, it hit me when Gerald made the pancakes and I was waiting for him. Everytime this morning it is all of the world I'm breathing. Does this make sense? It is there in my head, solid, spinning slow for me to see all sides. Or it's the little voice Reverend Watson talks about, that comes to you. But it's too far away can't be touched. Oh and then he made me take it doggy style. I mean, Gerald, after the pancakes. I saw my eyes in the chest of drawers mirror while he did it, they were shining. Also the moon over the dam is very pretty. I'm waiting at the park for you.

But this was not what I came home to see. I had no time for Richard, his little fucked-up epiphany and crisis. I tossed the cardboard into the yard. I slapped my hands together, held them there, as to pray. I didn't go inside. Someone slammed shut a screen door down the street. And someone yelled for her husband or dog or son, Ralphie, to come home: here was supper. Somewhere, Ralphie, a tenor, yapped. I leaned on my shoulder on one of the front-porch columns: flecks of paint crunched, stuck to my skin. Those trees, they were not dead after all. Sudden pointed leaves, flat as folded gum-wrapper, cluttered and flapped about the black knots of the branches. Calm, a fist, hit my stomach. I had to eat, I had to think, I had to shit.

I called, "Thomas?" into the quiet common room. I knew better but called, "Keller?" anyway. The new blinds rattled right back down against the sill. Empty furniture, striped with slants of light, sat.

Donna-May Dean smoked his most sardonic cigarette, and lounged on the lounger. He didn't say anything, seemed to be ignoring invisible others on either side. A pointed, vertical exhalation, to symbolize inner strength. Then he muttered, "Trashy bitches," with affection. Maybe he was reliving the party ten years ago, maybe he was pretending to, for my benefit. I don't know. But he was wearing that fur coat, natty and leprous, and that blue jockstrap, that pearl choker. He made reluctant titters, then clomped his high-heels one at a time on the coffee table. He crossed them at the ankles, a challenge: he looked at me. Beside his feet, Keller's picture album, still open to whatever story it was he had been telling Mother.

I gathered it shut to my chest, guilty thrill, as if anybody cared, or could see. I went with it to the bathroom, turned the key locked in the rusty gothic useless hole, then settled sinking on tiptoes against the door. I didn't open the album, not yet: what's the use? My arches ached, I shifted further down, let the album drop open on the Scrabble tile before me.

Then I fell onto and past it, and slid into the commode, because Donna-May Dean had slammed open the door: in-human strength of the ghost, or the drag queen, or both. I turtled onto my back to look. "Oh! *Beg* pardon," he said, but with a dangerous look, "you pitiful boy." He traced the outline of a muscle in my leg, the upper one, with his pump-toe. When he got to my crotch, he stopped, pressed, ground it in, circling: but gently. As if putting out a cigarette butt on the street. "You devastato of the trailer park set."

I laughed. "Donna-May Dean," I said. Meaning, Stop. He whipped his remnant of an electrical cord at my face.

"I love it," he said, apropos of nothing, with Katharine Hepburn's dry but overpowering enthusiasm. He removed his foot, stood bowlegged above me, as to shit, or give birth, or get fucked; he kept on sinking.

But I kicked the door shut.

It just went through him. He stood, with dignity, turned the key, put it in his pocket, and left his hand there, rummaging. He said, carefully, "Damn." Then he made a loud wince, brought out his hand to show me: one lifted index finger, a prick of blood. Beneath that, in the loose awkward fist of the rest of his fingers, two open safety pins.

I lifted up onto my elbows, but there was the pump, more firm, on my chestbone this time.

"Oink Oink Sack?" he offered, testily. "Hungry Worm?" He smacked his two cinnamon lipstick smears. "Oh how perfect. I'll bet you used to finger the scummy rim of the toilet bowl. And—don't lie!—suck that finger the rest of the night. Anything dirty, is that correct? Because you're too much for the world, not good enough for the world. Am I right? And you thought I was dead? Why, my darling, my darling, my dearest: you've been a Donna-May Dean from the first." Then he was squatting above my crotch again, and made it all the way down, because I was scared. But there he sat, light as nothing. "Self-hatred," he whispered, and made a happy shiver. "That's Donna-May Dean!" In a show-biz tone of voice, like "That's Entertainment." Then he said it again. "Donna-May Dean will never die. Not with such fine spontaneous followers as you."

I didn't say anything, though he seemed to want me to. I said, "What do you want? What do you want me to say?"

"I mean, really," he went on, then held his breath, frowned. "What's all this business with your mother? Admit it. That you despise yourself. Or else you wouldn't have left the house when she found out, right? Or when she let you know she knew." He unbuttoned my shirt. In a deeper voice, but less serious: "Admit it." He tossed the safety pins, after shaking them, like jacks, or dice, onto my chest. But they didn't roll. They didn't do anything but gleam in the medicine cabinet light.

Bruce Lee touches his fingertips, almost with affection, to the victim's lower abdomen, where the ribcage flares away from the chestbone. Then plunges, and there's the heart in his hand. The victim's face, looking down, that was my face, I was watching those pins. I was fine. I was breathing in and in and in through my nose, making noises.

Donna-May Dean, with the bloody fingertip, rubbed the pins, sexily, as if they were some part of my body, up and down.

I don't know, this is odd: I was purring. But I said, "No."

He stuck both safety pins into my nipples, at once, together, which didn't hurt; then one at a time he squeezed them clasped, which did. Blood, mine, spurted out of the left one, to join his on my chest. The right one remained impassive. So he bent down to lick it, but I thought he would bite. He did. But I was fine, I was fine.

"Never guilt," I said to him. "Never fear. Not what you think. Why did I have to leave my mother? I don't remember. And you're wrong about the Hungry Worm, and the Oink Oink Sack. It was beautiful, what they were. Too much for the world—yes. But good enough, too fine, and you're wrong. And why did I have to get away from Mother? I don't remember." Finally, I said—I laughed, then I said—"Embarrassment."

He clapped stiff hands ceremonially together. "Yes! Embarrassment! The most crippling and madcap of the self-hatreds! I! Love! It!" He snapped open the silver lid of the lighter. "Cigarette?" he said.

"No thanks. I'm trying to quit." A joke, but I didn't laugh.

He smirked. "Don't worry. It will be your last." He lit one of his, attached it to my lip, left the lighter burning to light his own. And left the lighter burning.

158

"It's my birthday," he told me. "Wish me happy birthday."
I did.

Then he fed one end of the copper cord into the flame, held it there, white-hot. Down came both hands, the cord and the lighter, toward my left nipple. "Hold still," he whispered. "This takes a damn while. To get it melted enough, you know." Then the lighter went out. He flicked it lit, started again.

"Okay," I said. "I admit it. I hate myself."

"No you don't. Not enough." He fluttered his eyelids, to show he was talking to some invisible other: "This new generation." Back to me, "Self-hatred, for us, it was perfect. It was a way of life. For you kids? It's nothing. It's a hobby. A habit you're trying to kick. No sir, you don't hate yourself. Not enough. Not enough to please me." Back down with the hand holding the lighter, the hand holding the cord, my right nipple this time. "Self-hatred? That's what made us beautiful, what made us *have* to be. But you don't understand, do you? Do you?"

But I didn't answer, I wanted to say, No. No, I don't understand. And, no, I don't hate myself. Or won't hate myself anymore. No: never never never. But I said nothing, because I was screaming.

Thomas, in the open doorway, "What in hell. What is this? What?"

"But the door was locked," I said, thinking that maybe he was a ghost, now, too. And Donna-May Dean was gone. The key that had been in the drag queen's pocket bounced twice on the tile: *tink tink*.

Thomas laughed. "That lock? It hasn't worked since I lived here."

I stood, brushed off my knees. "Nothing's going on," I said. "Fell in the bathtub, that's all." But there I was with my pants on. And there was the dry bathtub. Donna-May Dean's cigarette sloping from my lips: menthol, 100's, but maybe Thomas didn't know better, would think it was my own.

He didn't even see it. He was watching my nipples, Donna-May Dean's safety pins in them.

"Do it yourself S & M?" he said.

"Yeah." I chuckled. "Kind of defeats the purpose, right? Think I'll stop now." I ran a hand through my hair, meaning, See? Still myself after all. No harm done.

But he stepped past me, with the distracted look of a man who hadn't wanted to be reminded of something. He picked up the picture album, then didn't ask me about it. I didn't volunteer. He folded it under his arm, went away, with light, somber steps.

I found him on the couch, flipping slow pages.

"I was wild as a buck," he said, as I slipped in beside him, head on his shoulder. "You know what they called me? Tommy Gun. Because I was always packing a stiff rod, they said. All the drag queens and such. Keller's crowd. I don't really guess I had a hard-on more often than anybody else, they had as many hard-ons hidden up their skirts and panties. But I never told them that. And anyway, when they started talking that trash, saying how hard I was always supposed to be—you know?—it would happen. And that's all they ever talked about. So I guess they were right, in their way."

"The only way that matters?" I said.

He nodded, as if to say, I get it. The joke.

"But you're not hard in that picture." It was the one Mother had described: Thomas naked in the kitchen, beer can tilting from his smile, two drag queens wrapped about his lower legs. One of them Keller. Donna-May Dean.

"You're right," he said. "I'm not. Oh well. But that's because they weren't talking."

He was right, there was an odd, ceremonial, silent quality to his pose, to the tight-lipped smiles of the drag queens.

"This was Keller's birthday party," he said. "Fourteen years ago."

I snuggled in closer to his shoulder, to look down, to see. I clasped my loose hands behind his neck. I said, "Self-hatred."

"What?"

"That's Donna-May Dean."

But he set his jaw, smiled. "Don't talk crazy. You've been listening to Keller too much." He peeled the plastic cover from the picture. "Let's see what I wrote on the back of this one."

I said, "Wait. No. Keller wrote that." Because Mother had already told me so. And the handwriting was too sissified for Thomas: dangerous curlicue.

"I'll bet he pretended to make the tea cakes, too."

On the back of the picture: *What comes next? Flawlessness and fear.* "What's that mean?" I said. "It's like a nellie fortune cookie."

Thomas, in a tone of voice to show he wasn't ready to change the subject, this had been bothering him for a long time, went on. "He just can't stand it, that's all. That I can make beautiful things, and he can't. That I'm a cook and a poet. That I'm as much a faggot as he is. More. Because all I like is to get fucked." He stopped, smiled, "Don't tell him I told you that. 'It just wrecks hell with our public personae,' he tells me."

"What's a faggot?" I said, not as a question, but a quotation, "Anything or nothing. A stepped-on cigarette butt in the street."

"Keller again," said Thomas, with a little dismissive wave. "He's so full of bullshit. You know that business, about me being straight? His idea. To save our public personae, he said. To put our role-playing back in its proper order. And because he wanted to have to save me."

I said, gently, "No." I took his hands, turned my widest eyes smack-dab into his narrow ones, "That's my job."

We didn't say anything for a while after that. "You're getting blood on the couch," he told me. "Go take out those goddam safety pins. Who were you trying to be?" But he knew. "Wash out the wounds with hydrogen peroxide, it's in the medicine cabinet. Also Band-Aids. And oh—clean up the bathroom floor where you were bleeding."

I blackened the Band-Aids—flat stripes across my nipples—with Keller's mascara, as a joke, to make him think of those girlie magazines. But he didn't say anything when I came back out. He'd set the album shut on the coffee table. The one picture he still held before him, but not to look at. Between two stiff, straightened fingers, he held it, as if it were a dollar bill, and he was waiting for some unpleasant cashier to take it away. He shut his eyes. "You know what else? Keller makes me call this pay phone. Dial-A-Queen, he calls it. 'Have you got an asshole?' I'm supposed to say. 'Because I've got a hard dick.' "

"I know."

He was surprised, afraid: "That I've got a hard dick—? No. Oh yes. Oh that. Last night."

I lifted one reproachful knee onto the armrest of the couch, and leaned into it, looking down at him. "Well, he wasn't home last night, God knows. When you made that phone call, when I picked up. He didn't make you call, not last night."

He brightened, slapped his knee. "But guess what? He doesn't have to anymore. Remember the hard-on, it's like that. He's told me the story so many times, how I am supposed to be such a stud, such a sleaze, that I let myself believe it now and then. The damndest thing. And I *do* have a hard dick. Right now. And a lot of the times. I just don't let Keller know." He looked down, grinned, ran a hand through his hair, embarrassment, as if accepting a compliment. "I want him to learn to love me without the hard-on, I guess. I want him to learn to love me for the opposite of what he's always wanted me to be. Even if I'm not, not quite. The opposite, I mean." He looked up, little boy, spread his open hands, a conduit between my face and his. "Does that make sense?"

All I said was, affectionately, "Tommy Gun." Meaning, I know you now. A threat. Then I went to my room, to the windowsill, took down two of Donna-May Dean's pixillated red pumps: a mismatched pair, it turned out, but that was fine. Magic works best with clash and oddity. I put them on. "There's no place like home." Because I didn't belong here anymore. The stories were coming apart, the ones I was supposed to be learning. I clicked the heels together, shut my eyes. With even more conviction, "There's *no* place like home, there's *no* place like home."

But when I opened my eyes, there I was, they had taken me nowhere, these magic pumps, they had taken me exactly here, by the windowsill, in my room. Donna-May Dean's.

Freshly shirted, barefoot, I came back downstairs. "I'm

going to see Keller," I said. Then I remembered to ask, "How is he?"

"Fine. I guess. He's got his arms folded on his belly button, and won't talk to me. It's like sitting with a corpse, or somebody in a coma. Except he's fine. He'll blow his nose, or cough into a folded napkin, or adjust the angle of the bed. He just won't say anything. But his eyes are open. I don't know, he might be mad at me. But why?"

I said, "What does it mean: flawlessness and fear?" I nodded toward the picture, where he had set it, writing-side up, atop the album. He took his feet from the coffee table, sat up, opened his eyes. "*That's* what a faggot is. What a faggot is made of. It's our snakes and snails and puppy-dog tails. It's our sugar and spice and everything nice." He grabbed me by a belt loop, pulled me closer. He forced my hand down, to press against his hard-on—no crochet dildo, this time. "Visiting hours are over, anyway. They won't let you in."

But I pulled away, went waltzing toward the door. Two hands, effeminate and bothered, I flapped behind me in his direction. "I'll just tell them I'm family. That I'm his daughter."

I didn't go to the hospital, not right away, because I saw my shadow on the sidewalk slap its back pocket, then crack knuckles, run them through its curly bangs. A sudden affection for myself overcame my attitude: not sexual. The kind of good feeling you get from the opening shots of *Funny Girl,* her little ways. What I did was find the river, and my place on the bank, where that rosebush still tended its raggedy uselessness among bottle caps and condoms. My own fucked-up crisis and epiphany: I wanted to jump up and up, shake and rattle my arms at the sky, shudder the rest of me down to my bare feet like a Congregationalist of God getting the spirit. But I didn't. I counted to ten, I stood there. I spun flat rocks and bottle caps across the water's cut, enamelled, turquoise surface. No, not turquoise, but an inexpensive jade, shot through with odd-color veins, curling whorls, milkinesses. A Styrofoam cup, half-sunken, floated stumblingly against the slow current. I took off my shirt, my shorts, swam butterfly out to get it, further than I had thought it would be. But then it was nothing: brittle, and too thin for me to have bothered. I crushed it in my lifted hand, which made me sink some. I was laughing. I treaded water more fiercely again. Between the black bars of the bridge above my head, the sun glittered neatly, five-pointed spangles.

Then it was over, and I had learned nothing new: epiphany for its own sake. "But aren't they all?" I said. I brushed off my clothes before putting them on, which was funny. They weren't dirty to begin with. I plucked four faded roses, then another: their sagging petals, firm green-white stamen and pistil. I told myself how weird I was getting. Then I decided I'd better not talk to myself anymore.

At the hospital, I didn't have to say anything. No nurses at their station. I breezed on past, checked the chart posted on the wall by the elevator: KELLER PHILLIPS—RM. 332. Above that: VISITING HOURS, 9–6. I should have remembered anyway, from Dad's cancer days. It was only three or four o'clock; Thomas had lied.

Coming out of the elevator, I met Bonanza Butt and Hell Thing, who were coming in. Bonanza scowled, lifted and wagged a scolding ring finger, to show he was pleased. "Flawless," he chanted at me. "Flawless, flawless, flawless."

I said, "Am I," not a question, an acknowledgement, and lifted my head. Maybe that's what had happened at the river: I was suddenly flawless, I was no longer afraid. Bonanza resentfully set aright the lace canopy of the baby carriage, as if to protect Hell Thing from whatever I was now. Then he pushed on past me. I was going down the hall, he hurled a mock sigh after me.

Dad's old room was on the third floor, too, and I went there without thinking. The door was ajar, I pushed it open. Just a lack of memories, and nothing: a hospital room, empty despite the sleeping, sheet-shrouded single occupant and the running television. *Truth or Consequences.* "Wrong room," I said. "Sorry." He was old, he had warts on his blinking eyelids. He turned, he snorted, went once again to sleep.

Keller's door was open, too—hospital doors usually are,

unless there's something serious—but still, I stood outside for a minute, checked the name, just to be sure. Because Thomas had lied again. I could hear Keller talking, cutting up. "Miss Thing," he whispered. Then a raspy giggle. "Oh you don't *mean*." So I went on in, expecting Wisteria or Lola Blow, and there was Mother, hands in her lap, eyes pointed—who knows how long, waiting—directly at the door, at me. My flawless- and fearlessness fell from me like a crystal tea set onto the floor.

"Wrong room," I said. "Sorry." Then I went running toward the elevator, but where was it? I heard her hard soles behind me, *clompity clompity,* like the Lone Ranger theme. "No," I said, aloud, "The William Tell Overture."

"What are you talking about?" called Mother. In the tone of voice you use when somebody is frantic, you are going to have to slap him. "What's gotten into you?"

I turned to her at the elevator, heard it open behind me. "Okay," I said. I surrendered, hands in the air, "I'll do whatever you want."

She laughed, but not seriously. As if she couldn't think of anything better to fill the pause.

"I'll come back?" I offered.

"I don't know," she said. "Is that what I want?" Not with distraction, but as a tease. She ran one fingertip across my imaginary smile, one invisible dimple to the other. "What I want is this. What it is, is—" Then she couldn't think of what to say. "Let's get something to eat."

"Not hungry," I said, pouting child.

She stepped past me into the elevator, then waited, wearing stern eyes. I handed her the roses across the threshold. "For you," I whispered, but a guilty smiling catch in my voice gave me away. I said, "Not really." I stepped in beside her, and down we went, watching nothing but the lighted numbers above the door: 3, 2, 1.

Meat loaf and mashed potatoes at the hospital cafeteria today, like every other day. We used to sit at the booth in the corner, close to the door, in case there was some emergency with Dad and we had to be found in a hurry. Toward the end of our two and a half months waiting, we almost didn't care,

165

we'd giggle and gossip, even wrestle our feet under the table.

That's what we were doing when the doctor himself came to tell us, flanked by two nurses, and another male one, holding a full syringe at his side, sharpshooter, I don't know why. If we got hysterical, I guess.

We didn't get anything, we got out of there. Mother, enflamed with fear and amusement, told me how she had always hated my dad. How he had never made her happy. Emphasis on the word *made*, as if it had been his job to fabricate for her some kind of life she could never make for herself. I didn't want to hear it, I told her so, she stopped. Still, I admitted, I was glad, too, that he had gone. That was the word *I* chose to emphasize: not died, just gone, as if he were one of those men you hear about, who step out to the store to get a pack of cigarettes. I said, "I'm relieved." But I didn't say, "Now he'll never have to know that I'm queer."

Anyway, it was our old table that Mother took her plastic tray to, her meat loaf and potatoes. I wondered if it were a conscious choice, if she meant to communicate something. Or if, just as I had gone to the wrong room, this had seemed the only natural place to be, she hadn't thought about it. Regardless: there was Dad's heavy presence, for the first time in forever. The presence of his death, rather. The first time I had thought about him since Mother and I had gone to the grocery store, trying to not think of him, and saw the town faggots. It was his dying that set everything spinning, in a way.

Having had this thought, I refused to hold it. I cleaned my mind of Dad, his little eyes and hands, a sensitive man trapped in a failing redneck's failing body. I sipped my lemon sparkly water—all I was having, thank you—and widened my eyes across the Formica at her.

Still, when she said, "He's the one who first put the thought in my head, about you," I knew who she meant. She shook her head, then lifted knife and fork toward the meat loaf, cut a slice, stopped, started to say something, then cut another. "One of the last things he said to me," she said, with her mouth thoughtfully full, "He just turned his head on the pillow, to look out the window, you had left the room. 'I'm worried about Jamie,' he said. 'Has he discussed his sexual preference with you yet?' " Her eyes gleamed above serious, serious chewing. "You wouldn't think he would say it that way, would you? Something about faggots, maybe. Something about 'No son of mine—' " She smirked, to show respect. "But no. It was 'sexual preference.' He loved you."

I didn't want to hear any more, to cry, so I said, "Bullshit." But she knew I didn't mean it, she just smiled.

"You were always such a seething, quiet child, locked in your own world."

Hungry Worm and Oink Oink Sack, but I didn't say anything.

"I called you my elfin prince, do you remember that? I said you were sent here to save me. Because everything bored me so, the trailer park, Waffle House, your dad. You were the one who knew how to get away from it, but you'd only take yourself. I thought someday I could go with you into your little magic world." She couldn't eat anymore, but kept looking at her food, smiling like crying. But not yet. Then she looked up at me. "But last night, I saw more of that world than I needed to know. You're right. It's not meant for me. The magic is too dangerous, and what am I? Nothing." She tossed her fork into her plate on this, then her knife, set her elbows on the table, face in her hands.

I told her not to cry, she said she wasn't, she wouldn't. But she was.

"It's going to be okay," I said. "I'm coming home."

And she, guttural, but friendly, "No you're not."

I opened my mouth, leaned back to look at her. I shut my mouth. I said, "What?"

"You're a total little shit about things. And yes, Keller and I have been talking." Her eyes were shut, aimed directly, though, at mine. "I can't do it. Raise an elfin child anymore. Out of my league." She shrugged, bit her lip, opened her eyes. "I'm tired of being what you want me to be, and not being what you want me to be. I'm tired of being hated because you hate what you are." She leaned forward, thumped her fist onto the table, "Learn not to hate what you are. I can't teach you that."

I said, "You could try." I reached to take her hands, but she didn't let me. I was begging now, "I love you. I'm coming home. I could teach you how. To teach me." Then I was just shaking my head, moving my lips, no words.

"Keller can teach you," she said. "Keller and Thomas."

"Keller doesn't know shit, Mother. Keller's so full of self-hatred he thinks it's an art form. Tragic and lovely, he says."

But she was smiling her know-it-all eyes at me. "You mean you haven't figured it out?"

I said, with trepidation, because she was as much as laughing at me, my stupidity, "Figured out what?"

Matter-of-factly, "He teaches by bad example. I mean, it's so obvious. Besides, he told me. Figures you'll eventually do everything the opposite of what he says anyway, might as well take that into account." Like a queen, with one hand in the air, coming slowly down, "Isn't it perfect?" Then, with reverence, catching the hand in her other, "Perfect magic."

I said, "Of course." I had forgotten to forget. I said, "Lesson number one. Always forget what I say."

But Mother ignored me. "Keller needs you right now," she said. "Go to him." She leaned back in her chair, to wait with wide eyes for me to leave.

So I did. I took the roses. She didn't mind.

"My mother kicked me out of the house for a faggot," I said to him, his shut eyes, his hands crossed over the belly button. "Tell any story often enough and it will come true," I said. Remember the hard-on. I said, "Talk to me." I sat down, turned the television off. "Talk to me now." I was giggling. "I'm flawless," I said. "I'm not afraid."

He opened one annoyed eye. "Flawlessness," he insisted, "*compels* fear."

But I had to laugh, I had to open the window, take a big breath. The parking lot, cars in it, every color. And past that, the bridge, our neighborhood. I gave him the flowers, but there was nowhere to put them. He set them plop on their sides on the nightstand. Dry petals fell, collected in and around the wide chevron ashtray.

"Have I told you how lucky you are? To have such a nice mother? Your mother, I mean. I don't mean me. She's nice."

I said, with sudden conviction, as if it were the funniest idea, I had never thought of it, "You know, you're right."

"The Phillips widow—I don't know—I wasn't flawless yet, but I must have been prettier than she. Nothing but sweet I was—a thin, sweet, fashionable boy. You wouldn't recognize me, my blue eyes, my dulcet tone."

"I've seen pictures," I said.

He coughed, reached for a Kleenex, then decided he couldn't reach them, didn't need one. I snapped four of them from the box, held them his way. But he didn't take them from me until the coughing was finished. He folded them, twice, set them on the bed at his side. "The Phillips widow? Have you seen her picture, too?"

I nodded, but he didn't look to see.

"That must have been it, I was prettier, she couldn't stand to look at me. Just lay in her bed all day, pill bottles on the floor, I mean carpeting the floor. Now and again, she'd get up, to cane me, for smoking cigarettes in the house. Not that I *smoked*, not even that I smoked in the house, but they were menthol, she said. Gave her some kind of headache. Then she'd go back to bed, shit all over herself, Spaghetti-O's and broccoli. Waiting with sly smiles and lifted eyebrows for me to come clean it up. I was a dedicated boy, the kind of faggot who has never sucked a dick in his life, never wants to. Just takes care of his mother, just wipes the red and green mess from her deep, dry asshole." He shuddered. "How she pretended to hate me for that. But I had no choice. How she pretended to be humiliated, when it was all her idea in the first place, me with my warm-water towels, her with her smooth white butt in the air, doggy-style. Her victory.

"Then one morning, she woke me, she was just up out of bed, she'd climbed the stairs by herself. 'No reason,' she told me. 'Let's get ice cream,' she said. 'Let's go for a ride.' " Keller hit the word *ride* hard, swoopingly, ironic breathless enthusiasm. "I just knew something had happened. But what? And what to do about it? She took me to the drugstore for Pure Process Rocky Road. And I never knew she knew how to drive! And she didn't. Fifty miles an hour down Coffee Street, then smack over the curb and the corner to turn onto Main. 'Don't talk with your mouth full,' she was saying. 'Don't drip on the Naugahyde.' It was like I had suddenly become the child again, she was taking care of me. And she was smiling.

"A triple cone, it was, that she bought me: the only act of generosity in her life. By the time I had finished it we were thirty miles south of town on some one-and-a-half-lane county road. Laundromats and trailer parks and liquor stores." He flicked apologetic fingers, quickly, to the back of my wrist. "Pardon. No offense."

I just said, "Go on."

"They were waiting for me at the cracker house, when we got to Tuscaloosa. It seemed she had been in communication with them for quite some time. The doctor, he was devastating, cocksure, blond, a regular Nazi. 'It's an experimental treatment,' he was telling her, past my head, where I was sitting before his desk. 'We cannot guarantee a cure, although there have been promising studies.' He pulsed his pencil in his hand, out and out, eraser tip indicating me, my obvious illness. And what was I? I was confused. It had never occured to me that something needed fixing about me—but still, but anyway. There we were, you know." He scowled, shut his eyes. "Not like a hospital, not at all like this one. No. Beautiful. Like the nineteenth century or something, all these moldering brick buildings, white columns, princess curtains. 'Here is the cafeteria,' he told me. 'Here is the commons.' With the Phillips widow following us around, her suddenly strong constitution, sturdy legs. It was like being sent off to college or something. And all the time, he had that pencil, was waving it, back and back and forth, like hypnotism. Don't laugh. He was that kind of a guy. Anyway, I finally couldn't stand it, grabbed the pencil, held some of his fingers there in my hand. 'Okay,' I told him. 'Where do I sign?'

"And all he said was, 'Here is your room.'

"Then I said something silly to him. Something, well, flirtatious. I can't remember exactly. 'How about a little stroll through the bushes?' He just looked at the Phillips widow, she nodded at him over my head. So they left me locked in there, my new room.

"Not a bad room, don't get me wrong. No padded walls, no bars on the window, nothing like that. A room you might rent in a boarding house. Flat white walls, a small stand-alone deco sink in the corner. One window that looked out onto nothing, the back end of some lunatic baseball field. But I came to value that window far more than anything. Not because it showed me the outside—silly notion. I didn't look that far. No, I inspected every evening nothing but its surface. Waiting for the precise moment, it was dark enough, I could see my face. Perhaps that's why Donna-May Dean chose to make herself known to me at that time. To complement the black outside, nothing more."

I whispered, "Self-hatred."

"Not at all. Not yet." In a satisfied, proving-his-point tone of voice, "Her coif was entire, and alive, and long, curly locks snapping about her shoulders. They had shaved my head, you see. Lice, they said. Imagine that. But Donna-May Dean, oh no, they couldn't touch her. I mean, the doctors. Those eyes: you were nothing, you could drop dead immediately, those eyes. The strength in them." He said, "Evil—"

"Strength isn't evil."

"But drag queens are. I mean, the best of them. And there's nothing wrong with that. With evil. A perfect response to what was being done to me. To us. Me and Donna-May Dean. And more than that. All of us." He chortled. "Even a tired old queen like me? I can indulge? Even so? In a little gay pride now and again?"

The first time I had heard him use that word: gay. Pride. I said, "Sure."

But then he blotted the side of his eye with a folded Kleenex. "Maybe not." He said, "Maybe it's too late." He said,

"Listen. I began to apply imaginary makeup. To pretend to emulate what I saw in the window. To become I don't know what."

I said, "Donna-May Dean?" To show I was learning my lessons well.

"Exactly," he whispered. "Evil and strength. Fear and flawlessness. I've told you about the treatments? What did he call it? Aversion therapy? The doctor, I mean?"

I said, "A little."

"Did I mention that I was in control? The button in my very hands. And more than that. You see, they might easily get in trouble. This was the late sixties, things like what they were doing—well. Word had better just not get out. Even in Alabama, they understood that much. Even I understood that much.

"The doctor, I have completely forgotten his name. And his bracing shoulders. His stolid nostrils. Anyway: he told me, the doctor, that all I had to do was say the word, it wasn't working. They'd leave me alone. His fleshy, vigorous earlobes. I've always been an earlobe man. I mean, girl.

"It was nothing, though, really: aversion therapy. Slides of naked men, naked women, alternating at random. The button in my hand to change the frame. 'Take your time,' he told me, the doctor. 'Enjoy the show.'

"A smaller room even than mine, and no window, no anything. One red chair, where I was. The doctor, his spread, beefy calves, in another. And nothing else: cigarette smoke, slide projector hum.

"The first one, he's on a beach somewhere. Pornography was fairly well—unadvanced, I guess. At the time. He's on a blanket on a beach, on his belly no less, one heel kicking up, toward his shoulder blade. Crew cut lifted, to show a bony smile. Kind of nice. Kind of brotherly. 'Take your time,' he said, the doctor. 'Do you like this picture?'

" 'Well,' I told him, 'It's a little too contrasty for my taste. I mean, the print quality—'

" 'Look again, though,' he said. 'Is there not something kind of nice? Kind of—'

172

"I said, 'Yes. Brotherly.'

" 'Take your time,' said the doctor, but there, in my bones, bones of both hands, came a slow, burning buzz. 'What is there to like about this picture?' he said, his most husky, most oh-so-patient intonation. He made you feel *this big,* center of the world. You'd fall in love, too: that voice. On an invisible table by his chair, an ashtray, a little black knob. He lit another cigarette.

" 'Could I have one of those?' I wanted to know.

"He inserted it for me, already lit, in the corner of my lips. The clunky electrodes on my hands, you know. He stood there, took it away after a while, to flick the ash. Dare I imagine? The beginning of an ethical crisis? 'You have to trust me,' he whispered, and lowered his face level to my own, turned to watch the screen. 'I need to understand,' he said, hard, almost compassionate emphasis on the *need*.

"At which point, in overpowered monotone, I whispered back to him, 'I'm in love.'

"He snapped about, went back to his chair, his little black knob. I had forgotten all about the ten thousand electrical pins in my hand, except that they got more insistent, he twisted the knob. But I was ahead of him already, pressing my button like madness itself. Because that's how it worked. You kept pressing the button until you found what he wanted you to look at, it didn't matter if you didn't look. Some woman. I never looked. I just wanted the hurting to stop."

Keller laughed, I looked: his crabby hands in his lap, he was rubbing them, rubbing them.

"Each evening, I went back to my room, there was Donna-May Dean. She came earlier and earlier, and more radiantly.

"One day, the transfiguration: I was the one trapped on the window's dark surface, she went walking around the room, striding, I *mean*. Cast her terrible, witty eyes this way and that. Washed my imaginary makeup off her face. 'Really,' she demanded, 'don't you know anything of beauty? Of foundation? Of ghastliness and glamour?' With a show-off attitude, pursed lips, flourishing fingers, she began to apply her own makeup. Imaginary as well, but on her, it became true.

"During treatment, that little room, the doctor was stunned, kept forgetting to turn his knob. Her beauty. His ruddy jawline. His lifted chin. When she asked him for a cigarette, he was afraid, he didn't come near.

"But who could resist her power, Donna-May Dean's? What I mean to say is this: he himself took her back to the room. And stepped inside. Donna-May Dean was down on immediate knees, her savagery, ripping with invisible Lee Nails at his stalwartness, his belt bucklet, his zipper. And out flopped all at once the most large and uncircumcised instance of manhood it has *yet* been my honor and pleasure to behold.

"The doctor, his trembling trembling, shut his eyes, pointed them to the ceiling.

"Donna-May Dean? 'Ooh,' she says, 'what do I like about this picture?' Nibbles with dry lips, puckering sounds, but he can't stand it. Still, she was the one, she was in control. Up against the door she had him, and was all at once slamming brutally down and down on his cock. He still can't stand it, he braces his knees, shoves her away, both hands on her forehead.

"Then he told her, 'No.' He said, 'Whew.' He said, "Go slow.' "

"So she just smiles, serpent-in-the-garden. 'Yessir.' And one more time, all the way down, and further down, to the bulky, pulsing root of it. She bites, I mean hard, I mean all the way through, and just like that, twists her head a little and bites again, her sharp shiny incisors, and bites again, to clear away the last clinging strings of cartilage. Blood up her nose and in her eyes, but still: it is with poise and cunning that she leans backward, to look up at him. She's still deep-throating it, she smiles around its bloody gray guts hanging from her lips.

"What did he do? What could he? He passed out. She doesn't want him to die, though: she stuffs tissue paper into his new cavity, dirty dishrags to stop up the kitchen sinkhole. She spits out his cock, wraps it in some more tissue paper, puts it away among her most private things. Then she's banging

174

on the door, banging and screaming until the nurses come.

" 'I think,' she tells them, little-girl voice, 'that it's time for me to go home now. The treatment, I'm sorry, doesn't seem to be working.'

"Best to keep it hushed up, they decide. The next morning, she has a new certificate of mental health or something, whatever they give you. And a one-way bus ticket to Genoa.

"The first thing she does, she's standing on the front porch now, is stare the Phillips widow down. I mean stare. The bitch. To literal. Death. Then she kicks her out of the way from the front door, into the common room, makes a timid call to the hospital. A stroke, it turns out.

"Then she preserves the doctor's penis in a pickling jar.

"Then she steps out, to the Salvation Army store, and knows exactly what to buy. She strides, aisle to aisle, just pointing: blue jockstrap, wolverine fur coat, electrical iron with a ratty cord. When no minions scurry behind her, she must all at once leave, to pose on the street corner, weeping. The realization: she has no minions.

"So she strikes toward the park, a slow Tuesday, to look for her minions."

Here Keller took the second of the folded Kleenexes, blew his dainty nose into it, tossed it on the floor.

"You have met their fading, genteel remnant. Wisteria Mercedes Magdalene. Bonanza Butt, that crowd. Also Little Nelle Helle, with the polio legs, who got her throat cut later by some redneck trucker trade. And a fag hag named Brenda, her dashing, gawky boyfriend. Tommy.

"They were sitting at the living room benches, silently, when she found them: as if reverent, as if bored. 'Follow me,' she whispered.

"She took them to the Salvation Army, instructed them to scurry behind her, grab the things she pointed to, pay for them: royalty is ever penniless. The pearl choker necklace was a surprise, Tommy's idea. He handed it to her himself, all curled up and tiny it was, on the flatness of a callus-covered palm. 'Ooh,' says Donna-May Dean, 'I just adore a working man.'

"Which sent this Brenda into no end of conniption fits. Turns out every man she's ever had goes queer on her. So tell me this—why does she take them to the park?

"But Donna-May Dean doesn't—couldn't—care. She needs time. Yes, even she needs a plan. With a brisk, flat-handed wave, she dismissed the minions. But not before inviting them to assemble at her house—the Phillips widow's, she gave the address—the following night. Her birthday, she told them. 'Everybody is invited. Bring your tricks and trade.'

"Then she specified, with her most imperious gaze, the working man, Tommy: 'Don't,' she said, 'bring your girl-friends.'

"Then she goes home, takes the cord from the electrical iron—"

"Keller," I said. "I know."

"Of course you do.

"Sure enough," Keller went on, "Tommy came by himself. And everybody else came as well. The accidental event of the season. But Donna-May Dean, she stands in the middle of the room, lifts one hand high, 'Stop the music,' she says. And gives this announcement, how everybody was invited to the party, but she can never invite herself. A little sozzled, she was. Also these were the days of LSD. She tells them she's sorry—she tells Tommy, his coltish grace, his awkward stare, his perpetual hard-on, that she is sorry—but she can no longer continue to crash such a fine gathering.

"That's where Bonanza pipes in, 'I'll invite you.'

"Our heroine, dispassionate as a knife, 'How dare you?'

"Then she turns back to Tommy Gun. 'All I demand,' she says, breathes, insinuates, three slow steps in his direction, 'is a little kiss.'

"But of course he cannot, he has this heterosexual reputation to maintain. But he'd like to. But who can resist Donna-May Dean? Even for the moment? She strides, ranting, to the bathroom. Yes, her most desperate fears are confirmed in the medicine cabinet mirror: no icy glamour, no ghastli- and fearsome- and flawlessness reflecting back at her. No." Keller stops, he breathes. Has he the strength to go on? He has the

176

strength to go on. "It's the timid pimply soul she thought she had imprisoned in the window of her room at the cracker house. It's Keller, it's me.

"She sticks the safety pins into her nipples."

But I stopped him. I took my hand to my chest. I saw him looking. "Keller, I know," I said.

"It's not herself she means to suicide, of course. That's why she tilts her hairdo to the left. She must, it seems, sacrifice her dignity, in order to reach me. She clambers into the commode, it's awkward with the heels and all. She bends, she reaches, she manages to plug herself in. A flash and a pop, the socket explodes. The lights for two blocks about expire. The minions—their tricks and their trade—mill cinematically about, a fey remake of *Ben-Hur* or whatnot. Nobody knows where to find her.

"Except that Tommy Gun, my working-class hero, shoulders open the bathroom door, he needs to piss, there's no stopping him. Then he just stands there, I don't know, and bellows, or something. Magnificent, the grief of a simple man.

"Donna-May Dean, on the floor, just enough moonlight from the textured window to see her by, her bloody black wrinkled nipples, her ghost-colored feet tucked one beneath the other, suddenly bare. Indeed, where is her nefarious fur? Blue jockstrap? French hairdo? The most ghastly sight of them all, a naked drag queen, a dead one. But wait!" Keller lifted a mock-suspenseful finger, "What is this?" And in a lower, more confidential tone of voice, "Yes, the pearl choker necklace remains.

"It is too much for Tommy, he takes her limpness into his arms, plants upon her that kiss."

"No," I said. "Don't tell me." I laughed. "Sleeping Beauty?"

"Not," Keller specified, "exactly. Because whose eyes fly open? Not her bothersome velvet ones. No: they are suddenly indigo, they are silly. They are mine." Keller sighed: irony. He folded his hands behind the pillow, lay back into them. "And happily," he said, "ever after."

"Impossible," I told him. I lit a cigarette, blew my pointed

177

skepticism directly into his face. Which I shouldn't have done, he was coughing. He settled his hands, fluttering, to the sheet, on either side, to show me he was fine. I said, "I don't believe a single word."

"No more impossible than the for-some-reason-blackened bandages I see shining through your hunky-dory T-shirt." He lifted a weak hand, his worried eyes, my way. "You've met her as well," he said, as if it were a question.

But he had me there, I didn't answer.

"It becomes obvious that I have told you that story far too many times."

With unexpected anger: "Why did you tell it again?"

"Simply to take you all the way, the happy ending. Because that's what you do with a story, you keep telling it, a little more every time. Any tragedy fades after a while into something else, into comedy. It's like pressing that button, the treatments, the slide show. You keep extending the story, pressing the button, until you come to a place where—at least for a while—it doesn't hurt anymore. And that's where you stop." He rolled a profound hand, "The death of Donna-May Dean."

"Yes," I said finally, "I *have* met her. So she's not dead after all."

"But in the story she is," Keller said, sitting up on *story*, to stare at me, hatefully desperately: will you never learn? "That's all that counts. Keep telling the story, all the way through, 'Ding dong, Donna-May Dean is dead.' You'll see."

Then we were gossiping, he mentioned Rex. "You remember the one from the party? Bonanza's just been to visit him. He's in the infectious ward." He smirked, self-hatred. "Another infected dicksucker," he said. "The wrath of an angry God."

"I'm worried about Jimmy," I said.

But Keller didn't want to talk about it. "I've done my best for that boy, always. Even paired him up with you. To see what might happen. To see if you could save him."

"Is that what you think I am? Somebody's salvation?"

He looked away, three-quarter profile, lowered lids.

178

"Maybe not," he said. "I don't know. I thought you might be the one."

I said, "The one what?"

"The one who could tell me what comes next. After self-hatred."

Maybe it was a drill. I quoted the back of the picture to him, to show how well I had studied. "Flawlessness," I said, so proud of myself. "Right? And fear?"

"No no no. That's the same thing. They coincide with self-hatred. I mean, after that."

I didn't have an answer. I told him about Richard instead.

He screamed, clenched the sheets, cowered—scandalized—into the headboard, away from me. "You think you might *what did you just say* him? Tell me no. That you didn't use that word."

But I, with ingenuous, lifted eyebrows, because this was my answer to his question all along, said, "Love?"

He got quiet after that one. Folded his hands across his belly button. I stared out the window—into it, I mean—waiting for dark. "Donna-May Dean is dead," I whispered. My breath mist pulsed on the vowels, on the glass.

Then the nurse came with his dinner. "Visiting Hours," she said, pronouncing the capitals, "ended forty-seven minutes ago."

But Keller, as she tied his bib around him, stopped me with one lifted hand. "You've seen the pictures. Tell me the truth? Was I prettier than the Phillips widow? It's what I like to believe. Why she sent me away? Do you think?"

"Could be," I said. "Who knows?" I said, "Of course."

I was all the way outside, down the stone steps, the light breeze from the river, when it hit me: I hadn't asked him how he was doing. But they'd never let me back up there, now; and he seemed well enough, didn't he?

Besides, I had to get to the park. Not that I wanted to see Richard. I didn't. What I had said to Keller scared me, I hadn't expected it, I needed time to think. But I also needed—burned—to know if he had waited this long for me. Just to know, that's all.

I found him leaning toward the water in the fountain, on his flat white hands on the rim. "I really do get a lot of money out of here." He turned, he sat, pulled one knee to his chin. "But you know what I really want? I want to get a wish come true. But after all the money I took out of here"—he nodded backward—"it would take a lifetime, a hundred years' worth of quarters, to make the fountain forgive. No good wishes for me here. Not to come true, anyway. Not from this fountain." He narrowed his eyes at nothing directly ahead. He still hadn't looked at me.

"What's gotten into you? You sounded so happy. Your note—"

"The little voice in your head? That tells you how good it is, how very very much you are? It wears off. I mean, you decide not to go home—fine. You dance that little dance awhile, walk, walk, walk all over town, every block, your mind is so keyed in to the beauty of anything that you can't stand it, you have to go see. But after a while you want some dinner, more than a Coke and a candy bar. And there's not but one dollar and seventy-five cents worth of quarters in the fountain. At least, except for the ones that are too gross and scummy for you to pick up. And you have to dooky, you have to dooky bad, the commode at the park probably has lice or herpes or AIDS or something."

I said, "You don't get it that way." I laughed. "Um. Sorry." But I couldn't help it: "You have to *dooky*?"

He just nodded, once, ponderously down, into his knee. "I have to dooky bad." He flicked his eyes at mine, then away. "You bastard," he said, but still quietly, "I didn't think you were coming."

Then he wouldn't stop looking at me.

I leaned in, I let him hold me tight around the shoulders, I couldn't breathe. "You don't know," I said. "You just don't know." I told him about Keller. I told him about Mother. I didn't tell him about Jimmy—even crying, even having him hold me. I knew to hold my moral trump card: Gerald. I told him about Donna-May Dean. He was patting my back—what else to do?—as if I had choked on something. But gently.

180

"Hey, come on," I said, "let's go to my house." Then I had to pull away, my burning nipples. He smiled, a vague nod, didn't seem to understand. I cuffed him on the shoulder. "Hey?"

"Okay, but just for a little while, though?" He flipped from his forehead long, imaginary, conspiratorial bangs. "Just, like, where's the bathroom, and can I have a ham sandwich or something?" He leaned in, to show me: his pleasure, his breathlessness, "Mustard only. Because listen—I've got a neat place to go, something to show you." He whispered, he stood, bounced on the balls of his feet, "Please?"

Thomas sat in puny light, stiffly, hostile, at the kitchen table, reading three-days-ago's newspaper. It sagged, we saw his eyes, he snapped it stiff. "Keller's fine," I said. "I think."

Again, he showed us his eyes. "We never said anything about bringing boys to the house," he said.

I just steered Richard on to the bathroom. "You have to get used to him," I said. "He's had a hard couple days, too." I stopped Richard directly in front of the commode, I stood there, leaned on my hands behind me against the medicine cabinet sink. "Let me," I said, "pretty please. Watch you *dooky*." I was snickering, he didn't say anything.

"Cree-py," he said.

But then he dookied, let me watch. I said, "I love you." He leaned forward, set his arms down aslant white, spraddled knees: concentration.

"What a total troll," he said. Meaning, Thomas. Or just to tease me.

Back in the kitchen, we were giggling, we crowded together inside the refrigerator door. Apples, bacon, hummus. "How about a Turkey Pot Pie?" I squeezed his elbow, to show him: how exciting! He wrinkled the smooth freckles around his nose.

Thomas, speaking from the authority of his flat hand trembling on the newspaper on the table, "Nobody can afford to feed all your goddam tricks, you know."

Richard whispered, "If we stop believing in him, will he disappear? As in Tinkerbell?"

181

But I cast a backwards look over my disdainful shoulder. Thomas's eyes gave him away, he had to look down, he had to smile. "I'm sorry. It's just. I got this phone call." Then he looked at us. Richard set a hand on my shoulder, we giggled. "Nothing. Never mind." He went to his room, slammed the door, quietly.

"What was that all about?"

"His interior," I whispered. "He showed it to me. He's not supposed to have one. Keller must have told him that I told."

So what if I should have been thinking more clearly?

"He has an interior," said Richard, narrowing vicious, awestruck eyes at the bedroom door. As if this were a glamorous crime. Then, to me, "Turkey Pot Pie is okay, I guess. If you have ketchup."

We didn't have ketchup, but he ate it anyway, he stood at the kitchen counter, eating. "What's for dessert?" He ran a sudden apologetic hand through my hair, "Just kidding." He said, "Fine. Okay. I love you, too."

But I wasn't thinking about that, I took his hand in my cold, distracted one. Because maybe I knew. I called, "Thomas?" I listened for a long time to his lack of response.

We took my car, I didn't ask where to, just obeyed his confident flitting finger at every turn. He showed me to park beside a low-key luminous kelly-green tennis court. "We have to walk from here. Don't want to wake up Dad."

"Wait a minute. No." But I opened my door, set one foot outside. "We're going to your house? I mean, he'll kill us."

"Don't be silly." Richard kissed his fingertip, screwed it into my invisible left dimple. "He'll never even know. Besides, he's a sweet kind of guy. And we're *not* going to my house. I mean, not inside."

A middle-middle-income neighborhood of development houses, television warble, chain-link fences. We sneaked through the next-door neighbor's backyard. "Watch out," he told me, "they put tacks out to keep you from walking on the grass."

It felt like Alcatraz, it felt like eloping. We came to a stop not two feet away from where his dad's bedroom window cast an elongated tic-tac-toe onto the raggedy grass. Richard smiled, lifted a magician hand in the air, "My tree house." He said, "Be right back. Um. Sort of stand on the other side of the tree, in case Daddy looks out."

He came back down with a burlap coffee-bean bag full of quarters. He handed it to me. His widest eyes. "I never spend them, you know."

"What is this?" I said. I hefted it up and down, to show annoyance: silver tinkle and flat, sliding sound.

"I never spend them," he went on. "And you want to know why?" He sat down on the grass, so I did, too. Somebody in the house moved shadows across the window, but Richard waved his hand at it. Meaning, Begone. But the window remained, the shadow stood still awhile. "I never spend them," he said, "because think of where they came from. Queer park, right? So who do you think's been throwing quarters into the fountain?" He nodded, once, with familiar emphasis, as if I had said something, as if I understood. "Exactly. Queers." He was watching from the corner of his eye: the shadow in the window went away. He took the bag from me. "I take them and keep them, because it makes me see how many of us there are." He dumped them onto the ground between us. They glistened in the light from the window and the moon and the streetlamp two doors down, dully. He rattled his fingers around in them. "I mean, I know. I know. There's that movie *Making Love,* and there's Frankie Goes To Hollywood, and there's Billy Crystal on *Soap.* But I mean here. I mean, in Alabama. In Genoa, Jamie—look at all the queers."

I said, because he was looking at me, "I see."

"Each quarter, I like to imagine, is another queer. It gives me that feeling, the one from my note—how splendid and totally queer you are inside. You know? That dance and that walk, when you're just too, too much. But there's being queer inside, knowing how good it is, and then there's having to go out and be queer in the world. I mean, what's really happened is you just got fucked bloody by some man who didn't give a damn. And he gave you pancakes and kicked you out of his house. Why can't it be like it feels in here?" He thumped his chestbone. I melted: his innocent innocence.

"But when I was waiting for you today, I figured it out. Think of this—nobody just throws a quarter in a fountain without some reason. Not even queers." He flipped one of the quarters on his palm between us. "I was wrong. It's not just a queer. It's a wish. The wish of a queer. I've been taking our wishes out of the fountain, they can't come true."

From the timidly cracked-open back screen door, "Ah— Richard?"

"You've got to put them back for me. We'll be happy, all of us. Our wishes will come true." He called over his shoulder, "Coming!"

"He's going to kill you," I said. "Right?"

"You want to know the truth?" He stood, slapped the front of his knees, bent down to slap the back. "He's used to it. I do it all the time, stay out, don't come home." He grimaced. "I guess I'm not the innocent little boy I like to pretend to be."

I said, my heart in my breath, "But you are, you are. You can be. Keep pretending."

We tell stories, we learn to live within them.

He toed the edge of the pile of quarters. "But will you do it? That's what counts."

"Why can't you? Why not tomorrow?"

"Because," he said, "tomorrow is another day." Then, less haughtily, "Have you ever thought about that line? How it doesn't mean anything?" He laughed. Then with a serious face, to show he was returning to the subject, "Because I'm evil, the fountain knows. Cancer: that's a water sign. Watch out for me." He turned, walked darkly to where his dad waited on the bright front porch, then stepped past him, inside. His dad: nervous, studious, round-shouldered. Slapped an angry hand through the air in my direction. But no: he had caught a lightning bug, that's all. He threw it directly to the ground, stepped on it, twisted his heel, to put it out like a cigarette. He shrugged, went inside after his too-much-to-think-about son.

184

In the window, there they were—Richard tossed his head to the left, grabbed hard, tearful hold of his dad around the shoulders.

I collected the quarters back into the bag. "Cigarette money for days," I said to myself.

Thomas was rolling slow hands beneath gray suds in the sink. I slammed the bag of quarters on the kitchen table before me, I sat. "It's three o'clock," I said. As if that meant anything. And with hostility. He turned a thin smile over his shoulder. I said, "It's Keller, isn't it?" Not because I wanted to know. "Something happened. I don't want to know."

So he didn't tell me. He said, as if he weren't sure he had heard the name before, he was trying to place it, "Keller?"

I lifted, one at a time, my cuticles. Thomas took from under the water a handful of forks and knives and dirty spoons, sprayed them with the Rubbermaid rinsing gun, then slammed them, wet, into the dry-drawer. He turned around, to show me: "I'm crying." But he wasn't. Or just invisibly.

"You never did love him anyway, did you?" I said, no recrimination, "It was always Donna-May Dean."

"Same thing," he said. That sounded so much like what Keller would have said that he had to sit down beside me, study his feet on the floor. He chortled. Then he kept on and kept on, not crying.

I slept in his bed with him—his and Keller's—we didn't sleep, didn't do anything, were careful not to touch or be touched.

"His throat collapsed," he whispered to the ceiling. "He was eating dinner."

I was thinking of the tire-changing tool, his gurgling moaning. I was thinking of his folded Kleenexes on the sheets beside him. The bib that the nurse tied around his neck.

"Malpractice?" I said.

"Of course it is. But who's going to sue?" He reached for a cigar on the nightstand beside the bed, then couldn't find one, didn't give a damn. "I'm nobody. I'm just a drifter, a

185

pirate, rough trade. They didn't want to let me see the body. But I made them let me. I *made* them."

He turned to the wall. I stood, slipped my shorts on quietly. "You know what else?" he said. "They ran an AIDS test on him. They're still waiting to find out." He turned to blink at where I had been beside him. "They can't do that, can they?"

"This is Alabama," I said. "Who's going to say they can't?"

He jerked up, wide eyes, then saw where I was. "Oh." He said, "Jamie?"

I said, "What?" Then I didn't say anything, he was crying. After flawlessness and fear, what comes next? Only this. Only fear.

"Where are you going?" he wanted to know.

"I forgot something," I said. "That's all." Because—how silly it was. And wishes have to be secret.

The quarters made a rushing slump into the scummy water. All our wishes: a flattened mound, almost visible, almost gray, hardly twinkling. Then one more quarter of my own, to send us into the black. I watched it slip, left and right, easily, down.

I thought I might give a couple quick blowjobs, but there was nobody there. And then I was glad.

Keller's short obituary notice in the *Genoa Lucid Observer* began, "A tragic accident." It ended, "Survived by: none."

"That's us," Thomas said. He stabbed his finger onto the word. "The nones."

He sat alone on the front row at the funeral service, the single convert at an otherwise unsuccessful prayer meeting. I sat behind him, between Mother on one side and Richard and Jimmy on the other. None of us had ever been inside an Episcopal church, but Richard, as the resident Christian, assured us that he knew everything about it. "I adore the dress, dah-ling," he whispered to me. "But your purse is on fire." Then, a sort of hiccup, "Dah-ling."

I said, "What?"

With more disgust and pity than five syllables should be allowed to secrete, "Tallulah Bankhead." He nodded toward the censer-swinging acolyte or whatever. "Don't you ever *read*?"

"I'm going to read you in a minute—" I threatened, but flirtingly. To get him giggling again, I turned all the way around in my seat, whistled, as if amazed, as if I hadn't already seen, "Look at all the queers."

Not all of them were from Genoa, surely—or lived here anymore—and not all of them were queer. But still, it was too much, all those paired-off mustaches. Even a veiled gaggle of drag queens. A brace of dykes. An exaltation of trade. Even a row of moldy trolls. Jimmy's eyes flashed cartoon cash-register dollar signs.

Mother slapped my knee, "Hush up. It's started." Then she was holding my hand. She got her fingers between mine, she smiled.

No sermon, just Thomas. "I'll read a poem. That's all." He announced, " 'To An Athlete, Dying Young'—"

Somebody, in the back of the—what do they call it?—sanctum, for all of us, screamed. But Thomas shot his most magnificent imitation of the grief of the simple, with slowly lifted eyes, directly at the perpetrator. " 'To An Athlete,' " he said again, more heavily, " 'Dying Young.' " But then he just shuffled his one paper before him. He said, "Fuck it. Just fuck it all." And finally released the stare, to put his face in his folded arms on the—what do they call it?—podium thing.

After the burial, I lost Richard and Mother and Jimmy, I went mixing. But nobody seemed to want to talk to me, I didn't know them, they were catching up on old times. When I found Mother again, she was surrounded by strange drag queens and Bonanza Butt. "Are you a friend of the bride," said Bonanza, "or the groom?"

Everybody tee-heed, everybody dithered. Mother's eyes,

her timid smile, hands to her side. One of her last visits to the elfin world, I could see her thinking. Where I saw drag queens, she saw dragons.

"*Do* you," said Bonanza, checking an invisible list, "have a reservation?"

That's drag queens, that's what they do best: find the one who belongs here less than they do. I was no longer afraid, I was flawless, I said, "Leave her alone."

Bonanza turned slow carnivorous eyes my way. "Ooh," he insinuated, "*it's* upset."

I didn't say anything, I overturned the baby carriage. To humiliate him. Also to make him see. "No Hell Thing," I said.

But he made a meager, lipstick-greasy smile. "Where do you think you are? The Emperor's New Clothes, or some such nonsense? Get a grip on the real world, honey, because this *ain't* fairy tales." He winked at me, witheringly. "Can I tell you a little secret? Hans Christian? Andersen? Lied! It was never the emperor everybody ended up laughing at. It was the blabbermouth. It was the silly. Little. Boy. Because anybody knows, we see what we need to see. Because you're a fool, if you don't leave us with that."

He righted the carriage. He slapped the pillow clean. "And furthermore." He popped his fingers, snap-snap-snap, in my face. And was gone.

Then I wanted to talk to Mother, but Richard came running up, he'd met Charles Nelson Reilly's furrier. He pulled me by the hand, I came, but then there was nobody. Richard was a *Match Game* devotee from way back when. I looked over my shoulder: Mother, hands folded on her purse in front of her, stepped a wallflower waltz across the parking lot.

Thomas never changed his clothes after the funeral: gray flannel pants, white shirt, black sweater, black bow tie, black eyes. I told him I loved him that night. We were in his bed again. He pulled his cock from his fly, fucked me hard, then cried, then slammed his fists into my face until I bled. He tucked his cock away. He said he loved me, too. I tried to hold tight to him, but he didn't let me. He told me to go to my room. I heard him walking all night, in the kitchen and the common room and the bedroom and outside. I got used to it.

A couple of days later, he loosened his tie for the first time. I was stunned. He smiled. I stood, where I had been going up the stairs. He sat at the kitchen table. "Here's this," he said. He handed me a check for more money than I'd imagined I'd ever have in my life. "It's Keller's, I guess." He looked at the ceiling, leaned back on two chair legs, steadied himself on his shaking hand on the wall. "Use it to keep the house up. I'm going away for a little while."

I sat on the stairs, looked at the check. "For a little while," I said. Meaning that I knew better.

"Pirate," he told me. "Poet. Drifter."

He didn't take anything with him, just walked out the door. He took one of those red high-heeled pumps. I saw it in his back pocket. I watched him all the way down the street.

WHAT COMES NEXT

I GO TO THE PARK, SIT AT THE LIVING ROOM benches, on my hands, shut my eyes. Before long, my minions have gathered before me, giggling, reverently. "Hello, Larry," I say. "David. Timothy. Mike." Because Keller was wrong, about this as about so much else: we do have real names, we must learn to speak them as often as possible. And because these are kids, pretty boys, they're getting fucked so much, so many guys who never bother to call them anything, who think they're nothing but slap-happy ass and silver-dollar nipples. And because this is the start of the ritual.

I am the storyteller now.

I spread open my hands, to tell them to sit. Larry, the smartest of them, the widest-eyed, grins. "Tell us that Keller story again. The Death of Donna-May Dean."

But I defer. Because Keller was right about this, as about so much else: the best stories, the ones we always want to hear, are bad for us. "No," I say to Larry. "Listen . . ." Then I shut my eyes, and am quiet for a long time. But smiling, like a man who knew a joke once, but does not remember the punch line: he waits. It will come. "I want us to make up a new story to tell," I whisper. "Where nobody has to die at the end."

My minions giggle, but they do not leave me. We sit here. We are waiting. It will come.